Praise for Ally Kennen's novels:

BEAST

WINNER of the Manchester Book Award
SHORTLISTED for the CILIP Carnegie Medal,
the Booktrust Teenage Prize, the Branford Boase Award,
the Berkshire Book Award, the Leicester Book Award
and the Bolton Book Award.

*"Rings with talent and compelling detail … a tense,
funny and touching tale. I really love this book"*
Amanda Craig, The Times

*"Beast has a tension that never lets up.
Ally Kennen is already a remarkably assured writer"*
Nicholas Tucker, Independent

*"An extraordinary imaginative achievement …this is
a compassionate story from an exciting new voice"*
Bookseller

*"Sharply and wittily observed …
An exceptional first novel"*
Books for Keeps

BERSERK

WINNER of the North East Teenage Book Award
and the Le~~~~~~~~~~~~
SHORTLISTED for~~~~~~~~~~~
the West Oxfor~~~~~~~~~~
the Coventry ~~~~~~~

*"This absolute nail-biter, written in clever and ~~~~~~~~
teenage vernacular, has an ending of stunning ingenuity"*
The Sunday Times

ALLY KENNEN comes from a proud lineage of bare-knuckle boxers, country vicars and French aristocracy. Prior to becoming a writer, she worked as an archaeologist, a giant teddy bear and a professional singer and songwriter.

Her first novel, BEAST, published in 2006, was shortlisted for the Booktrust Teenage Prize and the Carnegie Medal, and won the 2007 Manchester Book Award. Her second novel, BERSERK, won the North-East Teenage Book Award and the Leicester Book of the Year Award 2008. Her third novel, BEDLAM, has been longlisted for the Carnegie Medal.

Ally lives in Somerset with her husband, three small children, four chickens, and a curmudgeonly cat.

No woman has ever beaten Ally in an arm wrestle.

BERSERK

ALLY KENNEN

MARION LLOYD BOOKS

Marion Lloyd Books
An imprint of Scholastic Children's Books
Euston House, 24 Eversholt Street
London, NW1 1DB, UK
A division of Scholastic Ltd.
Registered office: Westfield Road, Southam, Warwickshire, CV47 0RA
SCHOLASTIC and associated logos are trademarks
and/or registered trademarks of Scholastic Inc.

First published in the UK in 2007 by Marion Lloyd Books.
This edition published in the UK in 2010 by Marion Lloyd Books.

ISBN 9781407117096

Printed by CPI Bookmarque Ltd, Croydon, Surrey
Papers used by Scholastic Children's Books are
made from wood grown in sustainable forests.

1 3 5 7 9 10 8 6 4 2

www.scholastic.co.uk/zone

For my parents
Edwin and Jenny Kennen

Thanks to
Ian at A1 Driving School
Dan Amos
Michelle Poulter at Bristol Alliance
Dr S. Odum at Frenchay A&E
Marion Lloyd

PART ONE

One

It was Devil who had my finger. We were hanging around under the bridge with the usual crowd: the Farrow twins, Connor Blacker, Devil's sister – Lexi – and her ugly mate Debs. It was the tip of my middle finger on my left hand. Imagine how embarrassing it is to lose your rude finger when you are a boy like me! How am I supposed to express myself?

So anyway we were messing around on the towpath by the canal. There's like, a million names tagged on the underside of the bridge. It reminds me of one of those war memorials you get, with all the names of the dead soldiers.

My name is one of the recent ones.

CHAS PARSONS.

I'm right below Devil but there are other names which I can't stop looking at. Right over the other side there's one which is sprayed in massive pink letters.

SELBY P and next to it in clear white curling letters it says **COLD BOY** and there's a fist drawn around both names.

These are my brothers' tags. They're not around.

The other tags I look at are dead centre of the arch, halfway up. They've got moss over them and are pretty faded but we don't let anyone spray over them.

J.JUBY   That's Devil's dad.
NAPPY PARSONS And that's my old man.

It's a family tradition.

Anyway, enough of the history lesson. It was a school night and it was getting dark and we were all messing around with Devil's knife and having intellectual discussions. Like this:

Devil: "Hey, Debs, why don't you show us your bra?"
Debs: "Tee hee hee."
Lexi: "Shut up, you perv."

I'd have rather seen Lexi's bra (or what's inside it) any day. But Lexi is Juby-the-Killer's daughter. Juby lives on our estate and his daughter is as untouchable as your schoolteacher's knickers.

We were playing "Knife", where you spread your hand on someone's skateboard and your mate stabs the knife between each of your fingers, slowly at first, then quicker and quicker. Connor Blacker had already scraped Devil's little finger so I suppose Devil was after some blood of his own. Anyway, the girls hated it, they were like, "Stop it, someone will get hurt." Girls are like that, I find. So the more they go on, the more we do it.

I'm getting bad vibes when it's my turn. I'm already annoyed because my box-fresh trainers have got canal mud on them. Devil keeps licking his bleeding finger and shooting shifty looks at Debs (the man has no taste, Debs hardly counts as female). But Lexi is watching so I put my hand down on the board and give Devil the knife. I decide to put down my left hand just in case. It was like I knew something bad was going to happen.

Connor's supposed to be holding the board steady but he's not concentrating.

"If dogs remember their ancestors were wolves, do ovens remember their ancestors were fires?" he goes.

He's always coming out with random crap like this.

"Shut up," I say. "Focus." After all, this is my hand at risk, here.

It's quite hard to cut off a finger. They don't just wave bye-bye to your hand and tippy-tap away. There has to be some sawing involved. But Devil keeps his knife very sharp and he reckons he's good at this game. So he's going faster and faster with the knife and not being careful enough for my liking.

THUMP THUMP THUMP THUMP. The knife jumps between my fingers.

"Stoppit," squeal the ladies and the Farrow twins start clapping in time to the knife falling. Then they start clapping faster. And I really don't like the look on

Devil's face (it's not pretty at the best of times). Devil's slamming down between my fingers now and Connor is having a job holding the skateboard steady.

"That's enough," says Lexi. "You children."

But it's too late. Connor loses his grip and the skateboard goes flying off into the wall. I feel this pinch and my middle finger is missing from the top joint.

"Oops," says Devil, and Debs lets out a scream.

I don't feel anything. This isn't so bad, I think to myself. Everyone is looking a bit freaked out so I raise my hand and waggle my remaining fingers at them.

Someone mutters something about playing the piano but no one laughs.

Then the blood starts pouring out.

"You bastard," I say to Devil, as the pain kicks in. It's like my finger has been slammed in a car door. I'm boiling hot, and then I'm shivering with cold. It hurts even though it isn't there any more. It's like shoving your finger into a red-hot oven.

"Ahhhh," I say and the world gets bits in it, like when the TV isn't tuned in properly.

"Chas," shrieks Debs.

"It's nothing," I tell her, though actually I don't think I can stand this. I don't know what to do with myself.

I pass out.

I wake up and I'm still under the bridge. Nobody has called an ambulance. Nobody has got me a bag of frozen peas to put on my stump. In fact, there's nobody here at all. I sit up. I feel dizzy and my finger REALLY hurts. All I want to do is get home and get some painkillers. It's like my finger is being turned inside out and I'm panting like a dog.

"Ouch," I say and try to breathe slower.

It's quite dark now and beginning to drizzle. The towpath is deserted except some old bloke and his dog, which is pissing up against a lifebelt. Where's the rest of my finger?

"Devil," I shout. "Where are you?" My voice breaks.

The old man looks in my direction, yanks his dog, mid-piss, and hurries off. My stump is oozing blood as thick as gravy. I haven't got a tissue so I take my cap off, fold it over a few times and press it against the wound.

The pain, strangely enough, comes booming in from my stomach before zooming up my ribs, down my arm and ending in an explosion in my finger. I don't cry though. I'm not the sort.

I start feeling around in the grass with my good hand, looking for my finger, but then I get scared about dog turds. I have to find it, or they won't sew it back on in the hospital.

To my relief, I see a shimmer of blue flashing lights up on the road. I bet it was Lexi who called me an ambulance. Maybe she'll be with them and will hold my (scary) hand all the way to the hospital. They'll have lots of lovely painkillers there.

But then this thing rolls out from behind the bridge and grabs my scruff.

Devil.

I swear at him and tell him I'm going to kill him. But I sound like a gasping old man.

"Run," he says, ignoring my death threat. "Some old biddy saw the knife and called the police."

So that's why everyone scarpered. We all got a warning about knives from Polly Panda about a month ago. And today, we've been drinking, and our cans and bottles are lying around everywhere.

"I can't run," I say, "I'm too weak."

"I didn't cut your feet off, did I?" says Devil, and drags me after him.

He's pretty thick, is Devil. But every now and then he comes out with a corker like that.

"But what about my finger?" I say as we are legging it over the grass.

"Forget it," says Devil. "It's gone."

I am in a bit of a dilemma. Do I go back to find my finger and meet the lovely kind policeman who will be interested in all the naughty stuff we kids have left behind, or do I keep my freedom and lose my finger to some tramp's mangy dog?

"What do you need it for anyway?" says Devil. "You've got nine others."

"Seven, Devil," I say. Then I feel really sick and I think I'm going to faint again.

"You've got to get me to hospital," I say.

"No way," says Devil. "I'm not getting caught up with them."

We make our way along the towpath. When we get to the trees Devil grabs my hand, and accidentally knocks my finger.

"Aarrgh!" I can't help yelling really loud.

"Let's see," says Devil. He holds my hand up and whips off the bloody hat. I'm too weak to stop him.

"It's nothing," he says, dropping my hand. "You don't need to go to hospital. All them nosey doctors an' that."

Devil hates anyone in uniform. I can understand his feelings towards police officers and traffic wardens, but he also doesn't like paramedics, nurses, postmen, shop assistants, even school kids.

"It's dark," I protest. "You can't see properly. My finger is missing, Devil."

"I'll take you home on the back of my bike," says Devil. "You wuss."

I am feeling really shitty now, so I just have to go along with him. I'm totally in his hands. Devil is sort of my best mate. But he's pretty twisted. He can be well lairy and isn't scared of using his fists. He's got a short fuse and when he gets annoyed, he takes it out on the weak, whoever they are.

This is why I act hard when I'm around him.

It's a few hours later. I've got my finger all padded up with bog roll and the bleeding seems to be stopping at last. I've found some ibuprofen in the cabinet and necked a couple. The pain is just about bearable as long as I don't touch the wound. Part of me wants to run downstairs and show it to Gran, and get her to call me an ambulance, but in a way I don't want anyone to know. I feel really weird about it.

It's the sort of thing that would really freak Mum out. She's got problems. She always has. But she's doing really well at the moment, and I don't want her upset. And to be honest, I can't quite believe it myself. I've lost my finger! And knowing Gran, she'd find out who did it using her granny underground and go round and try to smack Devil one round the head. I don't want Gran going round Devil's house, not because of Devil, though he is dangerous in the wrong hands (he's dangerous with any hands – especially mine) but because of his dad.

Have I mentioned Juby?

Devil and Lexi's dad is about five foot eight, the same size as me, but that's where the similarity ends. He's not human. He's nails. It's like he's made of bricks and wood and metal. He's square all the way down and he hasn't got a neck. He's got HATE tattooed on his knuckles. He's moody and, according to Devil, can be very, very mean. He's not around that much and Devil and Lexi spend a lot of time home alone. I shouldn't think they mind too much. Juby delivers cars for people but Devil told me this was a cover-up, and really he's part of a ring that knocks off stuff from stately homes and mansions. He's a middleman. So he's not exactly straight but neither is he a major-league criminal. I don't go round to Devil's house if I know Juby's in. Apparently he's known my dad since they were kids but my dad has made sure he'll never be welcome back in this estate again. If I meet someone and they find out that Nappy Parsons is my dad it's like they're sympathetic and disgusted at the same time. I've seen it over and over again. He's a total alky waster and would steal the shoes off his own grandmother. No one seems to miss him. Anyway, back to Juby, two years ago, Devil, me and Connor were messing around out near the bus stop. Me and Devil thought it would be funny to hang Connor upside down from the bus shelter. Connor wasn't happy but we were only mucking around. Juby turned up and went bananas.

"So you think you're bully boys, hey?" And he slapped Devil round the head and shoved me out of the way so hard I tripped backwards on the pavement and landed on my bum. Juby got out a knife, cut Connor free (which ruined all our school ties) and lifted him down. He pointed his knife at me and said if we ever did that again he'd teach us a lesson we'd never forget. It was only a laugh. Anyway, afterwards Connor said he was more worried about Juby than being upside down. So now I stay well out of Juby's way and I don't want my grandma going round his house yelling her head off.

I need to eat so I have to go downstairs. I get up off the bed feeling like an old man. My arm aches because I'm holding my hand at a funny angle so I don't knock my finger. And my shoulder feels stiff. I make it to the stairs before I take a breather. I'm dizzy. I don't know if it's because of my finger or because I've been a bit trigger happy with the painkillers.

Unfortunately both Mum and Gran are in the kitchen.

I hide my injured hand in the loose pocket of my big, baggy hoody. There's probably no need – Gran is half blind and way too vain to wear glasses, and Mum wouldn't notice if I was missing a whole arm let alone a fingertip.

The food cupboard is open and I aim for a red and white packet of cakes.

"We've not seen much of you today, young man," says Gran, taking off her apron and folding it away.

I grunt. Nothing is going to stop me reaching the cakes.

"They look like thieving pockets," says Gran eyeing up my hoody. She takes a step towards me. "And you look like you're on something."

I can't deny that.

"Oh, leave him alone," says Mum from the kitchen sink, where she's sucking sherbet lemons and scraping burned chips off the tray.

"As long as he lives in my house," says Gran, "I'll never leave him alone."

I smell her bread breath and I feel weak and sick. It's probably because I've lost a lot of blood.

"You shouldn't criticize my clothes," I say, "I'm at that sensitive age."

Gran leans close to me.

"What are you up to now?" she says.

I cast a needy look at my mother and she bangs the tray in the sink to show her support.

"If you get into trouble one more time, you're out, do you hear me?" says Gran.

I roll my eyes.

"I SAID DO YOU HEAR ME?"

"Yes, Gran, the whole estate can hear you."

"Cheeky little bugger," she says, and swipes me round the head pretty hard for a woman in her sixties. My instinct is to put up my hands to protect myself but I only use the one, for obvious reasons.

"Child abuse," I protest.

"You need a firm hand," says Gran. And she gives my mum a dirty look.

I take advantage of the lull to grab the cakes and get out of the kitchen.

Gran would never throw me out. At least, I don't think she would. After all, she finally busted me out of Care four years ago. She wants me here. She loves me. She didn't boot me out last winter when I got arrested for thieving. And she told me I had "just one more chance, my laddie" when I was caught abseiling off the canal bridge in the spring. The cops came to our door three weeks ago about the burned-out Toyota in the next street and she saw them off quicker than Devil could chop off your finger.

Ah yes, my finger.

I still don't know if I should go to Casualty or not. I'm the sort of person who likes to keep his head down.

They're bound to ask lots of questions at the hospital. It might go down on my records. I'd be instantly identifiable for the rest of my life, like the muppets with tattoos. But my finger still hurts and I'm worried about it going bad and getting gangrene or something. I might end up losing my whole arm!

Anyway, I've got other things to think about, like the next job me and Devil are planning. It's got to be bigger and better than the last one. We've set the date, Monday, next week. I'll have been at school every day for a whole month by then so I'll be due a day off.

School. Don't go there.

It's just gone eight o'clock in the evening, there's nothing on the telly and I'm lying on my bed examining this manky flap of skin where my finger used to be, when there is a thump at the door.

"What are you doing in there?" screeches my gran.

"Having some private time, Gran, a man has his needs."

"Pack your bags," she snaps. "I won't have that kind of talk. I want you out in the morning."

"Right, Gran."

I hear her muttering to herself and turning herself around.

"Gran?" I call.

"What?"

"What did you come up for?"

There is a pause while she tries to remember. Then the door handle slowly turns, like in a horror film.

"Why is the door locked, Chas?"

"I told you that, Gran."

"Oh." She clicks her tongue against her (false) teeth and I hear shuffling sounds and the click of an old back as something is pushed under my door.

I swing my legs round and sit up. I rub my eyes, but only with one hand. If you had lost a finger a few hours ago, you probably wouldn't be rubbing your eyes with it either.

There's a yellow envelope on the carpet.

I pick it up.

There's no stamp, but there is a franking jobby. Which says, "Louisiana, USA."

I hold the envelope and bite my lip. I never thought it would come so soon. To be honest I thought it would never come at all. Right now I wish it hadn't.

"Oh God," I whisper. What have I got myself into now?

TWO

I didn't want to write to a woman. I wanted a proper killer and preferably one who had mown down innocent bystanders with a sub-machine gun, Rambo stylee. Someone who would go down in history; a mass murderer with bodies in the basement. Now what fifteen year old can say they have a killer as a pen pal? Me, Chas Parsons, that's who. I may look like a skinny teenager from the estate, who only just goes to school and whose ultimate fantasy is to snog the face off the daughter of the resident hard man, but I have a few little secrets and this letter is just one of them.

Sometimes I have funny ideas. Like when I went into school pretending I'd lost my memory. (The teachers didn't notice.) Or when I freaked out the kids by the canal because the only word I said all day was "**Death**". Those are just the small things. And of course, there's the stuff me and Devil get up to. My teachers call me A Ringleader. But I prefer to work in a small organization. That's not to say I haven't got mates, I've got loads, but only Devil is allowed into the inner circle, it's only him who gets to come with me on my campaigns and magical mystery outings. It's only him who knows the truth behind the police canteen maggots or the supermarket sheep. Take Connor Blacker, he's a good kid, we hang out a lot, but he's a bit, I don't know, off the wall. He's always going on about stuff that doesn't matter, like pygmies living in bungalows, or giros for children or whatever. Devil, however, can be pretty unpredictable, but he has his uses:

1. He's ALWAYS up for a bit of fun. No matter how illegal.
2. He's strong and he's not afraid of anything except his dad.

But I told no one, not even Devil, about my quest for a killer pal.

I'd found out about the pen-pal organization a while ago, but didn't do anything about it until recently. I was wasting time, searching the net, and I typed in *murderers* just for fun and all this scary stuff came up: stories of nasty killings (which freaked me out) as well as boring news items and names of weird rock bands. I also found a site which invited people to write to prisoners on Death Row in America. How cool was that! I decided to go for it, even though I'd never written a letter in my life.

I imagined my new buddy would tell me all about his life. All the riots and stuff, all the screws who were scared of them. I was also interested from a professional point of view. (Not that I'm a killer, you understand.) Twice, I've nearly been sent to a detention centre for young offenders. Once for burglary and another time for a load of stuff that ended up in me graffitiing the walls of the pig station with shocking pink car body spray. (The fuzzies really hated that one . . . oops.)

The website went on about *offering a window into the outside world* and being a *friend in a place which is often dark*. I didn't think about that. I just liked the idea of having a killer for a pal. And what would a killer's handwriting be like? Would it be written in blood or something? I couldn't wait to find out. The organization wanted people to commit to writing for at least a year. Well, I didn't know about that, but they're hardly going to come after me, are they?

I had two problems. The first was that you had to be over eighteen to apply. The second was that you actually had to write something. Don't get me wrong, I can write. I'm the only one in my family who ever went to school. My brothers were into other things. Gran is always going on about how I'm the only son who will ever come to anything. Selby, my eldest brother, is dead and Stephen, who is twenty, fired up to Scotland very fast a couple of years ago. He must have something to hide. I don't expect he'll be back for a while.

My problem was I didn't know what to write about. My friends?

Dear Killer,
What wonderful weather we are having today.
My mate Devil (real name Devlin Juby) is a
wonderful chap. He just peed for three whole
minutes . . . and filled two pint glasses.

My family?

My Dear Mr Murderer,
How are you today? (That is, if you are still with
us.) Let me tell you about my family. My
grandmother is setting a trap for next door's cat
so it doesn't crap in her flower bed. She says she
doesn't want to kill it, only break its back legs.
And my mother is in a wonderful mood because
a white butterfly nearly drowned in her
cornflakes this morning. Apparently it's "a sign".

I couldn't write about school because I was supposed
to be over eighteen. And I couldn't write about my
mates, because mostly all we did was get into trouble,
hang out by the bridge or mess around in the
allotments, chat up girls (oh, Lexi) sleep, eat and maybe
sometimes go to school. I couldn't see my killer man
being interested in that.

So I'm too young and I have nothing to write about,
so what's the logical conclusion? Pretend to be someone
else. So, and this may sound a bit spooky, I decided to
write pretending to be my mother. That would get over

the age problem, and I could talk about all sorts of stuff like an adult and not have to stick to the kiddy subjects like astronomy or fox hunting. I didn't write pretending to be my dad because I thought letter writing was a woman thing. And I don't want to think about my dad anyway. He's useless and I haven't seen him for about five years. I don't know where he is. Nobody does. And nobody seems to care either.

I got myself a brand-new email address, filled in the online registration, pretending to be my mum, sent the whole lot off, and waited.

I got an email back really quickly. These people must be desperate. They had accepted my form and said I sounded like I would be a good pen pal, seeing as how I led such a busy, active life with a big, happy family. (I'd let my mind run wild on the application form.) They offered me a choice of three killers.

1. Gordon McBurn
2. Lenny Darling
3. Aneka Haden

Like I said, there was no way I wanted to write to a woman, so Aneka was out of the picture. So I looked the other two up on the internet. Gordon McBurn had murdered his wife. Now even I found the details of this killing a bit too much. It was scary seeing what the man had actually done. It made it all more real. I began to wonder if I should get involved at all. This bloke was due to die very soon and the charity really wanted supportive letters. This was too heavy for me. I didn't want to do it. It felt wrong. So I typed LENNY DARLING in the search engine. The name had a familiar ring to it. I must have seen it in the papers or something.

Lenny Darling, 40, a British tourist, murdered a fifteen-year-old boy, nine years ago, by holding him underwater at high tide on the coast of Florida. Lenny was sentenced to death but he hadn't got a "termination" date yet because of a series of ongoing appeals. I got a massive shock when I read the next bit. Lenny Darling is from London, but he spent most of his childhood in Harrington, which is only four miles from here. How mad is that? I decided to write to him. He might appreciate hearing about life at home and it would give me something to write about. So I tore a page out of my school English book (I thought it was appropriate seeing as I was about to make a work of fiction) and began. . .

Dear Lenny,
Hi, I hope you don't mind me writing to you.

Do I sound like a woman? I think so. Women are politer than blokes.

My name is Caroline Parsons, but my nickname is Chas. Please write back using my nickname. I'm 37 years old and live with my son, Mark.

21

My second name is Mark so that's fair enough. My mum's name is Caroline.

I read from your details you are originally from Harrington. Well that's a coincidence because I live in Bexton, which you probably remember is the next town along. You're not missing anything, believe me. Harrington is a right dump these days.

Lenny is around the same age as my dad, which makes him old. I chew my pen and try and think what old gits might be interested in.

Mark is into bodybuilding and has just won the national competition for his age. He's also captain of the school football team. We think he's going to go to university and become a doctor. He's tall and very good looking. He's going out with a lovely young girl called Lexi Juby. I do worry about what they get up to, but young people have to go their own way, don't you think?

I'm talking too much about my family.

It must be tough being on Death Row. Did you mean to murder that kid? I can understand wanting to murder someone sometimes. My own mother is very annoying. (Not that I would try to take her out!!)

22

I hope you'll write back.
Yours truthfully,

(Truthfully, isn't that what people say?)

Chas Parsons

OK. It was a pile of crap. But I wasn't writing it all out again. And Gran was getting all suspicious at my door, asking why was I being so quiet and I wasn't up to anything, was I?

I was pretty fed up by the time I'd finished. It's hard making stuff up. Anyway, it was a letter, wasn't it?

This brings me on to the post office. It was pretty embarrassing going in there. I hoped no one was there from three years ago (Devil and I tried to rob *all* the sweets and got cornered by four old biddies, but I'm not going into that now) but although the bloke behind the counter gave me a bit of an evil look, no one said anything, and he took my letter and dropped it in a brown sack.

Then I forgot all about it. I've had a lot going on, you know, looking at Lexi, going to school, skiving school. Doing my little jobs for kicks. I forgot all about it until Gran shoved the letter under my door.

Louisiana State Penitentiary
Dear Chas,
You have an intriguing nickname for a woman.

23

*Of course, you modern women can call
yourselves what you wish. Until I received your
note I was very downhearted but its arrival has
raised my spirits considerably. The common
understanding is that I should not write to you
until I have received at least two letters in order to
show your commitment. However, I am always
desperate for a friendly voice so I'm bypassing this
rule and writing back straight away. I oscillate
between dreams of oblivion and despair and
your charming letter has done much to reignite
my interest in the world I have lost. Now, by my
reckoning you owe me two letters to satisfy the
two-letter rule, so tell all!*

*Knuckle down, my dear Chas, and tell me about
your life and everything in it. I was amused to
learn of your family. Mark sounds like a model
child and sadly you don't get many of them these
days. And it sounds like he has a good
relationship with his girlfriend. Fallible
creatures, young women, so you must keep an
eye on their behaviour. One question, did you
say her surname was Tuby or Juby? Only I
couldn't make out your handwriting and I used
to know someone called Tuby from your area.
Lovely to hear from someone British. I wish I'd
never come to this country and always dream of
returning home one day. Sadly, those dreams
have now died. Every minute brings my death*

closer. Each second passes too fast and too slow.
You have a warm voice, Chas, and I have to hear
from you again. Open up and tell me about your
world.
Unusual though it is, I like your expression,
"Yours truthfully," so I'm adopting it as my own.
Yours truthfully,
Lenny Darling.

PS In answer to your question, I'm still trying to
prove my innocence.

Is he cracking on to my mother? (Even though he's not
technically writing to her.) Does that mean he's really
cracking on to me? He fancies me through my writing.
Does that make me gay? Or maybe I'm just a fantastic
actor. What was that he said? *You have a warm voice . . .*
Eek. I don't know if I'm going to write back. Mind you,
I might feel tight if I don't. He sounds like he's having
a hard time. If I was in there I'd have to find a way to
bust myself out. I've been locked up before and I
managed to escape. Of course, it wasn't an American
maximum-security unit. I was only seven or eight and I
was living with this couple, Midge and Guy, and their
four kids. This lot were right-on; they put their jam jars
out for the council to collect and took us to Pizza
Express instead of McDonald's. Anyway, when any of
the kids were bad, they'd shut them in the attic. That
included me. Social Services said to treat me like one of

their kids. So they did. I wish they'd have treated me like a long-stay guest instead. I was in that bloody attic more often than I was anywhere else. Even in winter. Attics are cold in winter.

There was only one light bulb hanging on a wire from the roof, and no proper floor so you couldn't walk around. Guy, the dad-bloke, had nailed some plywood to make a narrow platform. A load of suitcases and crap tennis racquets and broken TVs and junk was crammed on to it. There was just about space for my skinny bum cheeks. I remember standing on tiptoe on a suitcase, looking out of the tiny skylight for aeroplanes. There was nothing else to do. But I only ever saw pigeons. I'd gone through the suitcases out of boredom and found nothing but old men's clothes. I'd searched the pockets but I'd only found coppers, an old pound note (weird) and a load of manky old tissues.

I was sent up there fairly often. Sometimes for a whole hour, which is a long time when you are only eight years old and a people person like me. How tight is that? Anyway like I said, I escaped once. Mr Chas Alcatraz. Except I wasn't very subtle. I was in a mean mood because I didn't think I deserved to be up there. All I'd done that day was:

1. Steal all the crisps from the cupboard.
2. Block the bog with three bog rolls.
3. Set fire to the living-room carpet to see how quickly it would burn.

4. Make my eldest foster sister cry (I told her she was ugly).

That's not so bad, is it? I was only a small lad. I was experimenting. I'd done far worse things in my time.

The trapdoor was bolted on the outside. I kept thinking to myself . . . what if the carpet fire wasn't actually out . . . but singeing away at the edges. And what if it caught alight when everyone was out the room and no one was looking? What if it spread up the walls and into the attic and burned me alive? I'd be trapped and fried. I had to do whatever it took to get out. My fear made me stronger than Juby-the-Killer.

I looked at the skylight but knew I would never get through it, and the drop down the roof was steep and deadly. The more I tried to work it out, the more I realized I was stuck and the more panicky I got. I stepped off the platform and balanced along the beams till I came to a spot which I knew was above my foster parents' bed. (Don't ask how I know; only I will say that I reckon they locked me up there sometimes for the slightest reason, so they could spend a bit of quality time together, if you know what I mean.) And this is what I did. I jumped off the beam, and crashed into the floor. It gave way quite a bit and I made a massive crack. A bit of plaster fell away and I could actually see the patchwork bedspread below me. Now this is where I was clever. I reckoned falling through the ceiling might hurt a bit, what with scraping my tender young skin on all those splintery battens and plaster crusts. So I balanced back over to the suitcases and made myself calm down in order to pull on two pairs of old men's trousers and two thick, smelly, itchy jumpers. The trousers were way too long so I had to roll them up. I even found a hat that looked like Gran's tea cosy, and pulled it low over my head. I must have looked mad. Then I walked back to the hole.

I jumped really hard between the battens, slamming my feet down and imagining I was a wrecking ball. I shut my eyes and heard splintering wood and cracking plasterboard. It smelled hot, like singeing. I felt something give beneath my feet. Dust flew up my nose and I was sneezing as I thumped down on the bed in the room below.

I landed face down and most of me was on the bed. So there I was, a small Chas Parsons, lying three quarters on his foster parents' bed, covered in plaster-board, wallpaper and polystyrene ceiling tiles.

It was the thing that got me evicted. By escaping from the attic, I escaped from the house.

Midge and Guy's youngest kid was a baby, Alex. I'm fifteen so he must be about eight years old now. He might be locked in that attic right now, waiting for an aeroplane to fly past the skylight. I bet he only sees pigeons too.

Three

I'm woken, as always on a Saturday morning, by the sound of Gran vacuuming the kitchen lino. The first thing I do is have a couple of paracetamol, then lock myself in the bathroom and unravel the wads of tissue and plaster round my finger. I don't want to touch it, but think I ought to wash it. The finger is swollen like a sausage and is a worrying reddish colour. It looks like a traffic accident. All this yellowy stuff is oozing out of the end. I make myself take another look. At least I can't see bone; it's all blood and flesh and tiny little stringy things. I have to sit on the bog seat because I feel dizzy. I catch my hand on the wall as I move and a drop of blood falls on to Gran's white lace toilet doily. I fill the basin with warm water, rummage in the cupboard for some TCP and slosh some in. Then I dunk my finger. It stings, but nothing like as bad as yesterday – Gran's painkillers are pretty strong. I dab my finger dry with a tissue and wad it up again. I need proper bandages, antiseptic ointment and plasters. Back in my room, I secure the tissue with Sellotape. Then I have to sit down again. It's nearly midday and I'm hungry again. I'm going to have to go down and face the mad women I live with.

Downstairs, Gran has finished cleaning the kitchen and is watching telly in the living room, which leads off the kitchen through a little archway.

Gran hates cooking. She says she won't buy fresh vegetables because they haven't been sterilized. She buys ready meals and sticks them in the freezer. They are delicious and I am seriously addicted. I choose a mince moussaka and set the microwave for three and a half minutes.

"Did you hear that?" squeals Gran. "Forty quid a week for teenage mums. They should make them work for it."

I go under the arch into the living room but don't say a word. No one ever wins an argument with Gran.

"I call looking after a baby work," says Mum, looking up from her tiny silver mirror. She's slapping on Fairy Dust eye make-up to match the Pixie Pink lipstick she found in the chemist. Mum's obsessed with fairies. She's got fairy tea towels, fairy socks, fairy T-shirts, fairy mugs, fairy ornaments. She'll buy anything that's remotely connected to fairies, even washing-up liquid. She says everything with a fairy connection has a little bit of magic and she needs all she can get. It's not surprising really; she's been away with the fairies ever since Selby died.

"If they're raising kids like yours, Caroline, they'd better be paid nothing at all," says Gran, her eyes sparkling at the prospect of a scrap. "Next generation, my arse. Next generation of spongers and thieves more like."

"Talking about me, Gran?" I nick a Werther's Original from Gran's pink-glass sweet bowl on the coffee table.

"Leave that, you thieving bugger," says Gran and slaps my wrist.

I pop it in my mouth, then spit it out and put it back in the bowl. I grin at my gran.

"Out of my sight, dirty boy," shrieks Gran, ferreting through the sweet bowl for the wet one. When she finds it, she puts it in her own mouth.

Mum gives me one of her smiles. It's like drizzle on a sunny day. Sometimes I wish she'd go off the happy pills. It's like she's wearing a big mask.

Gran turns to the telly. In just a few seconds she's swearing at the screen. My mum takes advantage of the ceasefire to have a go at some mothering.

"Hello, Chas," she says.

"Hello," I say, The microwave pings in the kitchen. I go and stuff my face. Afterwards I come back, intending to nick another sweet. I'm about to dive into the glass jar when I notice something.

"Mum," I say, "what are you wearing?"

"A waste of good money, that's what she's wearing," says Gran.

Mum's wearing a dark red skirt and a black blouse with frilly sleeves. It hides her flabby gut. She looks a bit better than normal.

"How do I look?" asks Mum, desperate for me to say something nice. Gran makes a small noise in her throat. She is desperate for me to say something nasty.

31

"Mum," I say, "you look like a queen."

Gran snorts and turns up the volume on the TV.

Mum smiles. "Thanks, Chas," she says.

"Don't go encouraging her," says Gran. "It will end in trouble."

Gran thinks everything will end in trouble. She thought the new kiddies' playground would be a centre for organized crime (she's half right there) and she and her best mate/worst enemy Dolores-from-down-the-road, organized a petition against the new Drop in Health Clinic, because they said it would bring all the drug addicts into the area. (They're already here.)

"She's got a date," Gran tells me.

"As in meeting with a member of the opposite sex, or a dried fruit?" I'm sounding cool, but actually I am very, very surprised. The only bloke I've ever known my mum to be involved with was my dad.

"Courting," says Gran. "At her age."

"I'm only thirty-seven," says Mum.

"Exactly," says Gran. "There's still time for you to get into trouble."

'What's going on?' I ask, a little concerned. Mum hasn't exactly demonstrated good taste in men so far.

Mum sighs. "Aren't I allowed to meet someone?" she asks.

"No," says Gran. "You're too batty, Caroline; no man wants an insane woman."

Mum looks really sad and looks at the carpet so I have to say something.

"Men think all women are crazy anyway, Mum," I say reassuringly.

"She's deluded," says Gran. "As usual."

"You're jealous," I say. "As usual."

Gran swipes at the air, obviously wishing it was my face. "Don't start on your lip, my boy."

But Gran can't be cross with me for long because she wants me to pick on Mum with her. She gets up, opens the drawer in the coffee table and fishes out a glossy brochure.

Mum is flustered. "You must have got that out of my room," she says.

"You're in my house," says Gran, "so it's my room."

"You should get a lock, like me," I tell Mum. "That should keep out Mrs Light-Fingers." But I take the brochure from Gran and read.

Heaven Sent Introductions
Meet your ideal partner. Just sign up and we will match you with many dates. The form is quick and easy to fill in and we have brought together many lonely hearts. Join today and give yourself the chance of true love.

"Oh, Mum," I say. "What if you end up meeting some freak?"

"He's called Jonathan," says Gran.

"He's a landscape gardener," says Mum.

"Dirty fingernails, then," says Gran.

"Where are you meeting him, Mum?" I ask.

"The Holiday Inn, I expect, looking like that," says Gran.

"Are you speaking from experience, Gran?" I ask innocently.

"Well, I'd better be off," says Mum, reaching for her handbag.

"Where are you going?" I repeat.

"Never you mind," says Mum. "I don't want you turning up and spying on me."

"I've got better things to do with my time," I say.

"She hasn't." Mum points at Gran.

"That's nice, that is," says Gran. "I put a roof over your children's head, and you repay me like this."

It's weird this thing with Mum. For years she's been ill, and not really able to do anything, that's why I got put into Care. That's why we moved in with Gran. Maybe that's why my dad left us. Mum had a nervous breakdown. I thought that meant she was mental, but a social worker said it just meant she couldn't cope for a bit. Like when loads of things get on top of you and close you down. But, like I said, recently Mum has been loads better. Not like a normal mum, I mean, she doesn't wash my clothes or cook my tea. Gran does all that, even though, like I said, she hates cooking. Come to think of it, Gran probably wouldn't let Mum do any of those things anyway. But Mum has been going to a club for people like her, and she's started applying for a few jobs. There was one where they needed a sewing machinist (at the bra factory where Gran works) but she didn't get it. They said she was overqualified. Mum has always made her own clothes. Before she was ill, she ran herself up these long skirts and weird baggy tops. Recently she's been buying material again and making herself dresses and skirts like the ones she's wearing in old photographs.

I think it means my mother is getting better.

I close the garden gate and step out into the street. People are out and about. It's sunny so everyone is in a good mood. People are washing their cars, going out for shopping trips. Little kids are bombing round on their bikes. A bee buzzes past my face and lands on a flower. There's loads of bees round here. They belong to Michael, who is Dolores's (Gran's-best-mate-and-worst-enemy's) husband. Michael keeps the bees in a hive at the allotments. He's always giving Gran these plastic boxes filled with honey, but she won't eat it because she says it's "bee poo".

I decide to go to the chemist's in town and get some bandages and TCP.

I wonder who this Jonathan bloke is. If he's a good bloke, he might sort Mum right out. Maybe he's rich. Maybe he'll buy me a motorbike.

But what if he's another nutter like my dad?

Four

About a week after my finger is chopped off, me and Devil hitch six miles out of town to the lorry driver's café just off the motorway. It's pissing with rain and we're sheltering under a bit of cardboard which isn't keeping us dry. We're hiding round the back of a lorry. It's loaded with paper. Now this would have been of great interest to my brother, Stephen. Apparently he had a bit of a thing for the matches, if you know what I mean. But I'm not into anything like that.

We don't go in the café. No way. Much too scary. We're here to get us a machine. A big one.

You know, when I'm on a job, it's like I've got fire running through my veins, but in a good way. It's like mega adrenalin. I feel sick and quick, like a fly. Do you know what I mean? I feel really clever. It's like, if there's a problem, I can solve it dead quick. I'm not being a big-head. It's true.

"It's not happening," says Devil. And for a minute I think he's going to give up.

"Come on, Devil, it's only a bit of rain," I say helpfully.

But then a huge juggernaut draws into the car park,

one of the really massive ones with blown-up photographs of green apples on the sides.

"This is the one," I say to Devil, and he grins. It's moments like these that make me realize he's worth all the hassle. He's a bad boy is Devil. He's got generations of quality thieving blood running through his veins.

The driver parks next to an oil tanker and jumps out. He splashes through the rain to the caff. He doesn't see us. He's wearing these little round specs with mirrors and a greying moustache. He's wearing a navy blue jumper and blue trousers and uncool trainers. He's got the most God-awful sideburns. If you ask me he deserves everything that's coming for crimes against fashion.

Devil gives me his evil grin. It's still raining, we're soaking and we're about to steal a forty-ton juggernaut. Am I not a naughty boy? Man, I love it.

Devil whacks the screwdriver in the lock – with all the racket the rain is making, they won't hear it in the caff. And nobody, I said nobody, is about. The lock clicks and we open the door, easy as anything. We look at each other and crack up. Then Devil goes to climb in. But so do I. This is where it starts to go wrong. We're messing around, each trying to get into the driving seat. We're sort of fighting, pulling each other back. Both of us reckon we're the man to drive this beauty out on to the open road.

"Chas," says Devil. "You're not into cars, you know nothing about them."

"I'm into lorries," I say, pulling him off the step, on to the ground, and grabbing the door. "Get out of my way."

"Get off." Devil pulls me down and, wham, I'm slamming into the wet tarmac. So I punch him in the legs. It's on the border of friendly fire and Devil is tougher than me and I've got a bad finger. But I'm on one, this is my baby and I want to drive. So I get up, climb on to the ledge next to him (he's in the seat now) and push his head, hard down on the plastic bit between the seats. The rest of his body follows his head.

Now Devil doesn't like being pushed around. But he doesn't immediately retaliate. I realize it is because I have actually hurt him. I'm so surprised I nearly let him drive. Though I don't of course.

"I'll tell my dad about this," says Devil, shuffling into the passenger seat. He sounds like a little kid and I laugh.

"Oh Daddy," I say, "Chas wouldn't let me drive when we were joyriding."

This shuts up Devil. Juby may be a lawbreaker himself, but he doesn't stand for it in his kids. This means he hates it when me and Devil get into trouble. A lot.

I prise off the plastic round the steering column with the Boy Scout contraption Gran gave me for Christmas a few years ago. It's very useful. It's a metal tube stashed with folding knives, a bottle opener, a screwdriver, and all sorts of other things a lad like me might need. I fiddle with the ignition wires. Devil decides I'm taking too long and decides to start the engine the old-fashioned way. He plunges the screwdriver into the ignition and forces it round. We start up nice and easy. The engine sounds loud but far away, even though it is just beneath us. Then I try and put her into first. But things aren't happening and I stall the engine. The clutch, brake and accelerator are all in the right places, the same as in a car, but the diagram which explains the gear stick is like something out of A level maths. There's eight gears on two different relays. I don't get it. More by luck than skill I manage to get it into what I think is second, and we pull slowly over the wet tarmac. My fingers keep sliding down the greasy steering wheel. The driver must have sweaty hands. I've never driven anything like this. It reminds me of walking around with a load of mud stuck to your shoes. I can feel the weight we're pulling. I can't see what's happening directly behind because there's no rear-view mirror, just massive side mirrors. I can just about reach all the controls but I feel like a midget driving this thing. Luckily I don't have to reverse to get out of the car park. The diagram does show where to reverse it, but I don't know if I'd be able to find it. We pull out from the car park. I don't want to go fast, because that would just draw attention to us. It's raining really hard now, and I can't work out how to operate the windscreen wipers.

I slam on the brakes. A bloke in a red coat with a

small dog has stepped out in front of me. I have to stop or I'll squash him. He clocks me. A fifteen-year-old kid, driving a forty-ton articulated lorry.

"That's it," says Devil. "You should have kept going, he's seen us."

"I'd have killed him," I say.

"We should kill him now anyway,' says Devil. He's only half-joking. I reckon maybe he could kill someone, if pressed.

But we let the man cross. The dog is a small, scruffy-looking terrier. I'd like a dog. Maybe we should kill him and I could have the dog. Only joking! I'm not Devlin Juby. I let off the clutch and manage not to stall as we set off again. OK, we're getting on the slip road and the engine is roaring. I have to change gears. I'm aiming for third but I mess it up and end up in what I think is fourth, but this doesn't seem to matter, we're still going. I'm pretty nervous about pulling out on to the dual-carriageway, but luckily there isn't much traffic about. I don't even know where the indicators are on this thing. But while I'm messing around with the switches I activate the windscreen wipers so at least we can see.

We pull off the slip road and a car zooms past, flashing and sounding its horn. Devil puts up his middle finger. I thought I had enough time to get out but this thing is so long, it's hard to judge.

I put my foot down.

"YEEHAR!" I scream.

We're bombing along. I keep checking my mirrors to

see if anyone is chasing us but it's hard to see because we're kicking up so much spray. I reckon our driver is tucking into his fried eggs and hash browns and hasn't even noticed we're gone. I'm getting a real buzz out of driving this thing. The driver has got all these cuddly rats on his dash. There's also a battered picture of a little boy, which is hanging from the radio above my head. My seat must be air controlled, because I'm having a smooth ride as it moves up and down with the road. Devil, however, is bumping all over the place. I change up a gear, or at least I think I do, and increase our speed. We're going at about 55mph and Devil is going, "Faster, faster," but the lorry isn't having it. I must be in the wrong gear. I'm glad I'm driving. It's wet and the visibility is bad. If this thing doesn't want to go any faster that's fine by me.

I feel mean in this beast. I should do this more often. I like to think this is my style. Not just a scummy little car thief, joyrider, but a lorry jacker. Now that's class.

"This is wicked," says Devil. "Wish I was driving."

A police car belts past in the opposite direction. The lights aren't flashing or anything but the countdown has begun.

Luckily our turning isn't far, just a few miles up the road. I put my foot down and end up right up the arse of a little Fiat.

I keep catching the eye of the little boy in the photograph.

"Your daddy is going to be in a very bad mood," I tell

him. I look across at Devil. He's picking the rubber from the window rim with his knife.

I keep thinking I see blue flashing lights on the horizon. OK, here's the turning. We bomb up the slip road so fast, even Devil grips the side of his seat. We slide round the roundabout and tank off to the left. This thing is pretty nippy.

Now we're on this country road. It's fairly straight, so I keep my foot down.

Then we hear sirens.

I go a little bit faster. The trees and hedges are flying past. It's like the middle of the countryside here, even though we are just a few miles outside Bexton. I slow down. There's a crossroads coming up and I don't want to miss it. Devil and me planned out this route some time last week. I know the turning is here somewhere. Near a tree . . . there it is. I try and turn in but I get the angle wrong and I'm nearly in the ditch. Now I have to back up. Devil looks interested now.

"Want me to drive?" he asks.

"I can do it, Dev," I say, and wonder how the hell I'm going to get the thing into reverse. I study the diagram; R for reverse is in the top-left corner. I knock the gear stick into neutral and push it up. I'll either land in reverse or fifth. I let the clutch off slowly and the machine slowly chunters back, making a bleeping noise. I have to steer to the left, to get the back end to go right. It's not easy and I'm sweating.

BEEEEEEEEEPPPPPP.

42

Some arsehole in a Maestro is right up our bum. Can't he have a little more consideration for us heavy-vehicle drivers? When I think I've got enough clearance, I put her into what I'm pretty sure is second and pull us round into the turning.

Done it! The Maestro flies past, still beeping.

"A lot of road hogs about today, Mr Juby," I say in my private-school voice.

"Damned out of order," says Devil.

We take up the whole of the road. If we meet anything, we're buggered. We're climbing now and I have to change down a gear as the engine protests. I'm getting good at this.

I stop just before a gate, and nod at Devil to open it.

"Nope," he says, and scratches the back of his neck.

When Devil scratches the back of his neck in this way, it means he is up to something. I'm pretty certain he isn't going to open the gate for me so I put the lorry into neutral and pull on the brake before I jump out.

When I look up from the gate, Devil's in the driving seat. I expected this and don't mind too much. Devil floors the accelerator and twists the jug into the field. The back end smacks into the gate post but he's through into the field, kicking up loads of mud. The tail of the lorry is just through the gate when Devil gets into a spin. Mud flies out everywhere and I can't get out of the way quickly enough. My trainers are ruined. I'm going to have to throw them out. Maybe there's a consignment of trainers in the back of the lorry. I tell myself not to be so stupid. This is a supermarket lorry. If there are any trainers, they'll all be shite own-brand ones.

Devil revs the engine and the wheels spin but he's not going anywhere, just embedding himself deeper and deeper into the mud. I reckon he was after a bit of joyriding round the field, but it ain't gonna happen. It's a wet field, full of nothing but grass. Leaving Devil to spin in the mud I walk to the corner of the field. I stick close to the edge even though it would be quicker for me to cut right across the wet grass. But I don't trust Devil. He'd probably like to chase me a little bit if he managed to get out of the gateway. In the corner of the field, in a ditch, I find a green tarpaulin. I pull the tarp to one side. Underneath, there's Connor Blacker's moped and, get this, two helmets. Am I impressive or what? The moped looks a bit damp, but I reckon it will start. I've got the keys in my pocket. Me and Devil left it here earlier, just before we hitched to the café.

Devil revs the engine all he can and the apples on the sides of the lorry look like they are going mouldy because of all the mud that sprays on them.

I wheel the scooter over the grass and prop it in the hedge near the gate. We may have to make a quick getaway. Anyone driving down the lane is going to see the back of the lorry stuck in the gateway.

I hear muffled swearing coming from the cab, in the pauses between the engine revs.

"Give up, Dev," I shout.

Dev's head pokes out of the window.

44

"Planks," he shouts. "We need planks."

"Bugger that," I say. "Let's see what's inside." And Devil's face changes from Devil-rage to Devil-interest. He switches off the engine and I start fiddling with the lock on the back doors. I'm a bit slow because my finger, wadded beneath rolls of bandage and sticking tape, is stinging. It's a mean padlock and I'm not sure I can handle it. I walk round the lorry to the sides and see they are made of a heavy plastic, strapped down and fastened with lots of metal clips. I'm tugging at the first clip when Devil comes to help; he takes one look at what I'm doing, tuts loudly and takes out my Boy Scout knife contraption. He saws through the plastic and pretty soon has made a hole big enough for us to climb through. I give him a leg-up and he drags me up behind.

Once inside, Devil hacks away some more of the curtain so we can see. There are pallets stacked high and wrapped in stuff like clingfilm. Devil takes out the knife and hacks away at the nearest pallet and unwraps boxes and boxes of biscuits. I'd hoped there would be TVs and stuff, but a lorry load of food is a lovely sight. We go around, yanking and slashing off the plastic wrapping and find boxes of cakes and chocolate bars and crates of tinned vegetables and boxes of cereals and pasta and everything. I climb up, break into a box of crisps and munch my way through two packets in three minutes. I'm like an animal. Devil has found himself a Deluxe chocolate cake and is ramming it into his mouth.

"Give us some of that," I say, but Devil spins away.

"You can have your own whole cake," he says, kicking a box full of them towards me.

The next ten minutes are embarrassing because me and Devil go insane, ripping open boxes, eating, eating, eating, stuffing sweets, cakes, peanuts, honey-crunchy cereals, biscuits, cola, everything.

"How's that?" says Devil through a mouthful of some kind of pink food, pointing to my hand. He means my finger.

"'S getting better," I say. I look at him. "Are you sure you haven't seen the missing bit?"

"Nope," says Devil way too quickly.

I shrug. I know this is a bit soft, but a part of me is missing and I want it back. I know Devil has something to do with it. But now is not the time to confront him.

We keep eating.

I'm deciding what to take home when I realize I forgot to bring any bags with me.

"DAMN." I'm really mad. I've got a lorry load of stuff. How can I get it home? For a moment I deliberate whether I could drive the lorry back to the estate, maybe in the middle of the night. I quickly forget that. It's too risky and the lorry is bedded in the mud anyway. I eat some more. Eventually I pause for breath. Devil has found a crate of vodka and is tucking in. I grab a bottle and have a swig myself. This is a bad idea. I think I'm going to be. . .

I puke all over my trainers.

My poor trainers.

Devil tuts and offers me back the vodka. "Want to rinse your mouth out?"

I shake my head and wipe my mouth.

The floor of the lorry is a slick of puke and alcohol, broken biscuits and cake crumbs, food wrappings and empty cans.

"We'll come back tonight," says Devil.

I nod but know we won't be back. It's too risky. This is gutting. There are crates of expensive-looking orange juice, boxes of chocolates and pasta sauce and rice and nuts and dried fruit and cans of soup and everything. And we have to leave most of it behind. I fit chocolate bars and miniature whisky bottles into my pockets, but there's not much room.

"I'm taking this," says Devil, heaving the crate of vodka on his back.

"It won't fit on the moped," I say.

"Yes it will," says Devil.

I'm about to jump off the lorry when I notice a box full of packets of Jammy Dodgers. I feel as sick as a dog but can't bring myself to leave them behind.

So we end up leaving the lorry in the field. We've made a mess, but most of the crates are untouched. I'm really annoyed that we forgot to bring any bags. We pull the moped out of the ditch and push it to the road. Devil lets me drive. He sits behind me, swigging vodka, the crate with the remaining bottles balanced on his lap. The plastic jabs into my spine. My Jammy Dodgers are tied to the back of the bike. I hope they don't fall off. I hate leaving that lovely lorry. The stuff inside could feed my family for years.

We motor home over the wet roads. We're in a good mood, shouting and laughing. What a job! I can't believe everything went so well. (Apart from getting stuck in the mud and forgetting to bring any bags with us.)

When I get home I leave three packets of Jammy Dodgers in the kitchen for Gran.

I leave a chocolate bar on Mum's bed.

See what a nice fellow I am?

The evening passed and no one came knocking on my door.

I thought we'd got away with it.

Five

I'm ill that night. I only puke a few times but my stomach hurts and I feel sick. I don't want to move. Why did I eat all that crap? Can you die of sugar poisoning? But when I wake in the morning, I feel fine. I think I might go to school. I'm not going to bump into any police there. Besides, I don't want to get behind, do I?

I open my door at seven thirty a.m. and pick up the pile of freshly ironed clothes I know will be waiting on the carpet: blazer, shirt, trousers, black socks, shiny black school shoes and tartan boxers. Gran does this every morning in the hope that I'm going to school. The boxers I can do without. I put on my black CK ones instead. The shoes I have never worn, ever. Gran came home with them two years ago and I haven't even bothered to try them on. They are three sizes too small now. Gran knows this. I reckon she likes to think that she's doing all she can to keep me on track, but there's no point in wasting money on shoes I'll never wear. I put the shoes out for the bin man a year or so ago, but the very next day they appeared back next to my pile of school clothes. I always wear my trainers to school. The teachers don't say anything about them. Mine are pretty skanky after yesterday so I have to make do with an older pair.

My finger looks messy this morning. There's white and yellow pockets of stuff on it and it's oozing pus. I give it a quick sniff but it doesn't smell bad. I wash it carefully in warm water and TCP and put a new bandage on. It's hurting less and I'm getting used to not using it. I'm managing on only a couple of paracetamol a day now. I'm not worried about Gran sussing out they're missing, she'll just think Mum's been at them.

I sit on the kitchen stool and give Gran my most charming smile as I want her to cook me breakfast.

"You need a shower," she says. "You stink."

"You look beautiful today, Gran," I say.

Gran tries not to smile. "Have a shower," she says.

"I will if you cook me breakfast," I say. "I'll have a bath this evening."

"Baths are a waste of the planet's resources," says my eco-gran.

She turns her back on me and for a moment I think I've lucked out. Then she bends and opens the cupboard.

"One egg or two?" she says.

I've brushed the baked beans out of my teeth and am about to leave when Gran stuffs something into my pocket.

"It arrived last week," she says. "I was going to give it to you when you started to behave yourself."

It's a letter.

"You can't do that, Gran. It's my property."

"Aren't you going to open it?"

Have I mentioned that there is absolutely no point in arguing with my grandmama?

"I expect you've steamed it open already, knowing you," I say.

"It's from America," she says. She's obviously dying to know what's inside.

"Gran," I say, stepping down on to the garden path. "I don't want to be late for school."

My convict has written again. I hope he's not sending me death threats because I haven't replied yet.

"Don't go falling for a Yank," yells Gran, from the doorstep. "A good English girl is what you need."

"Later, Gran."

The thought of the letter in my pocket makes me feel slightly sick. I wish I hadn't started this. I thought it would be a laugh, but already I feel like I owe this bloke something and I don't like it.

There's loads of people about this morning; kids on their way to school, mums with buggies. I walk in the road so they don't get in my way.

I spy Lexi Juby stepping out of her house. She looks great, all done up in her school uniform. She smiles when she sees me.

"LEXI."

And there, in broad daylight, is Juby-the-Killer standing on the doorstep. "Don't forget my fags," he says. He sees me and gives me such a look that I keep right on walking. I don't want to be looked at by Juby. It's best to remain unseen and undetected. Particularly if you are interested in his daughter.

Lexi is a year younger than me and I may have mentioned she's very fit. I was embarrassed the other day. I was round at Devil's (when his dad was out) and I was only wearing my shorts because Devil had poured ketchup down my trousers for a laugh, and Lexi came in. She saw my skinny legs. I nearly jumped out of the window. I hate my legs. They look like they belong to a little kid.

"Hullo, Chas."

I turn round, pretending I've only just noticed her. I glance back at her house but Juby's gone back inside.

"Where's Devil?" I ask, because I don't know what else to say. Lexi shrugs, a movement which lifts her fantastic boobs.

"In bed," she says. I bet she thinks I can't do anything without my big sidekick. She eyes up my uniform. "Are you going to school or is this just to fool your gran?"

"Nothing fools my gran," I say, falling into step with her.

She removes her blazer and catches me gawping.

"Hot, isn't it?" I mumble, my face burning.

"Can I see your hand?" asks Lexi.

This might put her off altogether but if she wants to see it, how can I refuse? I hold out my hand, pleased I put the nice fresh dressing on it this morning. Ever so gently, Lexi takes my hand and holds it close to her face.

"How come it hasn't gone bad?" she asks.

I shrug. She's touching me! She's holding my hand! Even so, I'm nervous. What if Juby-the-Killer sees?

I whip my hand away.

"I think Devlin's got your finger," she says. "He was messing around with some vinegar the other night. I saw something small and gross in a jam jar. I asked him what it was, but he hid it." She looks at me suspiciously. "He was drunk last night."

I nod. I knew Devil had it. It's the sort of sick thing he'd do. I'm not surprised. But I don't like Lexi Juby telling me my finger is gross. It is, after all, a severed finger. Anybody's severed finger would be gross, even Lexi Juby's. I'm not happy with Devil. If he'd handed it back to me at the time, I could have gone to hospital and they'd have sewed it back on for me. Now I'm going to miss a fingertip for the rest of my life.

We arrive at the school gates at five to nine. Several bystanders watch jealously as I stroll in with Lexi. Lots of women are quite ugly when you get up close, but Lexi has this amazing clear skin, apart from one tiny zit on her cheek which looks like a beauty spot anyway. She's got long dark hair which swings around in a sheet. It shines and smells of perfume. Lexi's got good legs and a tight ass. She's smart too, and friendly. She's not put off walking into school with me because I'm mates with her brother.

"So what's special about today?" she asks in her sexy voice.

"Whaddya mean?"

"This." She points at the school building. "How come you're here today?"

I nod and smile. "I've come to learn, young woman," I say. "What else?"

I sometimes wonder what it would be like to be one of the kids who comes every day, on time, clean and tidy, in proper shoes. Someone like Connor Blacker, who goes to chess club and studies extra maths at lunch times. However, I show up most weeks because I want to get some exams. I quite fancy the idea of college. I don't want to leave school one day and sign on the next.

First thing, I have an art lesson. I like art, even though it usually ends up with a paint fight. Today, we are given two pots of paint, I get blue and red, and we are told to paint the simplest thing we can think of. I think of a circle. But it's hard. I'm covering this sheet of paper in blue and red circles. It's fun. I like the sweet smell of the paint. I like the way the paint leaves my brush. I even like my wobbly circles. They're off kilter . . . like me. And as the teacher doesn't have any smart remarks, and no kid tries to paint my face, I leave everyone alone and get on with my imperfect circles. I hope I'm not turning into a hippy.

I decide to bunk the next lesson. It's geography. The only geography I'm interested in is a map of Lexi Juby's body. I don't want to skip off the whole day and I want to read my letter, so I go into the girls' loos and lock myself in. It's all right in here. There's flowers painted on the walls and, unlike the boy's bogs, the locks on the doors work. They've even got proper soft bog roll in here. You only get tracing paper to wipe your bum in the boy's bogs. That's sex discrimination that is. I settle myself on the pink and purple bog and reach for my letter.

Lousiana State Penitentiary
Dear Caroline, I mean Chas,
Looks like you're not going to write back. Each
morning when the guard comes round my first
thought is, "Will there be a letter?" As I expect,
there never is. Very well, I shall give up hope.
Ergo, unless I hear from you, this is my last letter.
Maybe you're finding it hard to write to a dead
man walking but just tell me about yourself.
Exercise your writing talent. Anything, no matter
how trivial, is of interest to me, especially about
real people living in the real world. Listen to your
heart and show me somebody cares. Otherwise,
I'm lost. Now I'm going to sign off. Exit Lenny
from the life of Chas.
Yours truthfully,
Lenny Darling

I feel like a right shit. It's not that I haven't been meaning to write to him. It's just that I've been busy worrying about my finger, nicking articulated lorries, and hanging out with Devil and his lovely sister. I've also been trying not to worry that my mother has started wearing lipstick. But I should have written back.

I've still got half an hour before break, so I tear out the back page from my English book and start writing.

Dear Lenny,
I've not written because I've been busy. (I expect time goes slower for you than for me!) My mother needs a lot of looking after. She's sixty-eight and pretty decrepit.

(If Gran knew I'd said this about her, she'd kill me.)

My son has taken up a lot of my time. He likes to take me to the cinema.

(Mum is scared of the cinema. She says the flickering lights and the dark mess with her medication.)

Mark is doing very well in school. They've made him captain of his year.

(My English book must be giving me inspiration.)

He's also entered a bodybuilding competition.
He's always doing his weights and working out. I
don't expect you get much chance to exercise in
there. You must be pretty annoyed if you think
you're innocent and you've been locked up for
ten years. What a bummer. Do you think they'll
actually go through with, you-know-what?

I thought I'd better not say it too bluntly or I might hurt
his feelings.

I hope you have a good lawyer. Do they have legal
aid in the US?

I know about legal aid because I've needed it a few
times myself and I reckon talking about it makes me
seem more grown up.

Did you have a car before you got locked up? I
drive an E-type Jag myself. I get some looks at the
traffic lights and it burns the gas, but it's a
smooth ride.

The morning-break bell rings and I decide that will do.
I sign off, but then remember something else.

PS Mark's girlfriend's name is Juby, not Tuby, so
it's not the name you remember.

I fold the letter away. I'll post it during lunch break.

I go to my maths lesson because I can't think of anything else to do.

"Do my eyes deceive me?"

My maths teacher, Mr Fuller, is in a witty mood. "Is that really you, Chas Parsons?"

"No sir, it's my evil twin," I say.

Fuller pretends he hasn't heard me. "Is there a blue moon?" He opens the blind and looks out. "Is the wind coming in from space? Is there an eclipse of two suns?"

"Ha, ha, sir," I say. "How about you do your job and teach us something."

A couple of the girls giggle.

"Mr Parsons. I'm honoured you could be with us for the first time in," he checks the register, "four days." He comes and stands next to me. "You've got to keep up," he says. "Especially with exams coming up."

"Well get on with it then," I say. I am feeling uncomfortable about all the attention. Usually I'd be smartarsing him and trying to make everyone laugh. Now I just want him to leave me alone. I wonder if it is because of the letter in my pocket.

Listen to your heart and show me somebody cares.

It's pretty sad. I can't stop thinking about it.

"What happened to your finger?" asks Fuller, clocking my bandage. He's the first person to notice.

"I wore it out doing my homework," I say.

"Have you had it checked out?" he asks.

God! I wish he'd leave me alone. "It's only a scratch." I add, "I'm not a girl, sir."

Connor Blacker sniggers and Fuller makes a noise like "Tssskkk," and to my relief he moves off and starts handing out revision sheets. I glance at mine. It looks hard, but not impossible. If I'm friendly with Connor Blacker for a bit, give him some fags, swipe him a T-shirt, he'd get me back up to speed. See what a swot I really am?

So here I am, looking studiously at my maths revision, working out ways I can catch up and having every intention of attending school again this afternoon, when I spot a bluish light flickering on the ceiling. I watch it dart all over the place. A patch of light wavers just above Fuller's head. I turn my head to look out of the window.

A panda car has pulled into the staff car park. The blue lights are flashing and it's not even rush hour. I look around the class to see if anyone else has noticed. Connor Blacker shoots me a grin and this kid, Daryl Peabody, looks terrified. Then I realize it's because Fuller is handing out the test results.

I watch the fuzzies get out of their car. There are two of them. Shit! It's Panda Polly and her buddy: The Stealth. I try to relax. If they're looking for me, they're hardly going to start in school, are they? It's not like I'm here every day.

Panda Polly is a police officer, and she has the honour of being the first person ever to nick me. (I was four years old and robbing an Incredible Hulk from the corner shop.) She's been on my case ever since. Her and her partner, The Stealth.

I watch them wind their way to the school reception. By now the other kids have noticed them and Maggie Allen and Emily Dogwood run to the window.

"All right, all right," says Fuller. "It's not like you lot haven't seen a policeman before." I swear he gives me this look. "Settle down. Let's talk about exponential curves."

But the girls don't budge.

"They're here for the stranger-danger talk for Year Seven," says Fuller. "So sit down."

Maggie and Emily go back to their seats and the lesson continues. I'm getting bored after ten minutes. I'm wondering whether I will stay in school this afternoon. But it's drama after lunch, and that's always good for a laugh. It's not really work. The teacher just makes us do all these little plays and pretend to be oppressed people and. . .

Panda Polly and The Stealth walk into the room.

I look around the class to see if anyone looks scared. But nobody seems worried at all. In fact, everyone looks pleased because this means the lesson will be interrupted for a few minutes.

Oh God. They're here for me. They've found out about the lorry.

Panda Polly goes and talks in Fuller's ear.

"Is it really necessary?" Fuller says. "Can't it wait? I'm trying to educate these kids."

Connor Blacker winks at me. The whole class knows that I'm the one the police are here for. I fiddle with my pencil and pretend to be deeply interested in my revision sheet. Oh yes, I am a studious boy, who loves his maths and never ever gets into troub. . .

"Parsons," says Fuller, and I swear he looks like he's sorry for me. "These police officers would like a word with you."

I don't move. "Fire away, chaps," I say.

The Stealth closes his eyes. I've seen him do this before. It means he is trying not to lose his temper. How did they find out? Nobody saw us except the bloke with the dog. They don't know I did it. I just have to stay cool.

"Outside, now," says The Stealth.

"You'd better bring your stuff," adds Panda Polly.

This isn't sounding good.

"I'm in school," I protest. "When I'm out, you put me in, and now I'm in, you're taking me out. No wonder the youth of today is confused."

I'm being mouthy, but I'm crapping myself. I put my stuff in my school bag, folding my revision sheet so the edges exactly match. What if something has happened to Gran? Or Mum? Or even Stephen, my other brother? He's working the fishing boats in Aberdeen. Maybe he's fallen off and drowned.

"Move it," says The Stealth.

No, he wouldn't talk to me like that if he had bad news.

For once the whole class is quiet.

"Nice knowing you." I grin and I am marched out by the pigs.

"What's all. . .?"

"Shut it," says The Stealth.

I can't shut it yet, though it would probably be wise.

"Hello, doll," I say to Panda Polly. "Fancy a date?" She looks at me. She's tiny but she's nails.

"Don't go there, Chas," she says.

I am about to make a witty reply, but instead I close my mouth. I don't go there. I'm marched through the school corridor. I get glimpses through the doors of all the other kids busy messing around and winding up their teachers. I even see Lexi Juby and ugly Debs having a history lesson. Lexi seems to be asleep, her head resting on her palm.

She looks beautiful when she's asleep.

The Stealth squares up in the car park.

"Chas Parsons, we are arresting you on the charge of vehicle theft and robbery. You have the right to remain silent. . ."

I can see all these kids lining the windows of their classrooms. I wave like I'm Elvis and I hear a cheer. But then The Stealth bundles me in the back of the panda.

Gran really is going to kick me out this time.

"Got anything to eat?" I ask, just for the hell of it. In

my experience, most coppers have a whole stash of chocolate and crisps in their pig-mobiles. Coppers do a lot of hanging around. You know old grannies that go, "Why isn't there a policeman round when you want one?" Well it's not because the police are underfunded or whatever, it's because they're all sitting in their nice air-conditioned motors scoffing sweets. Why else do you think they're so hyperactive?

But The Stealth isn't giving me anything. He swerves to avoid a supermarket delivery van.

"Want me to drive?" I ask. "You seem to need a hand." Despite my bravado, I'm terrified. "What's all this about?" I ask innocently. My finger is hurting. I've been picking at it under the bandage.

"You tell us," says Panda Polly. She twists her small body round in her seat to look at me. "You've been doing so well, Chas, and now you've messed it all up again. A lorry? What came over you?"

I decide to exercise my right to remain silent.

PART TWO

Six

I get a sea view. I watch the waves hammering the pebbles through the reinforced glass window of my cell.

It's one week later and I'm on remand in a young offenders' institute. There wasn't any room in a proper Youth Remand prison so I've ended up here. No one has told me what has happened to Devil. He didn't turn up at the Youth Court, so anything could have happened. I think I'm going to be here for a long time because they haven't given me a date for my court case and Gran is refusing to cough up the bail money. She hasn't spoken to me since I was arrested and she didn't come to court for my initial hearing. I've spoken to Mum on the phone and she said Gran puts her fingers in her ears whenever my name is mentioned. Gran doesn't like it when I get into trouble. She tries to blank it out, whereas I think Mum expects me to get up to stuff.

I'm in secure accommodation because I've got a bit of a record behind me. To be honest, I've been in trouble so much I'm surprised I haven't been sent down before. This is what happens when you go to school. I should have stayed at home; Gran never lets the police in. I gave

Panda Polly my letter for Lenny Darling and asked her to post it for me. She gave me a bit of look when she read the address, but didn't say anything. I hope she does post it. But you can never trust a policeman – or woman.

The escort officer drove me here and I admit I felt pretty scared as we passed through the electronic gates and up the driveway towards this massive ugly building. At reception another bloke took my name and showed me into a room with brown walls, a tiny barred window and a stained green carpet. There were three chairs. I picked up the one which wasn't broken and dragged it to the corner of the room. Then I sat and waited. I had nothing to eat, nothing to drink and nothing to do. I pulled my chair up to the window and tried to look out, but the glass was all frosted and dirty. I got back down again. Sat back on my chair.

There was a poster stuck to the wall.

BEVANPORT HAS **ZERO TOLERENCE** TO BULLYING

IF YOU ARE BEING BULLIED

TELL YOUR KEY WORKER OR

TELL SOMEONE YOU TRUST

IF YOU ARE A BULLY

YOU WON'T GET AWAY WITH IT

IF YOU ARE THINKING OF HARMING YOURSELF

DON'T DO IT

TELL SOMEONE

WE CAN HELP YOU

Things didn't look too promising.

I must have read that poster a thousand times before I decided to find out if they had forgotten me. I opened the door, but before I had even put my foot out, the reception bloke yelled:

"GET BACK INSIDE."

I stepped back and chose a different chair for a bit of variety. Was this my cell? I wondered. Was anyone ever going to come? Wasn't I even going to get a bed?

After one long hour, I opened the door.

"I SAID GET BACK. . ."

"I need a piss," I said, putting my head round the door as slowly as if I was worried about snipers.

"YOU NEED A PISS, WHAT?"

That was easy. I could do that one. "I need a piss, sir," I said. At least school was good for something.

"LEFT, LEFT, FOUR MINUTES," shouted the bloke.

I hesitated. Did he mean it was four minutes away or did he mean I only had four. . .?

"NOW," shouted the bloke.

So off I went. I wondered why he was shouting at me. I was, after all, on remand. I was innocent until proven guilty. Maybe he had me mixed up with someone else.

I was back in that room in three minutes and forty-eight seconds. I paced up and down the room and listened to my stomach rumble. I was so hungry I felt faint. I would have given anything for a burger, or a chocolate bar, or even, God forbid, a plate of Gran's microwave pasta.

I don't know when I fell asleep, but I remember dreaming about drinking lemonade from a massive bowl. Anyway I opened my eyes, looked at my watch and it said 17:45.

I opened the door.

"Can I help you?" This time, there was an old bloke with a silver moustache behind the reception desk. He seemed a bit friendlier than the other bloke.

"Yes," I said, looking around for the scary one. "I'm Chas Parsons, I've been waiting for three hours and I'm starving."

Moustache-man checked his clipboard, gave me a cup of tea and a bag of crisps and sent me back to the waiting room. I drained the tea and ploughed through the crisps, turning the bag inside out, looking for crumbs. Then I screwed it up and threw it at the window. I examined my finger. It looked pretty gross and the skin was all pale where I had kept it bandaged. It had this massive scab thing on the end. But it had stopped pussing and wasn't swollen any more. The nasty white pockets of fluid had dried up and I couldn't see the stringy bits. I shut my eyes and tried to go back to sleep.

I was in that room for five hours.

When someone finally came to collect me, I was really pissed off. I was hot, scared, tired and very hungry. The prison officer led me through loads of doors and corridors and he had a mass of keys hanging from his belt, just like in the films. He took me to another room and I had an interview. One of the questions was *Have you ever tried to harm yourself?*

Jeez. This place was freaky. The prison officer took my watch, my money, my keys, everything that I had left.

Then came the really horrible bit.

I was strip-searched.

I don't want to think about it actually. But there were two blokes, one doing the searching and one just standing there. They tried to make a joke of it, but I wasn't laughing. I've never felt so shit in my whole life. They took the dressing off my finger and everything. When they'd finished, the plaster didn't stick back properly so I had to keep smoothing it down. When it was all over, I was so relieved, I admit, I nearly cried. But I didn't.

They gave me prison clothes to put on. It's like these grey trousers, a T-shirt and a sweatshirt. I even got prison shoes, socks and pants. It's all disgusting. I look well lamby. I hope Lexi doesn't ever see me like this.

Next I had to have a medical examination. It was about eight o'clock in the evening and I was knackered.

Doctor (looking at my hand): "What's this?"
Me: "Nothing."
Doctor: "Take it off."
(I take the dressing off.)
Doctor: "Urrgh."
Me: "Thanks."
Doctor: "When did this happen?"
Me: "Dunno, three or four weeks ago."

71

Doctor:	*"How?"*
Me:	*"My hamster bit it off."*

PAUSE.

Doctor:	*"Do you think you're funny?"*
Me:	*"Yes."*
Doctor:	*"You're wrong."*

He said I was very lucky it hadn't got infected, and asked me if it still hurt and I said, "Yes," even though it isn't that bad any more. And he said he couldn't give me any paracetamol in case I hoarded them and took an overdose. Then he said to let him know immediately if it went red, or hot, or hurt a lot, or started weeping, or if I felt dizzy. I was surprised he was so cool about it. I thought he'd be rushing me to hospital and having plastic surgeons make me a new electronic finger or something. But no, he washed it, and re-dressed it, and gave me a pack of bandages, TCP and plasters and said to keep looking after it the way I was doing and it would be fine. I suppose a prison doctor has probably seen worse than my missing finger.

I thought after all that I'd finally get shown to my cell, but yet another prison officer led me to another room with wall-to-wall lockers and cupboards. This bloke looked like he could be Juby's older brother. He had the same build and the same "don't mess" look in his eye. He asked if I was a smoker. I said no, because I didn't want a lecture, and he went to this cupboard and gave me this bag.

"Here's your welcome pack," he said. "Make it last."

Inside was a Mars bar, a Snickers, £2.50, a phone card with the value of £2.00, a toothbrush, a small bar of soap and sachets of toothpaste and shampoo.

I learned later if I'd said I was a smoker, he'd have given me some baccy instead of the sweets. I was really hungry and started to unwrap the Mars bar.

"Put it away or I'll bin it," said the guard. The way he said it made me put it straight back in the bag.

I was led outside through a courtyard enclosed on four sides by five-storey buildings with rows and rows of barred windows. It felt nice to have some fresh air on my face after my time in that waiting room. It was a warm evening and the sun was just beginning to go down. All the gang would be hanging out by the canal. The girls wouldn't be wearing very much because it was so warm.

"WHAT YOU IN FOR?"

I looked up. I saw an arm waving out of a high window.

"WHO ARE YOU?"

Another hand was waving at me from a window on the corner of the building.

Then something hit me and a massive cheer went up. Then it was like people were shouting from all the windows.

"WHAT'S YOUR NAME?"

"ARE YOU GAY?"

I looked down and saw I'd been hit by a Coke can.

There was cheering and jeering and shouting all around me. Hands waving from windows, knocking on the bars.

"GOT ANY BACCY?"

"FRAGGLE, HE'S A FRAGGLE."

I quickened my step behind the prison guard and dodged another missile. This time it was a bog roll.

"GIVE US A SONG."

I could feel all these eyes on me and I felt my cheeks turning red.

It was like that film, *Gladiator*, when the bloke is in the arena with all the crowd screaming for blood.

"WHERE'VE YOU COME FROM?"

I was glad to get back inside.

Finally I was shown in my cell. To my relief, there was no one else in it.

The door locked behind me and I slumped on the floor. I sat there for ages. I didn't feel like myself, my legs and arms ached and felt heavy. I put my head in between my knees and shut my eyes.

It wasn't a good night for Chas Parsons.

I come away from the window and sit on the bed, which is bolted to the wall. It has a thin, lumpy mattress. My room contains: a metal bog with no seat, a sink with one tap (cold water only), a desk and chair, strip lighting which hurts my eyes, and a couple of shelves for my stuff. I have two pairs of prison trousers, three T-shirts, three pairs of prison boxers, ditto socks, one prison jacket, and one postcard (shaped like a puffin) Blu-tacked to the wall.

I also have a plastic cup and a paper plate with a ginger biscuit. There is no TV and no hi-fi. Loads of kids have got radios, I haven't. Everyone plays theirs so loud I don't need one anyway. I also have a pen and some paper, a box of bandages and some TCP. This is all I have in here apart from the stuff in my "welcome" pack. I'm in "Cotswold", one of the four blocks which enclose the courtyard. There are about fifty lads in my block, aged between fourteen and eighteen. Some are remand prisoners, like me, but most are serving sentences. I'm so bored I'm going bananas. I've been here one week and so far I've managed to keep my head down. I've tried to make myself look invisible. I don't want any trouble. All I have to do is survive. I hate to admit it, but I'm scared. I don't know how things work in here. The other kids know I'm new, but nobody has tried anything. Not yet. I'm not as depressed as I was the first night, but I don't seem to have any energy and I can't think of anything to say to anyone. It's like my sense of humour has shut right down and all I want to do is sleep. I'm getting my days and nights mixed up because I spend so much of the day asleep in my cell that I'm wide awake at night, pacing my cell and watching the navy boats sail out of the harbour.

I thought I would just get another Youth Justice order or some nice fun time with someone right on, who would teach me to be a better person while we fixed stolen bicycles together. Instead I'm banged up here at Bevanport, which has the reputation of being one of the nastiest young offenders' institutes in the country. One of Devil's mates got sent here a year ago and apparently he had a really hard time. I still haven't got a date for my court appearance. Remand prisoners are supposed to be treated better than those who have been sentenced. I haven't seen any evidence of that yet.

I keep thinking about Devil. My solicitor said he would probably get off lighter than me because he didn't actually drive the lorry on the highway. That's so unfair; he was gagging to drive it. I just wouldn't let him. This is the reward I get for standing up for myself.

In three hours' time is Soc, which means I can either take a shower, go to the gym, go to the library, or make a phone call.

I decide to make a phone call. You'd think it would be easy, wouldn't you? You just put your card in, and tap out the number and hey ho, off you go. Not in prison you don't.

When the bell goes for Soc, my door is unlocked and I belt out of my cell and along the landing. There are three phones on my block and they're on my landing but only two of them work. There is already a queue of eight lads when I get there.

I look behind me, and see more people coming so I join the end of the queue. No one says much. We are all too busy listening to the lads' phone conversations, which aren't very interesting but there's nothing else to do.

This morning I had my drugs assessment, which I quite enjoyed because I met Snoopy, the sniffer dog. He's a brown mongrel with massive eyes. The screws were going on about how he can sniff out blow from three blocks, but he just spent the time licking my hand when I scratched his belly. I was quite sad when they took him away. I had to give them some of my piss so they could check it. I wonder if all the paracetamol I've been necking for my finger will show up. I wasn't too worried about the assessment because I'm not really into any of that. My older brother, Selby, he was a bit trigger happy with the class As, Bs and Cs and look where it got him.

There's only two people in the phone queue now and we've still got ten minutes of Soc. I should make it.

"You've had your four," says this boy to this kid who is on the phone.

The kid presses the phone closer to his face and puts his finger in his ear.

"I love you, baby," he says and the rest of us snigger. Imagine that was me, talking to Lexi.

You'll stay true to me, won't you, Lexi?

Oh yes, Chas, my darling, you'll be out soon.

Just then a boy pushes in front of me.

"Oy," I say.

He turns to face me and I bite my lip. It's Simon Avery. He's a head case and the buddy of Kieran Greedy, who is the Big Man round here. I've seen these two at recreation. They stick together. They make trouble. They are bad news. Kieran is in for robbery (same as me) and grievous bodily harm (definitely not the same as me). He did over a schoolteacher for his credit card. Nice. Simon is in for being an accessory to an armed robbery. His cousin took a gun into an amusement arcade and Simon was on lookout. I've found out a lot of information in the last week. I've had to. It's necessary for my survival. No one likes to get on the wrong side of Kieran. But this is Simon, and he has just pushed in front of me, and everyone is waiting to see what, I, the new boy, will do about it. Everyone will make their minds up about me based on what I do next. If I let him in the queue, I will be a target for everyone and I won't make it out of here alive.

Besides, I want to talk to my gran.

"Are you confused?" I ask politely. 'This is not the end of the queue.'

Everyone goes quiet. Even the lads on the phones are watching. I check Simon's pockets. I can't see a knife, not yet.

"Get stuffed," says Simon, and turns back.

I tap him on the shoulder.

He turns back with his fist ready but I'm too quick. Now one good thing about being mates with Devil is that you learn how to fight. Dev is always getting into scraps in town. He has also had to defend himself from his old man when he's pissed and looking for a fight. And I've been standing alongside him too many times myself. I'm not the kind of boy to run away. I hate running. So I smack Simon hard in the nose with my fist (the one with all the fingers intact) with an uphander. Simon's face does not like this, and it starts to bleed even before Simon falls over.

I wonder if Simon will pound me to death. I am expecting him to come back at me and I square up. Everyone clears a space and waits. But Simon doesn't go for me. Instead he coughs, straightens up and gives me a look.

"You're a dead man," he says.

And he's gone.

Silence.

"Respect," says this big guy in front of me, and he gives me a smack on the back. "He's had that coming." He gives me a look. "Wouldn't want to be you though."

I feel brilliant at first. I've come off well and now people will think twice before having a go. But my buzz quickly goes. I know the comeback won't be very pretty. Ronald the screw comes ambling by, and checks us over and we all stand nice and polite as Girl Guides at the church fête.

I get to make my call.

– Hi Gran, it's me.
– Who's me?
– Chas.
SILENCE.
– Is that you, Chas?
– Yes, Gran.

79

– Where are you?

– In the nick, Gran.

SILENCE.

– You've disappointed me, Chas.

– I know, Gran. How's Mum?

– She split up with the gardener because she's so embarrassed about you. I'm ashamed to go to the club any more. You should hear Dolores going on. I'll never hear the end of it. I didn't bring you up to behave like this.

– Right, Gran.

– Don't bother coming home, Chas. No grandson of mine gets locked up.

– OK, Gran.

– You're a lorry jacker, that's what Dolores said.

– You ate the Jammy Dodgers though, Gran.

– What's that?

– The Jammy. . . Oh, don't worry.

– I won't.

– Have you seen Devil?

– Devil by name, Devil by nature. He's the one that got you into this. I mean it Chas; I won't have you back in my house after this.

– All right, Gran, I won't come back. Bye.

– Chas?

I put the phone down and walk back to my cell.

I wish I hadn't bothered.

Seven

It's recreation time, but after tea I came straight back to my cell. I don't fancy joining the crowd in the games room. There's TV, table tennis and table football, but it's always really busy, and everyone's talking so loud you can't hear the TV anyway. Besides, I haven't made any mates yet, everyone is still sussing me out, and I want to keep out of the way of a certain double-act. I'm beginning to get used to the routine. After breakfast in the canteen, we get twenty minutes' Soc before we're locked up for a couple of hours, then it's gym or education for an hour, then lunch. Then the long afternoon lock-up, which is the killer. Tea is at 5.00 p.m., followed by one and a half hours of recreation with the night lockdown at 7.30 p.m. As I'm new I'm getting extra outings for all the tests they do on new inmates. My educational assessment was a laugh. The questions were so easy I nearly didn't do them at all. But mainly I sleep. I open my eyes and don't know if three hours or two minutes have passed until I make myself roll over to look at the clock. Most of the time I don't bother. I just close my eyes and go back to sleep again.

Today, however, I am more alert than usual. I think

something is going to happen. It's not going to be good. I hear shouts coming from the games room. Someone has probably nicked the ping-pong balls. One thing I have learned is that the screws here have even less humour than the police at home. You have to call them sir (or ma'am) and they're big on stuff like having a tidy cell and clean shoes. It's like being in the army without any of the fun.

I'm thirsty. I'm just working myself up to getting off the bed and fetching a drink when my door is pushed open.

I've been waiting for two days for this.

Kieran and Simon walk in. The moment has arrived.

I look up from my magazine, pretending to be Mr Cool.

"Hello, gentlemen," I say. "I'll ring for some tea."

"Got a fag?" asks Kieran, ignoring my devastating wit.

"Nope," I say swinging my feet round to the floor.

"He hasn't got a fag," says Kieran to Simon. He sticks his hands in his pockets and starts looking round my cell. According to my watch it is ten past seven. In twenty minutes the bell will go and that will be the end of Rec. After that, we'll be banged up in our cells for another hour until tea time. I have to stay alive until this time.

"You ain't got much stuff," says Kieran.

"No," I say.

Simon sits on my bed and puts his feet on my pillow. "Got a girlfriend?" he asks.

"Yes," I say, and I wish I hadn't.

"Name?"

"Lexi." (I wish.)

"She a tart?"

I grin. "Sometimes."

God, Juby would kill me if he knew.

"Lexi, who?" asks Simon.

I stand up.

"Take your dirty feet off my bed," I say softly. Listen to me. Really I'm terrified, but you can't be a flower boy with nutters like these.

"What's that?" Simon really can't believe what he just heard.

"Do you want me to say it again?"

I wish I was bigger. I'm not small but I'm way too skinny. These two are going to paste me good and proper.

"He was disrespectful," says Simon, looking up at Kieran, who is pretending to look out of the window.

Kieran sighs and turns. He looks at me and I wonder if the last things I'll see are his crazy eyes.

I get off the bed slowly. I never meant it to end this way. I'm holding my stomach tight, like if I hold it hard enough, when they stab me they won't be able to get the knife in. Maybe I should crack another joke to loosen them up. Then they'll realize I'm just one of the guys and. . .

Whatever hilarious thing I am about to say is lost as my lips are pushed into my mouth at the end of a big hard fist.

I taste the blood before I feel the pain. I have white

rectangles in front of my eyes. I need a minute or two before I can even begin to think about fighting back. OUCH. Another punch. This time, in the guts. I am winded. I gasp for breath, but I can't let myself fall to the floor. Kieran kicks me in the legs next. It floors me and I'm in pain. I curl up in a ball to protect myself.

"See you around," says Kieran and walks out of my cell.

Simon looks hard at me.

"Think you're a hard man, eh? Next time, you're dead."

And he clears his throat and makes to spit on my pillow.

But I don't let him.

I fly up off the floor and push him away.

"GET OUT," I shout, through all the blood. "GET OUT, GET OUT."

This is when the screw, Ronnie, comes along to see what all the fuss is about. He sees us standing there: me with my face all bloody and Simon with his fists out and he blows his whistle.

In seconds the cell seems to be full of screws and I am pinned on the floor, my arms forced behind my back and locked in cuffs. They knock my finger as they are doing this and it hurts worse than where Kieran punched me. The concrete floor is biting into my face. This is called a "restraint". I'm shocked at how helpless I feel. Also surprised how violently the screws react.

So I'm on the floor next to Simon. We eyeball each other.

"What happened?" asks Ronnie.

"He tripped," says Simon.

My dodgy finger is hurting. I want to check it out. It feels like it is bleeding again.

I am pulled into a sitting position.

"So you tripped?" asks Ronnie. "What on? Thin air?"

Usually I'd come out with some smart-arse remark at this, but I can't. It's like there's nothing inside me. I sigh heavily.

"I tripped," I say.

It's night time. We're all banged up and everything's quiet except Ronnie is playing his bloody awful music in the staff room. He has terrible taste. He plays all this creepy stuff. Like Des O'Connor or something. Stuff even my gran wouldn't like. It's sick. I hate listening to it. There's this one song Ronnie plays over and over again. There's this line in it.

And maybe one day, I'll be in your dreams again.

It goes high at the end, on the word "again". I find myself humming it all the time, especially at night, when I can't sleep. I just have that one line going round and round my head.

And maybe one day, you'll be in my dreams again.

And maybe one day, you'll be in my dreams again.

And then I swap it round, for variety.

And maybe one day, I'll be in your dreams again.

And maybe one day, I'll be in your dreams again.

I try to stop myself thinking it and singing it to myself, but I can't. And even though Ronnie isn't playing that particular track right now, I can't stop hearing that line in my head. I wonder if this is all part of the punishment. They're trying to break us down. I'll be as mental as my mum when I get out of here.

I don't like prison. There's nothing to do, nowhere to go, and no Lexi Juby. I have been here three weeks and I have one fat lip, one bruised stomach, and zits like you wouldn't believe. It's the food. It's even worse than Gran's cooking. I swear I've lost a stone already. I keep thinking about Gran, how she said I wasn't to come home. I know she didn't mean it, but I was so fed up, after all the strife I'd been through, she didn't have a nice thing to say to me. It would serve her right if I didn't go home. But maybe she doesn't give a shit anyway. She hasn't written to me, no one has. And no one has visited me either. I look like a right loner. It's hard to make any mates in here because we're banged up for most of the day. I get on all right with Marshall, the bloke from the phone queue, but we're not exactly mates. He's just someone I can kick the ball at in gym.

When you're stuck in a place like this you really want some proof that someone in the outside world gives a toss. Since I've been banged up the only thing I've had is the puffin postcard, which I swear smells of fish, from Stephen in Scotland, saying, "Don't hang in there." Har har. I suppose he's referring to the two suicides that have happened here earlier this year. Stephen always had a pretty sick sense of humour. Even I remember that and I only really knew him as a kid. The youngest suicide was fifteen, same as me. The rumour is, he didn't hang himself. The rumour is the screws did it, because he was a cocky bugger, also like me.

I'd like to see someone. Even Mum. She'd talk about blind dates and Gran's knees. She'd talk about Stephen as if he was next door and Selby as if he was still alive. She wouldn't mention my dad or ask me what my plans are when I get out. She'd forget to bring me any money, food or fags. But I'd still like to see her. It's not her fault she's useless. What I'd really like is a visit from my brother, Stephen, but he's not going to come back. I'm on my own.

A screw snaps open the door viewer, and looks me over. I can tell it's Ronnie by his breathing. The flap snaps closed and I turn over. There's no privacy here. I play with the knobbly end of joint where Devil cut off my finger. It's been bothering me ever since the fight. It worries me. The wound has begun to weep again. There's yellow pus and it throbs. I pick at it, squeezing the pus.

The door is being unlocked. Hey ho, maybe someone has come to see me. God knows, I'd even be pleased to see my social worker. I must be desperate. My social worker is a very strange woman. She used to be my brother, Stephen's, social worker, and my brother Selby's before that. She's called Mindy. I don't like her.

She's old and wears too much perfume. She has bad breath. She doesn't let me smoke in her car. She's full of shit. Mum and Gran hate her too. Gran won't let her in the house. But even Mindy would be a nice change from Mr Nobody.

Ronnie comes in, so I sit up. I don't want another smack round the head. We have no rights in here. It's a different world.

The lorry wasn't worth this.

Ronald stands there in his ironed white shirt and black trousers. He's got his steel toecaps on. Any kid here can tell you about those regulation steel toecaps. They're for protecting the screw's feet while they kick us down the stairs.

"Can you read, Parsons?" he says in a sarcastic voice.

"Yes," I say.

"Yes?"

"Yes, sir." I hate calling anyone sir, but it's better to have teeth, I find. Think I'm exaggerating? Well you nick a supermarket lorry and find out for yourself. I'm not stopping you, am I?

"Well then, you can have this," he says and he throws something on the floor.

It's a letter. Amazing! Someone out there is bothered about me. I'm chuffed.

It's got an English stamp on it and has handwriting I recognize from somewhere. I don't want to bend down and pick it up because I'm worried Ronnie might kick my head in.

"Go on, Parsons," says Ronnie. "Pick it up; it's making the place look untidy."

"Think I'll leave it for later, sir," I say.

Bravado might work with my kiddy cohorts, but not with these people. They're like Gran, you can't argue with them.

"No you won't," says Ronnie. "Pick it up now."

I swing my legs off the bed and slowly climb down the ladder. They don't like anything out of the ordinary here. Hardly anyone gets letters. I decide to pick it up really quickly, take Ronnie by surprise and avoid the inevitable boot in the side of the head.

I pick it up. I am not kicked. The paper is slightly damp, like it has passed through too many hands.

"Open it now," says Ronnie. "I need to check there's no drugs inside."

I open it.

"Shake out the pages," says Ronnie.

I immediately recognize the handwriting. I bite my lip and let out a little squeak which makes Ronnie raise his eyebrows. How does he know I'm in here? It's all wrong. He thinks I'm my mum. But it's here.

The letter is from Lenny Darling.

Lenny Darling the convicted murderer, apparently incarcerated on Death Row.

But the address at the top of the page says something different. The top of the page says Bexton.

Lenny Darling is in my town.

Eight

Marsh View Hotel
Bexton

Dear Chas,
I expect you're surprised to hear from me of all
people. Fantastic news! On April 26th, the court
released me with immediate effect. Unexpectedly,
the evidence against me collapsed when mortuary
records were reviewed and revealed the drowned
boy had a heart problem. Never mind the detail,
but other witnesses have come to light and an
existing one has since been found to be unreliable.
Decisions were made in the light of the other
evidence which had always prevented my sentence
being carried out. You won't believe it, but
because of a legal technicality, I'm a free man.
OK, it's time to be honest. Until now I've been
playing along with your game. I know you are
not a thirty-seven-year-old woman. Actually, I
guessed from your first letter you were just a
child. Maybe I needed a friend so badly, I
tolerated your deception. Now, unfortunately I
haven't got many friends. Only a homicide

conviction has that effect. To make a long story
short, I came to your town hoping to find you in
person. Amazingly I happened to find your
mother, the real Caroline Parsons, and she told
me what had happened to you. Fill me in, is she
single? Right now you must be having a hard
time, believe me, I know what it's like. Anyways, I
hope this letter gives you something to think
about: why not try and stay out of trouble? I hope
you are learning your lessons. Don't ruin your
life.
Yours truthfully,
Lenny Darling.
PS Do you mind if I ask your mother on a date?

A massive chill runs right through me. It's like he's here in the room. I screw the letter into a tiny ball and throw it into the bin. I don't want to touch the pages. Ronnie the screw grunts and I nearly jump off the bed. I'd forgotten he was here.

"Something you want to tell me?" he asks. I hardly hear him.

He's come to find me! Why? Oh my God, I've got a killer on my tail. And he knows I'm just a kid and where I am.

This can't be real.

And then there's the PS.

Do you mind if I ask your mother on a date?

Of course I mind. This is not, I repeat, not, what my

91

mother needs right now. She's only just beginning to get better.

This has to be a wind-up. Hasn't it?

I check the envelope. It's Lenny's handwriting but the postmark says BEXTON. Maybe someone saw one of Lenny's letters and copied the handwriting and, and. . .

"Are you all right?" asks Ronnie.

"Yeah," I say, and wait for him to leave but he's not going anywhere, just staring at me.

It's all my fault. If I hadn't been such an almighty nobbins and got a kick out of having a murderer for a pen pal, none of this would have happened. I should have stuck to lorry jacking and skiving school. I'm in real trouble now. I can feel it. I have to tell Mum. She can't go out with him. She might never come back. He's a killer, isn't he? She had enough trouble with my dad. She doesn't need any more.

I take a deep breath and try and think clearly. He's been released, so he must be innocent. That's logic. The thought makes me feel a little bit better. Only a little bit.

The bell goes for gym.

I have to find out more.

"Can I visit the library instead of gym?" I ask, pulling on my trainers.

"I'll take you," says Ronnie, looking surprised.

I haven't visited the prison library since my initial tour. It's in a small room in a hut behind "Mendip" Block. Ronnie drops me off and the librarian gives me a nod as I walk in. There's nobody else here.

92

The library has five bookcases of books, three tables with a computer on each, and a sad-looking spider plant. There's a rack of newspapers and the librarian sits behind a huge old-fashioned computer monitor. The books look pretty easy to read. Loads of them have graffiti on them and there's Sellotape holding half of them together. They have titles like *Fried Heads*, or *Crazy Boy*, or *Malcolm's Journey*, and the covers are all black and orange and red sunsets. The problem is, half the kids in here can't read.

I lift the newspaper from the stand. It's attached to this wooden pole, which would make a good weapon. I leaf through, looking for anything that will tell me why a convicted killer has been released and is in this country, stalking me and my mother. I can't find anything, though I look at every single page.

"You seem agitated." It's the librarian. He looks younger than he dresses if you know what I mean. He's wearing old man's trousers and a nasty jumper like your gran would buy you from the bargain rail in some scabby charity shop. He needs a haircut and his glasses look about fifty years old. His shoes are, you've guessed it, old man's shoes. He can't be more than twenty-five.

"I am agitated," I say. It's true, and I figure that by admitting it, I have nothing to lose. I face the strange library man. He's got funny eyes. They're too big. He could easily be a killer too.

"I can help you if you are looking for information," says Library Man. That's my job."

This man is offering to help me so I take him up.

"I want to know," I say, "why Lenny Darling, a convicted killer, formerly on Death Row and due to be put to death by lethal injection in March next year has been freed.'

The librarian nods. "It's been on the news," he says. "It's a major victory for human rights and those opposing the death penalty—"

"All right, all right," I interrupt. "I don't want a lecture. Just tell me why he got out."

Library Man isn't fazed by my lip. He just switches on the nearest computer and goes to the BBC's website. He wheels me up a chair.

"Help yourself," he says. He stands over me for a minute or two. I suppose he's checking I'm reading the news and not looking up tits on the Internet.

This is what I learn. Lenny Darling has not actually been proved innocent, but it has been decided at his latest and probably last appeal that those who said he was guilty, were unreliable. (Aren't all witnesses unreliable?) A new witness, a girl aged seventeen, said she saw Darling put his mouth on the dying boy, before he seemed to slip out of his hands. She says she couldn't see that well because she was some distance away, also she was only seven years old at the time and never really thought about it until she heard about Lenny's appeal on the news. The boy who said he saw Darling hold the dead boy under, turned out to be unreliable. He was drunk at the time on Geech (some retro kiddy booze).

The prosecution had up till now withheld evidence that the drowned boy suffered from a heart condition. The cold water could have killed him, not Lenny. A tide expert testified that the waters on the beach were treacherous, and no one could come up with a motive for Darling doing the drowning. Also, Darling had already served nine years in maximum security jail, for a crime they could no longer prove he committed.

The authorities had to release him, although there were major protests from the police and the victim's family. It was decided to deport Lenny back to England as soon as possible.

Just because they can't prove he did it, doesn't mean he is innocent, does it? And what does it all mean for me?

"You need to get back," says Library Man. "Or you'll be in trouble."

"Mr Library Man," says I, "I'm fifteen years old and incarcerated in a youth prison for nicking a juggernaut full of groceries. Two of my fellow prisoners are planning to kill me in the next few days, my mother is insane, my gran has disowned me and my only living brother has abandoned my family. My father is the scum of the earth, my best friend is called Devil and I am in love with a woman whose father would remove my head just for looking at her. Also I have a killer writing letters to me, wanting to date my mother. And you're telling me I'm going to be in trouble for staying too long in the library?"

Library Man shakes his head. "Who's writing letters to you?" He looks concerned. "We can sort it out, you know. This place isn't just about punishment."

"Yes it is," says I. I am feeling brave with this chap. I'm not such an idiot to believe that he really wants to help me.

I'm on my own. I always have been.

I'm wandering back to my cell, my head full of Lenny Darling, when I hear a commotion coming from the Soc area below. I lean over the banisters. A crowd is gathering; some kids are still in their gym gear. There's cheering and shouting. Two lads are fighting. I can't see their faces, but one is much bigger than the other. Oh my God, it's Simon and Kieran.

WAYHEY! I can't help joining in with the shouting. A bust-up between those two is good news for everyone. I hope they manage to do each other some damage before it gets broken up. I settle on the banister to watch, and groan as a pack of screws pile into the crowd.

It's quite interesting watching it all from up here. Some of the screws obviously don't know what to do. Ronnie and his mate Harold have waded right in, sending lads flying as they get to the fight, but Gilbert and Francesca are just waving their arms around and shouting. No one is taking any notice of them, even though Gilbert is a pretty big bloke. They've even dragged out Snoopy, the drug sniffer dog, for the occasion, but he's so chuffed to see all his old mates he only gives a little woof and wags his tail.

As they are dragged apart, I notice Kieran has a bleeding eye, but Simon doesn't have a scratch on him. Even up here, I can see he's gone really pink, like his face is about to explode.

The bell goes for lock down and I get myself back into my cell before the screws get too jumpy. I fish the letter from Lenny out of the bin and smooth it out. I read it over and over again.

I came to your town hoping to find you in person.

Why does he want to find me? Does he want to thank me for writing to him, even though my letters were all lies? Or is it something else?

For the next week, the fight is what everyone is talking about. No one seems to know what it was about, only Simon has been put on special watch, and Kieran isn't talking to him any more. Hallelujah! It means I can worry about Lenny Darling and my non-existent court date without having to watch my back all the time.

And I do worry about Lenny Darling. I just can't get my head around why he has come here, and why he is still interested in me. I lie awake at nights turning it all over in my mind. I remember the stuff about the victim's family protesting when Lenny was released. What would they say to me now?

I get a scare a few days later; Ronnie comes into my cell with a massive parcel. For a moment I worry it is from Lenny, but when I open it up I find it contains a maths textbook, some geography reading, a book called *The Catcher in the Rye*, which we're supposed to be reading at school, with a whole list of essay titles attached to the cover with a paperclip. There's also two new exercise books, three biros, some stamps and a note.

Bexton Community School
Canal Road
Bexton

Dear Chas,
It would be worth your while to continue your school work while you are at Bevanport. I have negotiated that you are able to use the library facilities for extra periods as long as you work at your studies. Don't waste this opportunity, Chas, you only get one chance. I expect you to reach page 56 of the maths primer by next Monday. Send me your work at the above address. Miss Cartwright is expecting an essay from you (1,500 words) about the enclosed novel at the same time. More work will arrive next week. You can still achieve some worthwhile GCSEs if you make the effort. We may even be able to arrange for you to sit your exams if you are still interred during the exam period.
Take care,
Mr Fuller

Someone, besides Lenny Darling, remembers I exist. OK, it's only a teacher, but it's still something. I'm so chuffed I decide there and then that I'll do the work. What's the point of going to school all these years only to blow it now? Anyway, I haven't got anything else to do, and I like the sound of extra time out of my cell.

I do some maths right after lunch. It's a bit hard to concentrate at first. I keep getting interrupted by all the shouting and banging that's always going on around here. But when the prison clock chimes I find I've done three pages and a whole hour has gone by. For the next week I do loads of work. I get way beyond p. 56 of the maths book and read the whole of *The Catcher in the Rye*. The kid in it is well grouchy. He needs to get a life. I write my essay about him – "*Is Holden Caulfield a hero?*" – which is mostly rubbish, and send it all off to Fuller. Two days later I hear Ronnie coming up the corridor at the time when letters are delivered. He's got something for me, but it's not school work.

It's another letter from Lenny.

> *Marsh View Hotel*
> *Bexton*
>
> *Dear Chas,*
> *Jail is hideous, isn't it? At least you know you're not going to be murdered by the State.*

(I don't know about that, he ought to see some of the screws in here.)

*Mind out for bad influences in there, Chas, you
don't want to drag yourself even further down.
Ever since I arrived in this town I've been
surprised and delighted by the friendly reception.*

(?)

*Sticking around for a while seems like a good
decision for me. Will you do something for me? I
haven't told anyone (including your mother)
about my conviction history, I've even changed
my first name. Let people get to know me as a
person first, won't you? Liberty is a double-edged
sword and I don't want to end up more
ostracized and lonely than when I was
incarcerated. Do you think you can keep quiet
about me for a few months? I've lost touch with
my old friends and my family are dead, so this is
important.*

(Dead! What! Why??)

*Embarking on a new life is a strange and often
frightening journey, so please help me.
Yours truthfully,
Lenny Darling*

I don't want to help him, innocent or not. I don't want
him in my life. My mother might be at risk. I preferred

it when he was safely locked up a thousand miles away.

I'm standing by the window of my cell, re-reading my letter for the millionth time, when the door suddenly swings open and in walks Francesca-the-lady-screw.

"You're being moved," she says. "Pack up your stuff."

"What, now?"

"Now."

She's trying to be hard. It's really annoying.

"I haven't done anything," I say.

"This isn't a punishment," says Francesca. "Come on, I'll help you." And she whips out a bin bag and starts chucking my stuff into it.

"Why?" I'm standing there like a lemon.

"You're being moved to a double cell," she says, taking my puffin postcard off the wall and chucking it in the bag.

"I've got to *share?*"

I don't know what to think. If I end up with someone cool, it could be OK, but what if they put me in with an animal? How am I going to cope being shut in a tiny room with another human for hours and hours, day after day? At least on my own I can relax.

"Hurry up, the cleaner is coming to do out your cell in five minutes," says Francesca.

It's surprising how much crap I've managed to collect in my time here. But it doesn't take much time to put it all in the bag.

"Am I going to a different block?" I ask. I hope not. Things are much easier now Kieran's gone and I've got a few people I can talk to in Soc. But I'm only going to the floor below to the double cells. Francesca opens the door.

"After you," she says and guides me in.

I drop my bag on the floor.

The cell is slightly bigger than my old one. And glancing out of the window I am relieved to see I can still see the sea, only not as well. I can see all of the prison yard really clearly. I bags the bottom bunk by putting my bag on it.

"Your room-mate will be here in a minute; he's just arrived," says Francesca. "Try and be helpful to him." And she leaves.

I lie on the bed for a bit, wondering what he is going to be like. Hopefully he'll be some quiet kid who isn't a complete numbskull. After about twenty minutes I hear footsteps outside. The door is unlocked and I feel a shudder of nerves. I hope this new bloke is cool. He has to be.

"Parsons, this is your new cell mate." Francesca steps into the room and a big kid follows. My mouth falls open.

It's Devil.

Nine

He looks younger in the prison uniform. His hair is slightly damp. Someone has made him take a shower. He looks tired. He's holding his prison-issue pack (he's got the one with baccy) and a plastic-wrapped duvet.

I am about to say something when he puts his finger to his lips.

"I'll leave you two to get acquainted," says Francesca, and locks the door behind her.

When her footsteps have faded away, Devil shoots me a grin.

"Nice pad," he says. He sits on my bed and takes off his shoes. "They haven't sussed we're mates," he says. "Let's keep it that way."

"But they must know," I say. "We're in here for the same thing." I look at him. "Aren't we?"

Devil nods. "I'm here on remand because of the lorry."

"I thought you'd got off," I say.

"So did I," says Devil.

There's a bit of an awkward silence after that. I get the feeling that Devil somehow blames me for him being here. Maybe he thinks I grassed him up or something.

"What's it like in here, then?" asks Devil.

"Crap," I say. I feel weird about him being here. It's great to see a friendly face, but on the other hand, this is Devlin Juby. "I'm trying to keep my head down."

"You would," he says.

He throws his shoes at the wall, which leaves a mark on the paint.

"How's Lexi?" I ask, trying to keep my voice casual.

Devil sniffs. "She's started seeing some bloke from town."

I freeze.

"He's a friend of Connor's," says Devil. "He's a big bloke called Benji. He's got long hair, like a hippy, and he's always playing football."

I've never heard of him. I want to kill him. Devil lies back on my bed and rearranges my pillow.

"Dev, that's my bed," I manage to say. "You'll have to take the top one."

"Oh will I?" asks Devil. He looks at me. "But I like this one."

I can't believe this. He's only been here three minutes and he's picking a fight already. I suddenly feel tired. If he wants this bed, I'll let him have it. I've got too much to worry about without taking on Devlin Juby as well.

"You can have it for a week," I say. "Then I'll have it. We'll take it in turns."

"Whatever," says Devil, and turns over to face the wall. I stand there looking at the back of his head. I thought Lexi liked me. Obviously not. I'm gutted. After a few minutes, I hear a snore.

We both know Devil won't be going anywhere near the top bunk.

It's night time. Devil is asleep again. I can tell this by the way he's breathing, which is long and drawn out. He's totally relaxed. Wow, maybe he'll sleep like this all the time, wake up for a few little chats, then back to oblivion – the perfect cell mate. He's lucky. I can't sleep. My mind is going round in circles. I've heard the clock chime four times since we've been shut away for the night.

I keep thinking about Lexi and this Benji bloke, and then Mum and Lenny. When I've worried about that for an hour or so I wonder how I'm going to survive living in a cell with Devlin Juby. I don't like thinking about him prowling around when I'm asleep.

I'm going to tell my mother all about Lenny, and soon. She'll go mad. I mean, I wrote to him, pretending to be her. If they get really friendly, she's going to start asking him questions about his past. I can't believe he expects me to keep quiet.

How am I going to tell her?

"*Ah, Mummy, I've been writing to a murderer, pretending I was you, and now he's out and he's your boyfriend!*"

There's no paranoid delusion about that, is there? It's all true.

I consider telling Gran about Lenny, even though the old bag isn't speaking to me. She wouldn't let him in the house if she knew his history. But it's tricky; I don't want her to give Mum a hard time about it. Lenny Darling has singled me out, from everyone in the world, to come and find after his release. But maybe, as he says, he just wants a friend. In which case I am being a bit of an arsehole over all this. But I wrote him fake letters. Is he mad at me?

Sometimes it's good being locked up in the slammer. At least he can't get me here.

As dawn breaks I desperately need to have a dump. This is very bad. If Devil wakes up he'll see me at it. It's getting light and it's only half past four in the morning. Maybe I should wait until he wakes up, then at least I could warn him. This cell is only slightly bigger than the one I had before, and the toilet is like, right in your face. It looks like it used to have a kind of screen round it which has been ripped off. I wish I was back in my old cell.

No. It's no good. I have to do it. Thinking about murderers has loosened my guts.

So I'm squatting over the crapper and watching Devil, hoping he won't wake up. I'm halfway through and beginning to think I'll get to the finish line when Devil yawns, rolls over and opens his eyes. He clocks me on the bog, closes his eyes and rolls back.

But the moment is lost and my business is left unfinished.

I hate this place. I pull up my trousers and climb carefully up the ladder to my bunk. My guts hurt, my head hurts and I don't know what to do about anything.

I sit at the desk, chew the end of my pen and listen to the clock chime. It's eight o'clock at last.

"Devil," I go, "'S breakfast."

Devil sits up and focuses on me through bleary eyes. He looks pretty terrible.

"You've been asleep for," I check the prison clock; "sixteen hours and forty-six minutes."

Devil yawns, scratches his head and gets up. He's not pretty at the best of times, but now, with his hair all stuck to one side of his face and huge swollen eyes, he looks like someone fresh out of a zombie film.

"Got any food?" he asks.

I tell him about breakfast, about how we are supposed to turn up at eight fifteen on the dot and how you load as much on your tray as you can and not to sit at the back table.

Devil holds up his hand. "Whatever," he says and clocks me sitting at the desk, scribbling away.

"What ya doing?" he asks.

"Writing a letter. Get your arse out of bed; you don't want Ronnie after you."

To my relief Devil heaves himself out of bed, goes to

the sink and splashes water over his face. I sign my
name at the bottom of my letter and read it all through.

> *Bevanport Correction Institute*
> *Bevanport*

Dear Lenny,
Now you're free you don't need any more letters
from me. Sorry I pretended to be my mother. She
has nothing to do with this and it would be better
if she was left out of it. She isn't very well in the
head and you shouldn't see her any more. If she
gets too wound up or excited she goes mental. For
her sake you should leave her alone from now on.
From,
Chas Parsons

PS Don't bother writing to me any more. It's not
like it's Death Row in here.

I'm on edge at breakfast because I'm expecting Devil to
kick off, but he takes his place behind me in the queue,
collects his breakfast and sits opposite me at a table
without any fuss. He mostly looks at his food, but now
and then he looks under his eyelids all round the room
and asks me questions in a quiet voice.

Who's the ugly blond kid with the black eye?
When's lunch time?
Which kid is the grass?
Who do I get my baccy from?

I answer his questions as best as I can and tell him about the day.

"We go to bed at eight o'clock?" says Devil. "Some days I don't get up till eight o'clock."

"You have to be in your cell by seven thirty p.m.,' I explain. "Most of the screws go off shift at eight and they get very annoyed if anyone is out of their cells."

I wish I'd had someone like me to tell me what to expect and what to do. Devil doesn't know how lucky he is.

At Soc, I expect Devil to swagger off and start making some contacts, but he just sits next to me on the bench asking more questions in his new quiet voice.

Who's done the worst thing in here?

Has anyone had a go at you?

Who's the hardest screw here?

I leave Devil to fend for himself for a bit while I go to the prison shop to buy an envelope. Simon is serving. I wonder how they make sure he doesn't nick all the cash. Simon gives me the once-over.

"I hear you've been getting letters," he says. "From a bloke."

If people in here think I'm gay then I'm done for.

"He's seeing my mum," I say. "Not that it's any of your business." I put down my money. "Give me an envelope."

"So why's he writing to you?" asks Simon. "And why do you want an envelope? Are you sending him a love letter?"

I can't have this going round. I need to survive. I

want to tell Simon where to shove it. But I also want to get out of here alive, so I show Simon the letter.

To my surprise he reads it aloud. He's slow, but he's not making any mistakes. I'm impressed he can read at all.

"So why were you writing to him in the first place?" he asks. He puts the envelope on the counter and I take it.

I can't think of a good lie, so I tell the truth.

"He was on Death Row in America," I say. "I wrote to him because I'm sick like that."

I have Simon's full attention. "Death Row. Cool." He licks his lips. "But why write to him?"

I think about that for a minute. Why did I start this thing off? Was it because I wanted a letter from a real killer? Or that my life is so boring I needed a bit of danger? Or that he seemed cool? That I wanted someone to write back?

I shrug. "He's a killer," I say. "It's good to have friends in high places. And I wanted to know what Death Row was like."

Simon raises his eyebrows. There's a queue of lads behind us now, all listening, but I don't care.

"Why, are you worried you're going to end up there?" asks Simon.

I decide not to answer that one. I pick up my envelope and give Simon a wave.

"See you, Simon," I say coolly. "Oh and tell your mate, Ronnie, not to look at my stuff, hey? Or I'll tell everyone you're a grass to the screws."

110

There are sniggers from the queue.

"He's not my mate," says Simon quickly.

I walk tall back to my cell.

Devil is there already, I can hear him snoring even as I walk up the corridor. I can't believe he is asleep again. I've never known him to sleep at all. Lexi must look lovely in bed: her hair all spread out on the pillow and her chest going up and down, up and down. . .

It's funny how kids can turn out so differently, even when they are from the same family. Like Lexi and Devil. Lexi goes to school every day as far as I know. She's never been expelled or excluded from anywhere. It's probably because Juby would go mad if she did start messing around. He's way too proud of that girl. I feel sorry for her. Who'd want a Rottweiler like Juby watching your every move? The girl needs to get out and have some fun (especially with me).

Later, during the afternoon lockdown when Devil is asleep and I am staring out at the seagulls out of the window, Francesca comes to our cell.

"You've got a visitor," she says. "But hurry up, she's only just got here and visiting time is over in fifteen minutes."

Me? Who would visit me? Gran would never come to a place like this and Mum is too sketchy to sort it out, so maybe it's Lexi.

Lexi, Lexi, Lexi!

Here I come.

Ten

I want to run all the way to the visitors' room, but I can't because Francesca is escorting me. Maybe they've got the wrong person. Would anyone really bother to come for me? I enter the visitors' room. Everyone has to sit opposite their visitor at tables. It's a big room with massive windows and screws patrolling round. I look down the rows of faces but don't recognize any of them. I'm beginning to feel stupid. They must have got it wrong. No one has come to visit me. But then I see her sitting at a table next to the vending machine. She looks completely out of place in a blue suit with high heels.

"Catching flies?" asks Gran. She looks mean. And as I reach her table she stands up and smacks my face. The noise seems to echo round the room and a couple of people cheer. Everyone's looking at me. Francesca looks over, clocks Gran, and goes back to her clipboard. I'm a bit shocked. That was a hard slap for an old biddy.

"My own grandson put away," she says, sitting down. "You should hear them go on about it at the club. The shame."

I put my hand to my cheek. I'm not going to cry. I'm not, I'm not. Oh my God, I'm going soft. I might as well kill myself.

"Nice to see you too, Gran," I say as cheerfully as I can. But my voice cracks, like it hasn't done for years. (Well, one and a half years at least.)

But then Gran leans over the table and gives me a hug, her arms lock round me and I look down on her stiff, white and blonde hair.

"Easy, woman," I say. But I feel better. I untangle her arms and sit.

"Chips," says Gran. "you smell of chips."

"And you smell of gin, Gran, no surprise there."

"Cheeky boy." And she hits me again, only this time it's pretend and doesn't sting.

We're back on track now, our little emotional outburst over with. I must admit, I'm chuffed to see her. I thought she'd washed her hands of me.

"How's Mum?" I ask as casually as I can manage.

"She's doing teacher training," says Gran, with a sniff.

Hurrah! No mention of Lenny. On the other hand, *teacher training*? She'll be eaten alive in the first five minutes. I was wrong about her getting better. She's totally insane.

"She's going to teach adults," says Gran. "She's going to teach Eastern Faiths and Philosophies or something."

I nod. That sounds more like it.

"And she's met someone," says Gran in a loud whisper.

Shit.

"He's called Henry," says Gran. She frowns at the couple at the next table who are off exploring down each other's throats.

"He's forty and has just moved here from America," says Gran.

It's him.

"They've been out twice now," she says. "Once to the garden centre, and once out for a meal." She rearranges her hair.

"Where did she meet him?" I ask innocently. "One of her dating agencies?"

Gran shrugs. "That's one thing I do not know."

"What do you think of him?" I ask.

Gran shrugs. "He's a man," she says.

All around people are starting to leave. But the kid on the next table is still exchanging a long sloppy kiss with his girlfriend. I bet that's not the only thing they are exchanging. He'll be supplying everyone with enough puff for the rest of the month the amount of time he's spending in his girlfriend's mouth.

"He's been ill, you know," says Gran. "Like your mother."

I must have given her a funny look.

"Oh no, not mental stuff," she says. "He's had this thing where he's had to be indoors for years and years, something to do with his skin reacting to sunlight. He's so pale. It's like he hasn't got blood in his veins."

It's definitely him.

The bell rings. Visiting time is officially over and the room empties fast. The visitors can't wait to leave. I can't say I blame them.

"Gran," I say, feeling panicky. "You've got to tell Mum the truth about him."

"What?" Gran is getting up and looping her bag round her shoulder.

"I used to write to him. His real name is Lenny Darling. He's just been released from Death Row."

The words are spilling out. The screws are coming round, like bouncers, chucking everyone out.

"Chas, don't start," says Gran, fiddling with the clasp on her handbag to make sure it's shut.

"I'm not lying. He was convicted for murder ten years ago. Look it up. He's got British citizenship so he's come back. I wrote to him in prison, and now he's writing to me here."

"I know he's been inside," says Gran. "So have you, your brother, your father, your uncles and your bloody grandad. The whole town knows this family is no good, so it's no great shocker that your mother can't find herself a half-decent fella. She hasn't had a boyfriend for years."

A screw I don't recognize ambles over. He doesn't look friendly.

"Visiting time is over," he says. He looks at me. "Scram."

You can't mess with these people. You have to do what they say. So I have to be quick.

"Gran, tell Mum to be careful."

"You should work for the telly," says Gran. She leans over and pecks my cheek.

And that's it. I am removed from the visiting room and frogmarched back to my cell.

Gran never hears anything she doesn't want to.

Devil is still lying on the bunk and doesn't look up when I come in. There's something wrong with that boy. It's like someone has cracked him one on the head.

I step over to the window and look at the sky. It's sunny outside. There's loads of little boats sailing around in the sea. I wish I was out there, not stuck here with Devil and all the freaks. Why can't they try some of their therapy on me instead? All this sitting around is just a waste of my life. It's not teaching me to be a better person.

I press my face to the window and twist my neck, and can just about see the street outside the prison. I see Gran; a little blue blob walking along the pavement towards the main road and the bus stop.

It's one hour later. Soon it will be five o'clock and we'll be let out for tea.

Me and my cell mate are lying on our beds, listening to the sounds of the prison. Devil is snoring again. I can't stand it. The noise grates worse than a shovel over wet concrete. Somewhere below us someone is

116

shouting. It sounds like he's one of the bigger kids. He's kind of crying and shouting at the same time. I dread to think what's happening to him. We also hear bogs flushing every now and then, and gurgling pipes. The heating sends out these little clanking noises. I hear a lorry drawing up in the yard, waiting to be let through the gates. This is an event, so I twist round in my bunk to watch. It's the frozen-food lorry. Our food comes every week in this way, ready for the cooks to defrost and put on our plates. The worst thing I can hear in this place is the staff room, which is directly over my cell. Sometimes you hear all the screws laughing (not very often). Usually there's some kind of argument going on. Today there's only a couple of men there, having quite a quiet conversation. The sort of conversation they don't want anyone to hear.

I hear feet come stomping down the corridor and try to remember the bad things I have done recently. I can't think of anything that would earn a visit from the screws, halfway through the afternoon on a Thursday. Maybe it's because my gran didn't leave quickly enough this afternoon.To my relief, whoever it is walks straight past the cell. See how jumpy I am in here? It's impossible to relax.

I'm lying on my bed, thinking, when I hear this kind of growl and then a loud thump as Devil rolls out on to the floor, kicking and punching the air. He flails around a bit, and shouts out a few rude words. Then he sits up and looks at me.

Uh oh. I think to myself, *Devil is back*. It's like the Devil who has been sharing my cell for the last two days was some kind of ghost.

Not any more.

Eleven

"Chasser," says Devil, getting up from the floor. He gives me a friendly thump in the stomach and I double over on the mattress. "How are we going to get out of here?"

He walks around the room, lashing out at the walls and yanking the bars on the windows.

"We can't," I say breathlessly. I watch him stalk around the room. He opens all the drawers and slams them shut. He kicks the table over, very gently, just for fun, then puts it back and climbs on it, in order to examine the light fitting. He aims a few kicks at the door and then gets his shoe and gives a few hard bangs to the heating pipes, which gets everyone else in the building going, and pretty soon the pipes are banging and tapping non-stop. Then he turns to me.

"What's this?" He holds up my folder of school work.

"Nothing," I say. I get down off the bunk and try and take it from him, but he holds it out of my reach.

"Devil," I say. "Get a life."

He opens the folder and takes out my latest English essay.

"What does it say?" he demands, pointing to the title.

"*Was Hal a Good King?*" I say reluctantly.

"What's this shite? Chas boy?"

"Shakespeare," I say. "I'm going to get me some GCSEs."

Devil tuts and shakes his head. "Waste of time, studying." He drops the file on the floor and I feel myself tense.

"Pick that up," I say as coolly as I can.

"Or what?" says Devil. He comes very close and I smell his breath, stale from too much sleep.

"Or I'll be rather annoyed," I say, putting on a funny posh voice.

"Can't have that," says Devil, instantly responding in the same tone. "Don't want to upset my room-mate, what ho!" He picks up the file and places it on the table. "Must get round to reading some Shakespeare myself sometime."

And that's it. The danger has passed. Pretty soon we're cracking mean jokes about Ugly Debs and reminiscing about eating the food in the juggernaut. Soon after this we're let out for tea.

For the past two days, Devil has shuffled behind me in the canteen queues, but now he's pushing ahead to grab a tray. He doesn't look back to see where I am.

"Excuse me, ladies," he says to a couple of kids as he barges past. I bite my lip. I know he is going to get into trouble, and soon. I only hope he doesn't drag me into it. Devil can't stand being shut up in one place for very long. He gets claustrophobic and starts hitting people.

At primary school, on one of his rare visits, he ended up jumping out of the window because the teacher didn't believe him when he said he wanted the loo.

Lucky it was the ground floor.

Devil is yakking away in a loud voice to the kid next to him, he's going on about how terrible the food looks and he wouldn't feed it to a dog. I notice a couple of the screws staring at him. I want to remind him to keep his voice down, that you've got to keep a low profile in this place or you've had it, but I'm too far back in the queue.

Everyone is looking at him. It's like he's come from nowhere.

Devil gets his food and goes to sit down and a few minutes later I join him. There are three other kids on the table: my sort of mate Marshall, a weedy boy called Dean, and David, a big slow chap.

"This stuff is total crap," says Devil, poking a mound of mashed potato with his fork.

Being used to Gran's cooking, I haven't really got a problem with the food, and I tell Devil so.

"That's you all over, isn't it, Chas?" says Devil in a nasty voice. "You haven't got a problem with anything, or anyone."

There is an awkward silence and everyone looks at me.

"I like to save my energy for what's important," I say, trying to keep my voice steady. But really I'm mad. What's he trying to say? That I'm a brown nose or something?

"And what's important?" asks Devil.

I know the answer to that, but I can't say it. Lexi Juby, that's what, and wishing Lenny Darling would leave me alone.

"You're saving your energy for your GCSEs, aren't you?" says Devil, and David and Dean snigger. "How about this," he tells the rest of the table. "In the afternoons, when the rest of us are banged up, this kid is let out in order to do his school work."

"So am I, so what?" says Marshall, and I shoot him a grateful look. But Devil is just warming up.

"Just cos these kids are arse-lickers, they get let out. It's not fair."

His voice is rising and I notice Ronnie edging over to our table.

"Shut up, Devil," I say and gesture over to Ronnie.

"He's at it again," says Devil, "Mr Peace Keeper himself. They wanna send you to Iraq, mate."

"Everything all right, lads?" asks Ronnie.

Everyone except Devil looks at their food.

"No," says Devil. "The food is shite."

The room goes quiet as he says this.

"I'm sorry you think so," says Ronnie, in his soft, dangerous voice. "Now you're on canteen duty, maybe you can help give some tips."

"I'm not on canteen duty," says Devil.

"Yes you are," says Ronnie. "Which means, you have to clear every single table in the place, starting with your own."

This isn't normally what happens, and Devil knows it. Usually we all scrape our leftovers in the pig-bin and stack the plates ourselves.

"Off you go," says Ronnie.

Everyone in the room is quiet, listening.

"Do it, Dev," I say.

"No," says Devil. "I'm not a fucking skivvy."

If possible, the room gets even quieter.

It's like watching two trains thundering towards each other. Devil hates being told what to do. And he never, ever backs down. But he doesn't know this place. He doesn't know what these blokes are like.

Devil's eyes are flashing, he's well wound up. He knows everyone is listening and he thinks he's invincible.

"I'll count to three," says Ronnie. "Three is a number which follows one and two, in case you don't know. If you haven't started clearing the plates by then, you'll regret it."

Devil swears at him, but doesn't move.

"One, two. . ." says Ronnie.

SMASH.

With a single swipe, Devil pushes his tray over the table and on to the floor, spreading mashed potato, gravy and meat all over the floor. He kicks his tray across the room.

Silence.

Someone starts cheering, and a few people join in, then it's like everyone is cheering. There's a crash from the next table. Simon Judd has tipped his dinner on to the floor. A couple of others do the same. Within seconds it's bedlam. Everyone is shouting and the screws are blowing whistles and more of them are piling in through the doors and the loudspeakers tell everyone to go back to their cells, but someone has started throwing mashed potato and, of course, not many of us have much self control, that's why we are in here in the first place, and who can resist a moment like this? So everyone starts chucking their grub around and laughing and shouting. Even I find myself caught up in the mood and manage to land a bit of meat in Simon's face. I know the comeback will be bad. But it's always bad in here. I figure we might as well have a bit of fun while we can.

Then the room is full of screws and I find myself dragged off and herded into a corner with four other kids. A big screw I recognize from Mendip shoves my little group out of the canteen and up the stairs to the landings. I'm pushed into someone else's cell and the door is locked behind me. I look around the room and consider nicking the chocolate bar which is lying on the table, but I resist. See what a good lad I am?

I can't believe Devil; he's only been here for two days, and despite sleeping through most of it, he's already caused a riot. I'm a bit worried about him. They make it their business to break people in here. Devil would be quite a challenge. I don't like to imagine what is happening to him right now.

After about an hour, Francesca opens the door and orders me back to my cell.

"But it's Rec time," I protest.

"Don't push it," she says. Going back to my cell I notice a buzz about the place. Things aren't as dead as usual. There are unfamiliar screws rushing around everywhere, taking us back to our cells. A pile of what looks like puke lies unmopped on the recreation room floor and a shoe sits abandoned on the stairs. I can hear Snoopy woofing somewhere in the distance.

I step into my room. There's nobody there.

"Where's Devil?" I ask Francesca and the door is slammed shut in my face. The banging on the pipes is so loud and furious it's like being in a club. Almost.

Even though I'm back in familiar territory, I can't settle. I walk up and down, feeling like an animal in a cage. I don't know how lifers can stand it. I make a note to myself. Never murder anyone and get caught.

There you are, you see, prison does work.

The floor is made of painted tiles. There are one hundred and fifty-eight of them from the window to the door. I count again just to make sure I didn't get it wrong. The pipes are still banging away and I can't resist booting my own pipes for a minute or two. It's like a victory song.

But gradually the pipes grow quieter as people give up. Eventually there's just one person left, tap tap tapping away. It's not cool any more. It's annoying.

"SHUT UP."

Someone else obviously thinks so too.

I stand at the window and watch the prison clock for twenty-five minutes. I try not to look at it too much. It's depressing. But today I can't help it. I'm still standing there and wondering whether to try and sleep when I hear someone crossing the landing.

The door is unlocked and Devil is guided into the room.

"Get off me," he snarls and shoves the screw's hand off his shoulder.

I don't recognize the screw. He's got muscles like The Incredible Hulk. He must be from another block. But I don't look at him for long because I'm looking at Devil. His head is bleeding and he's got the beginnings of a massive bruise on his arm.

"I'll report you," croaks Devil. "I know my rights."

"In here, you have no rights," says the screw. "Tomorrow you're being moved down The Block. You'd be there now if we had the space." He gives me a scary look, and leaves.

Devil goes straight to his bunk and lies down.

The cell is very quiet.

I am listening to see if I can hear him breathing when he lets out a great big girly sob.

"Shit," he says.

I don't blame him. How embarrassing. I don't know what to say, so I don't say anything.

Eventually he gets up and comes to look out the window and I stand aside to give him room.

126

We watch a stream of screws arrive for the evening shift.

"What happened?" I ask.

"Four of them were having a go at me," says Devil. "All shouting at me in this little room, then one of them pushed me and I fell over and someone else said, oops he tripped." He shakes his head. "Then this bloke grabs my arm really hard and says that kids like me don't last very long in here." He holds up his arm. "Look at the bruise."

"What about your eye?" I ask. "Who did that?"

A grin suddenly breaks out on Devil's face. 'Some kid chucked a plate at me during the food fight. Wicked, wasn't it?'

You can't keep a Devil down.

'I can't believe those screws did that,' says Devil. "I'm on to my solicitor as soon as I get a chance."

"I tried to warn you," I can't help saying. "These people are animals. And no one ever messes with Ronnie."

Devil says nothing.

"There's too many of them to fight," I say.

I'm expecting to get a tirade of abuse about what a goody-goody I am, what a brown nose and all that, but Devil is quiet for a bit.

He sits back on his bunk.

"There might be something in that," he says, to my surprise.

He lies down.

"My head hurts," he says, and shuts his eyes.

It's one o'clock in the morning and I'm awake. I listen to Devil's breathing. It kind of goes like this:

SHEEEEEEEEeeeeee, SHEEEEeeeee, SHEEEEEEEeeeeee.

There's no curtains in our cell and the moonlight is pouring in. This place looks better with the lights turned out. The prison, for once, is quiet. There's usually someone worrying at the pipes or having a bit of a shout somewhere. Not tonight though. It seems like everyone is asleep. Everyone except me.

And maybe one day, I'll be in your dreams again.

Twelve

It's tomorrow. Tuesday to be exact, though in this place, days of the week hardly matter. It's very hot and nothing has happened for four hours. They shut us up before morning recreation and I'm seriously looking forward to my two hours in the library this afternoon just to get out of the room. Kids have been banging on the pipes all morning.

It's so hot me and Devil are wearing only our shorts. There's no air because we can't open the windows. Dev's been pretty quiet this morning, except to ask me questions about what happens when you get sent down The Block. Luckily for me, I don't have first-hand experience, but from what I hear, it's like being at the bloody Hilton here compared to there. The Block doesn't have a name like Mendip or Cotswold or Quantock. It's just The Block. I think Devil's freaked by the treatment he got yesterday. It's sad to say it, but life is definitely easier when Devil is down. It's weird, he's been my mate for years, since we were little kids, but I don't know what to say to him. I'm annoyed with him for having a go at me in front of the other kids yesterday. It's not exactly how your so-called best mate is supposed to behave, is it?

At two p.m. I'm collecting my files together and looking for a pen when Devil looks up from his bunk.

"Off to school again, Chas boy?"

"Yep," I say. "Bet you wish you were being let out for a couple of hours."

"Not so I can brown nose the screws," says Devil, and his voice is all hard. "Can't have you failing those exams, can we?"

"Oh, get lost," I say. "You're just jealous because you're not going to get any exams, ever."

There is a silence and I wish I hadn't said anything.

"There's more to life than exams," says Devil, eventually. I don't like his tone. It means trouble.

"Such as?" I ask, finding a biro wedged between the desk and the radiator.

"Freedom," says Devil, "from pricks like you."

I'm pleased when the door is unlocked and I am escorted to the library. It's cooler in here and it's a relief to get away from Devil. I spend one hour doing a practice maths exam sheet and another really boring hour, reading about science experiments.

When I get back to my cell, it's hotter than ever and I find Devil sitting at the desk, rifling through my stuff.

"What you doing?" I ask, and snatch my English book out of his hands.

"I'm just bored, and looking around," says Devil. He gives me a look. "Been enjoying yourself?"

"Not really," I say. I start stuffing my maths exam answer paper in an envelope.

This cell is so airless, I can hardly breathe.

"How's that?" Devil is pointing at the place where my missing finger ought to be.

"Pretty crap," I say, though I've hardly noticed it the last couple of days.

"That was well funny, wasn't it?" says Devil. "One minute your finger was there, then wham, I'd chopped it off."

"Hilarious," I say. "Perhaps I should do it to your finger and we can all have a good laugh about that."

"It's rotting," says Devil.

"What?"

"Your finger." He looks at me closely. "You knew I had it, didn't you?"

"Where is it now?" I ask.

"At home," says Devil. "I thought it might come in handy. Get it? Handy?" And he laughs.

Stay cool, Chas boy, I tell myself. Don't let him get to you.

"It looks like a tiny shrivelled prick," says Devil. "No surprise there."

"I want it back," I say, sounding far calmer than I feel. I want to kill him.

Devil shrugs. "I thought I might feed it to a dog or something."

"You're sick," I say. My hands work themselves into fists but I make myself stay calm. I can't let him get to me.

Devil watches as I find my English essay and a

131

science worksheet I'd done the day before, and add it to the envelope.

"You've changed," says Devil, watching me. "You were never into all this exam stuff before."

I say nothing.

"If you think you're going to impress my sister with all this, you haven't got a hope," says Devil. He gets up from the desk and leans back against the wall. "She thinks you're gross."

I hesitate. Is this true or is he winding me up?

Devil gets a lighter out of his pocket and starts flicking it on and off.

"That's mine," I say, recognizing the design on the side.

Devil knocks on the window through the bars. "This isn't glass," he says. "It's reinforced plastic. It would burn."

"Your point is?" I put the envelope on the table, climb up to my bunk and turn to the wall. I feel tired. Does Lexi really think I'm gross? I shut my eyes. There's still one hour to go before tea.

"And what are you going to do with all these exams?" ask Devil. "Are you going to be a professor or something? Do you think it means you'll be too good for the rest of us?"

"Shut up," I mumble, looking at the wall.

"You're full of it," says Devil. "You're going to be in and out of places like this for the rest of your life. You'll never get anywhere."

"Shut it!"

He's getting to me. I've got to ignore him. But he's saying all the stuff which, secretly, I think is true. What difference will a few exam grades make to my life? No one's ever going to employ someone with my record.

I hear paper rustling.

"And what is this?" Devil bursts out laughing. I turn over and see he is holding a leaflet Fuller sent me about working in the travel industry. On the front there's a picture of a holiday rep in a nasty blue suit with a bubble coming out of his mouth saying, *Can I help you?*

"Is this what you want to do? Oh Chas, there's no hope is there?" Devil cracks up and waves the leaflet in front of my face.

"You only want to go so you can look at the girls in their bikinis."

I lurch out from the bunk and swipe away the leaflet. It tears down the middle.

"Diddums," says Devil, looking at my face.

"Devil," I say, sitting up. "You are supposed to be my mate."

"Not now I know what a lightweight you are," says Devil. And he starts on about how I've "crossed over" and now I'm "nothing but a creep" and a "policeman's wet-dream".

I'm getting more and more wound up, but if I fight him I won't win. We both know this. I lie on the bed and try to ignore him. I haven't even got the energy to laugh it off like I usually do. I'm too mad and hot and tired. Eventually Devil shuts up and I try and calm down. If he says one more thing, I swear I'll kill him. I wipe the sweat from my forehead. It's quiet for about three minutes, apart from Devil striking my lighter over and over.

Then I smell burning.

I'm still for a moment or two. Devil is trying a new approach to wind me up. But when a cloud of grey smoke wafts in front of my face I have to sit up.

"Devil, you loser, what are . . ."

I stop talking. Devil has set fire to a load of paper and crammed it into the space between the bars and the windowpane. Orange flames lick up the walls.

Devil himself is grinning manically, his face lit up by the flames.

"I thought I'd try and melt the window," he says, "so we can get us some air in here."

I recognize some of the burning paper as the envelope with all my work in.

"You bastard," I scream, and jump down from the bed. I pull at the burning papers and my maths exam paper and all my exercise books fall burning to the floor.

That's it. I slam my fist into the side of Devil's head and knock him over. He's getting up, really quick, but I'm ready for him. He's had this coming a long time. He runs at me and we're almost hugging only we're kicking each other at the same time. Lucky for me Devil isn't wearing any shoes, and as he draws his leg up to knee me in the bollocks I pull back and he misses, but he manages to land a massive thump in my guts. I'm gasping for breath as the loud screech of the smoke detector erupts overhead.

I hear shouting from outside . . .

"FIRE, FIRE."

I don't care about the fire. All I care about right now is killing Devlin Juby.

I am about to go for him again when he picks up the chair.

"Come on then," he says softly.

I run at him and get the chair wrapped round my head. To my surprise, it doesn't hurt. It just makes me angrier.

I can't see so well out of one eye, and the room is filling with smoke, but the fire itself is dying down.

I throw a punch, miss and end up sprawling on the desk. Devil laughs and kicks me over. I'm lying on the floor, with Devil standing over me.

"You've lost," he says calmly.

I spring up and headbutt his chin, and over he goes. I feel fantastic, though the smoke is making me cough. He's on the floor and if I was anything like him, I'd whack him with the chair leg. But I'm not like Devil. I'm Chas Parsons. Right now I hate this kid. But I'm not going to sink to his level.

We're about to spring at each other again when the door flies open. Ronnie takes one look at us and blows his whistle.

He comes wading in with his bat.

It's three hours later. I'm in a different cell, on my own. My lip has just stopped bleeding. My head hurts. I haven't been given anything to eat. This fight will go down on my report. I'll be stuck here for ever and go as mad as my mother.

And maybe one day. I'll be in your dreams again.
And maybe one day. I'll be in your dreams again.
In your dreams again.
In your dreams again.

Thirteen

'll be out in approximately three hours! Out, out, out! It all kicked off yesterday. I was lying on my bed admiring my new bruises, when Francesca came in to tell me the Youth Court had had a cancellation and they wanted me in there at three o'clock that afternoon. I didn't have time to get nervous because I was sent off for a shower, given an early lunch and bundled into the escort car before I could get a grip on it all. I wore a long-sleeved shirt, even though it was hot, to cover up my Devil souvenirs. In court I put on my innocent face for the judge and to cut a long story short they're shipping me out later this afternoon so I can go back to school! I knew education was good for something. When my case came up, Mindy, my social worker, said that I had a *workable* record of attendance, which ought to be maintained for the *sake of stability* and that *my personal development* was *best served by my immediate reintroduction to school and family life.*

She always talks like that.

I'm not sure about the family life bit and I've got to do some sort of community service, but who cares? I'm getting out of here! I'd love to see Devil's face when he learns my school work is the reason I'm being let out. I heard that he has been sent down The Block. I'm not happy with him but I wouldn't wish that on anyone.

Here I am back in the waiting room. It seems like ages since I arrived, but it was only five weeks ago. Everything is the same; the anti-bullying poster, the smell, the broken chairs, the chewing gum stuck in the carpet. I've got to wait for them to process some paperwork, then they said Mum will collect me. I'm wearing my own clothes. My trainers are so comfortable and my T-shirt is nice and baggy and kind of soft. I put my cap on and feel a bit weird, so I take it off. Maybe I'll get some new clothes this afternoon. I can't sit still, I keep fidgeting and messing around. I can't wait to get out of here. I want to just break down the walls and run and run. All this waiting is unbearable. I twist my cap round and round in my fingers.

Hurry Up!

But I know I'll probably have to wait for ages. I'm prepared. I've nicked a book from the library (*Ballistic Street*) and I've got a can of Coke and a cheese and onion pasty. (I'm too wound up to eat it.) But I've only just opened the Coke when the bloke comes to tell me I can go.

I amble past reception and there, waiting for me, is my mother, looking tanned and wearing a big smile on her face. I can't believe she's actually managed to get herself here.

I feel fantastic.

"Hello." She pats at my shoulder. I'm so high about getting out; I lean over and give her a kiss.

"Right, thanks," says Mum, not looking me in the face. "Come on, let's go." She seems edgy. This outing is a big deal for her.

The receptionist presses a button and the doors swing open. I'm out of there before anyone changes their mind. I step outside on to free soil. It's warmer than it is inside. I look up at the grey sky and watch the seagulls and swear I'm never coming back.

Mum's heading off over the car park.

"The bus stop's this way," I call, pointing in the other direction.

"We've got a lift," says Mum. "I couldn't come all this way on the bus."

It's most likely to be Michael and I'll have to share the back seat with a load of vegetables. But Mum's hovering by a black Escort. I don't recognize it. Maybe Mr Fuller has come to pick me up. The man has been full of surprises recently.

Instead, a tall, freakily thin man gets out. He stares at me under half-shut eyelids. I'm not a hippy or anything but right away I get these really bad vibes off him. It's like shock waves are pouring out of him into me. It's him. I know it. And his face is like, I don't know, empty. My good mood vanishes. I feel like I've been kicked in the guts and the doors are slamming shut around me.

"Chas, this is Lenny Darling." At least she knows his real name now. "This is his car." She says it like that's really something.

Lenny is whispering something to my mother. I look up and see silhouettes of bodies against the windows of the prison.

We eye each other. Mum is jabbering on about the traffic and the journey here but neither of us is really listening.

He's the sort of person you'd notice even if you didn't know him. For one thing he's so pale it's like he's barely alive. It reminds me of when I get cold and the blood runs out of my fingers; they go all white and thin and wrinkled. This is what this bloke is like all over. And he's really tall. Freakishly. But so skinny. He's wearing a belt that makes his waist look tinier than Lexi Juby's. But it's his eyes that get me. They just stare, not blinking, like some kind of reptile. I know this isn't very nice of me to say, but he's one ugly bloke. Has my mum ever got bad taste. My dad wasn't exactly a looker, he'd been drinking too long for that, but he was in a different league to Lenny Darling.

"So this is the legendary f-footballer." Lenny's got a quiet, whispery sort of voice with a slight stammer. "I see you weren't able to keep up the bodybuilding while you were locked up. And I do hope this won't affect your chances of getting into M-Medical School."

On impulse I turn to my mother. "I'm getting the bus," I tell her.

Her face falls. "Chas, don't be like that."

"Sorry we didn't bring the Jag," calls Lenny.

I leave the pair of them alone in the prison car park. I can't handle this.

I'm at the bus stop. I've been here for twenty minutes. I know because I can hear the bloody prison clock chime. I really, really don't want to hear that noise AT ALL. It's started to rain, I need the loo and I'm hungry and there's no effing bus. I've chilled out a bit though.

A car draws up next to me and the window is wound down. The smell of chips wafts into my face and my mouth waters.

"Chas, come on, stupid, get in." My mother leans out of the passenger-seat window.

"We've got you some chips and they're getting cold."

They smell amazing. I haven't had proper food for weeks. Suddenly it seems mad to sit out here in the rain.

"There's no child lock, is there?" I ask and the two of them burst out laughing.

I climb in the back, watching Lenny carefully. Mum hands me a paper wrapper full of fat golden chips and I stuff my face. Oh Lordy, chips!

"Ketchup?" I grunt, and Mum hands me a sachet. I squeeze the stuff on the paper and dip in a stubby fat chip. It is the best thing I have ever tasted. I happen to look up and see Lenny eyeing me through the rear-view mirror. His eyelids cover most of his eyes so I just get the glint of his pupils. I'm so freaked out I freeze, a chip mid-air on the way to my mouth.

Mum turns in her seat to look at me. "Don't worry. Lenny's explained all about his troubles, and why he had to use a different name And guess what, he even used to go to Bexton School! But he left before I started."

I say nothing, but stare out of the window until my mum turns back. The thing is, when she was ill, she thought everyone was out to get her, and rob, rape, beat her up. And now she's better, she's going out with a possible real-life kiddy killer, and she says, "It's OK.'

I've always felt I had to protect my mum – from the Social, from Gran, even from Dad, years ago. I probably crawled out in my nappy and screamed at him as he was beating her up. She's delicate. She just doesn't do relationships and I'm glad. I don't want another waster like my dad hanging around the place. She definitely doesn't need Lenny Darling and neither do I. The back of his neck is as pale and wrinkly as an old man. There are these nasty little purple spots, like warts, sprinkled over the skin. A few straggly hairs sprout out from the back of his head. He looks like a bloody zombie.

"You want to do up your seat belt," says Lenny." 'I don't want you inadvertently killing me. Though in your letters you said you often did feel like m-m-murdering someone."

"Did you, Chas?" asks Mum. "Who would that be? Gran, I expect."

I ignore her and keep stuffing my face. Has Lenny

come all this way just to wind me up about my letters? I try and remember what other lies I'd written.

"Gran's baking," says Mum. "So leave some room."

Gran. She'd sort Mum out.

"Your progeny appears to be f-f-frightened of me," says Lenny. He sounds pleased. What the hell does progeny mean? Is that some Bible-bashing stuff?

"He's not himself," says Mum, sounding apologetic. "He's just been released, after all. He's a good boy really."

Why's she making excuses for me? He's the one with the teenage skeleton in his closet. I finish my chips, wind down the window and chuck the wrapper out of the window. Then I belch.

"Chas," says Mum in a laughing sort of voice which also means "you little bugger". "Don't do that."

"It's not nice," says Lenny. "But it's biodegradable. Like him."

Is this like, a hidden message? Is he going to throw me out the window and leave me to rot by the roadside?

"His trainers aren't," says Mum thoughtfully. "Not with the amount of plastic they have in them. . ."

"Mum, please," I say. "Can we change the subject?"

"And I expect all that hair gel would preserve the hair," she carries on, looking across at Lenny to make sure he's listening.

"Mum, shut it," I say and they both giggle away like they're having the funniest conversation ever.

I don't say another word all the way home. But Mum doesn't notice. She's too busy talking to Lenny about some party at her college. Her voice is higher and squeakier than normal and whenever he says anything she gives a really irritating laugh and touches his arm. She's so obvious it's embarrassing. Maybe she'll scare him off by being too keen.

"It's a funny feeling, being set free," says Lenny.

"I expect I'll get used to it," I say.

"No you won't," he says. "Once you've had your freedom s-s-stripped from you you're never the same. But the question is: have you learned your lesson?"

I'm tempted to tell him where to go, but for my mother's sake I just shut my mouth, fold my arms and look out of the window, trying to make it obvious I'm not up for chit-chat. I don't understand why Lenny is interested in my mother. She's not particularly good looking and she's pretty thick. And he sounds like he's read too many books. He's not our sort.

The estate looks colder and scabbier than I remember. There's loads of rubbish lying in the gutters and graffiti on every wall. The grass is full of turds and litter blows around the pavements. Every shopfront has metal grilles. I look at all the little kids out on their bicycles. They should be indoors by now. The world's a dangerous place.

We pull up outside our house.

I have a funny turn when I spot Gran's plastic flowers on the kitchen window sill. She gets new ones every year in the January sales and takes the others to the graveyard. She puts them on Selby's, my older brother's grave, and takes away the old mildewy ones. Grandad's grave isn't far away and I once asked her why she didn't give him some flowers. She'd said, "He doesn't deserve them, the nasty old sod."

I go to my brother Selby's grave for a chat sometimes. I never really knew him though. I have a photograph of all three of us, Selby is holding me, I'm just a baby, and Stephen is sitting next to us. We look like three normal kids.

And they say the camera never lies.

I pick up my bag and get out of the car. I slam the door and say nothing to Lenny.

"Thanks, Len," says Mum, and kisses his cheek. "Sorry about Chas."

"I won't come in," says Lenny, to my relief. He doesn't kiss her back.

I'm not hanging around for all this sentimental shite so I go in the house and leave the lovebirds to it.

Gran is waiting in the hallway, with her hands on her hips.

"Gran," I say. "Have the fire engines gone, then?"

"What?" She looks startled.

"Mum says you've been baking."

"Rude boy," says Gran, stepping forward to hug me. Mum stands behind us. I wonder if she's thinking that maybe she should have given me a hug too.

"I've made tea," says Gran pulling away. "Fish fingers and waffles."

"But we've all had chips," says Mum.

Gran's mouth screws up into a little knot. "That's all the thanks I get? Here I am worrying what's left of my life away and that's how I'm treated. . ." And she's off, nagging and picking at my mum like I'm not even here.

Mum sighs. "I wish you'd leave me alone," she says.

"And that's how my own daughter speaks to me," says Gran. "My daughter, who I gave birth to." She looks at me. "Fifty hours I was in labour with her you know."

"And you don't let me forget it," says Mum.

I nip off upstairs and look out under the net curtains of the landing window. Lenny's still here, sitting in his car. I can see his long white fingers on the steering wheel. It's quite easy to imagine them round the throat of some kid. Pushing him down into the water, tightening their grip, pushing down, down. I get a start when Lenny sticks his hand out of the window and gives me a wave. I drop the nets as quick as if he was a sniper and stand back as the car pulls away. I watch until it is out of sight.

I go into my bedroom.

Gran's cleaned it! All the clothes have been washed and put away. She's stuck up the Man U poster that was falling off the wall, hoovered the carpet and put all my stuff on the shelves. It's too tidy for me, it reminds me of prison. I want to tear down the poster and kick the piles over the floor, to restore a little chaos back to my life, but I can't be arsed. I lie on the bed on my side. My digital alarm clock shows me the time in large green letters. 20:46.

I turn over, trying to get Lenny's face out of my head.

And maybe one day, I'll be in your dreams again.

That evening, after Gran has gone off to the social club, I decide to have a word with Mum about Lenny.

She's standing in front of the hall mirror, examining her hair. She's wearing a massive bead necklace and each bead is a different colour. My mother dresses like a hippy. She should go to New Look and get herself some proper clothes.

"I've got a grey hair." She rummages around her head. "I've lost it. Chas, help me find it."

"No," I say and stay where I am, which is sitting on the bottom stair.

"You have to," she says. "You put it there."

I say nothing.

"I've been so worried about you it's killing the cells which are responsible for my hair pigment," she says.

Is that why you visited me in prison every chance you could?

"Gotcha." But a whole clump of hair comes out in her fist.

"Don't," I say. "You look much nicer with hair, even if some of it is grey." I don't want her shaving her head again. She did it for years and it looked awful.

"I'm getting old," wails my mother.

"So am I," I say.

I don't like this. This sort of behaviour is what my mum used to be like. I hope she's not heading for another one of her episodes.

147

"I'd be fine you know, if I lived on my own," she says. "If I didn't have to worry about you and Gran eating away at me."

"Why don't you leave then?" I ask. But Mum just shakes her head.

There's all these warning bells going off inside me; Mum doesn't like showdowns, but I can't miss this opportunity.

"Mum, why are you seeing Lenny? You know what he was accused of."

"He's an innocent man. You, however, are a thief. It's you I ought to be dumping."

"Mum, you can do better."

"He's kind to me," says my mum. "Anyway he wasn't accused of murdering women."

Oh God. She's right into him. And I can't shake off the feeling she *likes* the fact he's got a dodgy history.

"He's been convicted of murder," I say.

"But if the courts of the United States of America believe he is innocent, why can't you?"

Because the courts of the United States of America aren't going out with my mother, I think to myself.

"If he's so innocent, why haven't you told everyone about him?" I ask.

"People round here are like you. They overreact. And anyway," she says, "It's none of your business."

"It is," I say. "It's my fault he's here."

"Trust me," says Mum. "He's a good man." And she gets a really soppy look on her face.

This is my mum talking. My mum who, two years ago, would scream the house down at the sight of any man in uniform. (The postman got used to it.) My mum who wouldn't eat anything yellow (bananas, pasta, crisps, potatoes, chips, sweetcorn, you name it) because it "took the colour from the sun", and "we'd all die of cold, because the sun would run out of energy" and she knows because she "nearly did an A level in physics".

See what I mean? She's barking.

"For goodness' sakes give me a chance of happiness," says Mum. "Don't mess it up."

I go upstairs and lie on the bed. I can't get my head round this Lenny thing. A little voice inside me is saying, Chas, the man has been freed. Maybe he really is innocent, give him a break. Imagine how shitty it would be if you'd been accused of something you hadn't done, and nearly paid the ultimate price for it, then have a muppet like me dissing you. But I got a really bad feeling about him yesterday. I didn't like anything about him. It's hard for me to put my finger on it. He's not big and hard like Juby-the-Killer, or a head case, like Devil. He's just got a way about him that isn't normal. And it's hard to understand why he's interested in my mother. Part of me is scared that he has a different agenda. But I don't know what it is.

PART THREE

Fourteen

The next morning I lie in bed for ages before I can work up the energy to face anyone. I'd woken at seven because that's when the alarm was set at Bevanport. At eight I imagine them all filing in for breakfast. I wonder how Devil is doing down The Block. I examine my finger and think about what Devil said in prison. About how my finger was rotting and how he might feed it to a dog. It's my property and I want it back. As long as he has it, it makes me feel like he has a hold over me.

When I get downstairs everyone is out. There's a note on the counter in Gran's crazy slanting handwriting.

I am at Dolores's; your mother is at college. Back lunch time. Don't mess the kitchen up. Cake in tin. Don't eat it all.

After breakfast (I have five slices of toast just because I can) I wrap a slice of Gran's cake (banana and walnut, home-made but edible) in kitchen towel and shove it in my pocket and go out. It's a really nice day, bright and sunny. I am heading for the canal, but when I'm on the bridge I get stage fright and walk round to the allotments instead. Maybe I'm not ready to see everyone yet. And anyway, it's a school day. I squeeze through the hole in the fence and into the allotments. There's only about ten plots left because a massive building project has taken over the site. There's all these dumper trucks and diggers and two of those massive cranes that tower right up into the sky. All of the remaining allotments are abandoned and overgrown except one.

I find Michael, Dolores's husband, sitting on his chair and having a cup of tea.

"Working hard, Michael?" I ask and make him jump and slosh tea over his hand.

"Look at that," says Michael, waving at the construction work. "This used to be my haven. Now look. It's a bloody mess. This council has sold us down the river."

What is interesting about Michael is that he doesn't say a word when you meet him on the street or when Dolores brings him round to Gran's. He grunts like a kid. But when he's at his allotment he's a different man. He's not exactly a chatterbox, but here he talks. His allotment is like another world. He's got bamboo canes covered in leaves and red flowers with loads of white butterflies flapping around them. There are long rows of vegetables and Michael's flowers look miles better than Gran's.

"Heaven, isn't it?" says Michael. "Only thing with

heaven, it's closer to hell than you'd like." He nods to the building site next door.

I agree. I've never been into all that Bob-the-builder stuff. You've only got to look at the poor buggers alternately frying and freezing as they jackhammer into the roads to see that building is hard work.

"How long have you got before you get evicted from here?"

Michael sighs. "It was supposed to be six weeks, long enough for all the fruit to finish, but now it might be longer. Nothing's happening," he says. "Building company is in dispute with the project management. No work's been done on this site for over a week. Gives me a bit of peace. All my neighbours have given up." He waves at the overgrown plots. "But I've always been the one to fight the good fight."

He looks at me. "Haven't you been inside, young man?"

"Yep," I say, with a bit of a swagger. Finding a tin mug from the shelf in Michael's shed, I pour myself a cup of tea.

"How shameful," says Michael.

He takes a slurp of tea and looks at me. I expect he's going to give me a lecture about wasting taxpayer's money or something.

"I'm worried about the bees," he says. "I think they're up to something. It's the heat. It's come up too sudden."

I sit on an upturned bucket and drink my tea. There seem to be more bees flying around than usual. But I can't really tell. Since I've been inside it's like I've lost sight of what's normal. I look at the neatly planted rows of vegetables. Michael's got all these sticks and netting and frames and things going on everywhere. It's like his own mini construction site. I hand Michael the crumbled cake from my jacket pocket.

"Your grandmother made this?" he asks warily.

I shrug.

"I might leave it." He hands it back.

My watch beeps the hour. It's two o'clock. All the kids will be going back into school after lunch. Devil, on the other hand, will be safely locked up in The Block.

I am beginning to get me an idea.

"Welcome home, lad," says Michael.

I go into the newsagent's for a bar of chocolate and some Coke. I'm going to need the buzz. The radio is playing a song by a girl going on about how cool she is and I notice a box on the counter full of sparkly toy wands. Mum would love one.

I shove three cans of Coke and the Mars bar at the woman behind the counter.

In the past, on Fridays, when I couldn't be bothered to go to school, me and Devil usually hung out at his house. This is because Juby was always away Fridays, regular as clockwork, either delivering his cars or doing over some mansion or whatever he gets up to to earn a living. He never comes back before dark. So in the old

156

days, on a Friday when I couldn't face school, Devil and me would grab some tinnies from the fridge and play the Xbox all day, or look at some of Juby's dodgy videos, which he doesn't bother to hide. Fridays used to be pretty good.

I swig Coke and stroke my stump with my thumb as I approach the Jubys' house. This is the best time for me to get my finger back. Devil has always had this nasty interest in blood and guts and stuff. He stops and pokes road kill, he's that sort of person. He watches all the hospital dramas and live operations on telly. It was his idea that we play the knife game. I have my suspicions that he might have tried to stuff my finger, or dissect it or something. I don't know why I want my finger back so badly, but I do. Maybe if me and Devil hadn't fallen out I wouldn't be as bothered. Maybe I'm scared he's going to do voodoo on me or something. Anyway, I'll be in and out of there in half an hour. If I can't find it easily, I'll just leave. There's no harm in having a quick look, is there? I know how to get into Juby's house. You go round the back, find the key under the loose patio slab, and let yourself in the kitchen door. Me and Devil have done it thousands of times.

I hang out on the street, waiting for everybody to disappear. I'm scoping out the houses, checking to see no one's twitching their nets and spying on me. I wouldn't want word to get round that Chas Parsons was seen breaking into Juby's house. I can't finish the last

157

can of Coke so I leave it sitting on the pavement. After two and a half cans I'm buzzing and totally hyper. *You can do this*, I tell myself. When the street is empty I creep down the passage, tiptoe over the concrete and scoot round the back to the garden. I say garden, I should say car park, because Juby has concreted over the entire area. There's nothing much in it, except an old bicycle of Lexi's and a rusty washer-dryer thingy. The patio has a white plastic table which is covered in black mould and two unsteady-looking chairs. A ragged wooden fence separates the Jubys from their neighbours. Before I look for the key I have to be certain Juby is not in. I've already watched the house from the bus stop and the vandalized phone box for twenty minutes and I've not seen any signs of life. But I'm not taking any chances. I creep up to the back door and look through the frosted glass. The kitchen is empty and quiet. I breathe out slowly.

It's Friday, I tell myself. Juby is never here on a Friday. Relax. To be honest, I'm more worried about whether I'm going to find my finger. I remind myself to look on Devil's bedroom window sill on the outside. My finger is bound to be a bit smelly by now. It's weird to think that part of me is decaying. Bloody Devil. If he hadn't legged it off with my finger, some sexy nurse would have sewed it back on. It's his fault I have to break in.

I lift the patio slab and feel around for the key. My (remaining) fingers close over cold metal. I have it.

Slowly, slowly, I unlock the door and step through into the kitchen. My rucksack catches on something in the door frame and I yank myself free. I leave the key in the lock on the outside. That way, it looks like someone just forgot to hide it when they let themselves out. I like to think it looks less suspicious. The Jubys have this bright yellow lino and yellow cupboards. It looks even worse than Gran's kitchen. The remains of Juby's breakfast, curling bacon rinds and crusty baked beans, stick to an abandoned plate in the sink. There's a dent in the wall where the plaster has come away. It's at fist level. It reminds me I need to move fast. I do a quiet recce downstairs, just to make sure. Living room: empty; hallway: empty. Downstairs bog: empty.

I go upstairs.

Devil's bedroom is a good place to start. I cross the landing and reach his door. I feel strange opening it. It's my mate's bedroom after all. I feel like I'm on a burgling job and I don't want to be burgling Devil. I remind myself I'm only going to take back something that is mine.

Devil was never the tidiest of kids, but his room looks like it has been hit by a dirty bomb. All the clothes have been pulled out of the drawers, the mattress is half hanging off the bed and a curtain has been ripped off the hanger. The rubbish bin has been turned upside down, and crisp packets and biscuit wrappers lie everywhere. It's a mess. In fact it looks like it has been burgled already. I think of how Gran tidied

159

my room for me while I was inside. No one's bothered to do that for Devil. I pick up Devil's lamp and clear a space for it on the bedside table. The lamp is in the shape of The Incredible Hulk's fist. Devil was given it years ago for his birthday. I remember at the time, I was going through my Incredible Hulk phase, and I'd really wanted that lamp. I'd still quite like it now. But I am NOT thieving from my own mate. I flick the switch on the lamp but the bulb has blown.

As I sift through the clothes on the floor I get the shakes. It's the caffeine I've got inside me but I had to give myself that buzz in order to go through with this. I open the cupboard. There's not much left inside, just magazines and computer games. No finger. I look on the window sill, nothing. I search under the bed, under the mattress. I look behind the stack of magazines and comics. I even try the carpet, but it's firmly attached to the floor and I can't see any new nails. I stand on the chair and look on top of the light shade. Then I look under the chair to see if Devil has taped my finger to the seat. But he hasn't. The crafty boy has chosen a good hiding place. I am beginning to get worried now. Maybe I should leave. This is only a spur of the moment thing. I don't want to be here when Lexi gets home.

I look under the chest of drawers and feel the linings of the curtains in case he has sewn it in there. I rip out the plastic backing of the bin and ferret underneath. No finger. I run my hand over the wallpaper to check for irregularities.

I don't enjoy rifling through my friend's stuff. I'm trying not to look at it, if you know what I mean. I don't want to know he has eight broken watches or a photograph of one of our neighbours asleep in her garden. I wish I hadn't seen the collection of shells in a jam jar. They're much too soft for someone like Devil.

I leave the room as I found it. A total mess.

So, if I'd stolen someone's finger, what would I do with it?

a) Throw it away?

b) Put it in my worst enemy's bed?

c) Keep it.

"Now Devil," I say aloud, "how would you keep a finger fresh?" Then I remember Lexi said something about a jam jar.

When I was in Year Eight the biology teacher had to leave the room. She was gone for so long that some of us more curious lads decided to have a poke around in her cupboard. She kept the keys in her desk drawer, this we knew from our keen observational skills, and the dafty woman had forgotten to take the keys with her. I admit, I was in charge of this operation, but I figured, this was my school, and what was in her cupboard was going to be educational. So we found the key and swung the lock, and walked in. Of course, we'd peeped in previously whenever she or the science technician were getting out extra beakers or test tube racks or whatever, and it had looked really interesting, like rows and rows of chemicals and jars and pots and books and sheaves of papers. So me and Devil (he never turned up at school at all after Year Eight) and some other kid went sneaking in and poking round and seeing if there was anything that might be worth nicking. I remember holding a vial of sodium hypochlorite and wondering if it could be smoked or sniffed when the other lad gasped and fainted. Just like that, on the floor. I remember the whack of his head on the ground. I remember who it was now, it was Eddie Mason. So he was lying there, all passed out, and a couple of the girls came rushing over to try out their bandaging or whatever. And me and Devil bent down to help Edward up, and then we saw what he'd seen. It was a pickled piglet. I mean it, a real tiny little pig in this massive jam jar. All dead and floating around in a jar of brown water. I nearly passed out myself when I saw it.

"Dare you to smash it," says Devil.

I told you he was an animal.

I didn't smash the jar, but I did drag Edward Mason out of the cupboard by his shoes, and we were caught by the biology teacher. Devil went on about that piglet for ages. He still mentions it sometimes.

"Hey Chas, remember that pickled pig? That was sick, that was. . ."

So that's why I know what Devil has done with my finger. He's pickled it, just like the little pig.

I'm in the kitchen. The wall cupboards are quite high so I get a chair and pull it up. Nobody ever uses the jars and bottles at the back of food cupboards, do they? It's the perfect hiding place. I search the first cupboard. Tinned beans, Frosties, packs of chocolate biscuits. I rummage to the back. Nothing. The next cupboard looks more promising. It is rammed with things like pickled onions and cider vinegar and stuff. I look on the top shelf and fight my way to the back through the sticky dust. A cloud of spicy orange powder wafts into my face. Then I see a small jam jar, right at the back in the corner, filled with a brown fluid. There's something which looks like a chunk of very small sausage floating inside. I am about to investigate when I hear someone coughing.

It's a man. A man who is very close. Someone who is walking down the path at the side of the house.

It can't be Devil. It has to be his dad.

Fifteen

*J*uby rummages under the patio slab for the key. I haven't got time to reach behind the packets and tins and get the jam jar. I have to leave it.

I leg it out of the kitchen. The front door is usually triple locked so I don't even attempt to go out that way. I run up the stairs and pause on the landing. I'm standing next to Lexi's bedroom door. I decide this must be the safest place so I dive in and close the door. She's changed her room around. When I've sneaked the odd look in the past, the walls were covered with posters of Robbie Williams. I remember Lexi saying, *Robbie isn't thinking woman's crumpet, but we all have our weak points*. She used to have a blue spotty duvet on the bed, clothes lying all over the floor, and female lotions and potions everywhere. This new room is tidy, with nothing in it except a bed, a chair and a wardrobe (too small to hide in). And this duvet is black.

I stand there like a lemon, and it's only when I catch sight of a pair of large white trainers peeking out from under the bed, it dawns on me that I am in Juby's room. He must have swapped with Lexi.

I've broken into the house of Juby-the-Killer. I'm hiding in his bedroom, and he's just come home.

He's climbing the stairs.

I look under the bed. The entire space is taken up by lots of wicker baskets full of neatly folded clothes. There's no room for me. The cupboard is too small and I can't hide behind the curtains because they only fall halfway down the wall, my legs would show. I've had it.

Juby must be nearly at the top of the stairs. I consider jumping out of the window, but it's a long drop to the patio. I would break my legs and then I wouldn't be able to run away. There's only one place left. I dive under the duvet, arranging it so it looks like Juby got out of bed in a hurry. At least, that's what I hope it looks like. I lie still. The smell of stale sweat coming off the duvet makes me want to retch.

Juby is walking across the landing. Oh hell. Why did I choose to hide here? He's going to think I'm a right perve. He'll show no mercy.

I hear a horrible little whine as the door opens. It's mid-afternoon, for God's sake. Why does Juby want his bedroom now? It's getting hot under here and I'm terrified I'm going to sneeze. I hope Juby just fetches something then leaves. But he gives a big sigh and sits on the bed. It's only through hard-core will-power that I don't scream.

Thump, thump.

What's that? Even through the pongy thick duvet a new rancid smell fills my senses. Juby has taken his shoes off. That's not good. No, no, no! The bedsprings creak as they give way to Juby's weight. He's settling down next to me. There's only a duvet between us. I'm not breathing but am in a sort of airless coma. I have two choices.

1. Stay where I am.

2. Jump up over him and hope he is so surprised he doesn't catch me.

But I'm so scared I can't move. And if I do escape he'll hunt me down. I'd have to move to Russia or something. But he'd find me even then. He'd send somebody after me.

I'm going to die. Soon.

I wait for him to roll over and find me. He pulls at the duvet, but when he finds it isn't moving, he gives up and lies back. Then, silence. He's never going to sleep, is he? Who goes to sleep in the middle of the day? I never do. Then I remember Devil saying that sometimes his old man sleeps all day when he's been out all night on a job. Oh no. I'm done for. Poor old Mum, two dead sons and one on the fishing boats. This is going to finish her off.

It's getting hotter and hotter. I have to make an air hole or I'll suffocate. Mind you, suffocation is probably a better way to go than whatever Juby's going to do to me. I'm sweating so much I reckon Juby's going to smell me before he sees me. I'm lying still, and my rucksack is digging into my back. It hurts like hell, and my arm is going dead where I'm lying on it. I don't know what direction Juby is facing so I don't dare risk the tiniest movement. I wish I was hiding in Lexi's bed instead. I bet it doesn't stink like an old man's underpants. Whew. My face is burning up. I am about to die of suffocation when I hear a noise, a tiny one, and then another, slightly louder. The noises build up in volume with each breath.

Juby is snoring.

I wait for ages and ages. This must be a joke. He's pretending. Oh my God! He's asleep. Slowly and silently I poke an air hole through the folds of duvet with my finger. A tiny waft of cool air finds its way in to me. The relief is incredible. I make the air hole a little bigger and see that Juby is lying with his back to me. He's fully dressed, except for his shoes. He's wearing a black leather coat. I look at the back of his stubbly neck.

He's moving around and the snoring has stopped. Instead he's making funny grunting noises. Please don't let him wake up.

"We didn't mean. . ." he mutters. *"Best get him out."*

I hold my breath. I think he is talking in his sleep.

"Get him out. . ."

Then I get the fright of my life as he groans really loud, close to my ear.

"Is he going to die?"

Oh man, what's he talking about? I'd rather be anywhere else in the world than here. I'm also worried about the pressure building up in my guts. It must be nerves or something but I am either about to poo myself or do the biggest fart ever. I will my bum cheeks to stay firmly clamped together. *Mind over matter, mind over matter*, I tell myself.

My stomach is hurting now. It must be all the Coke. I also need a pee.

I can't . . . help . . . it. . .

PAAAAAAAAARPPPPPPPPPPPP!

I am going to lose my life because I did a fart at the wrong time.

Juby is stirring.

I freeze as he turns over. I don't even dare cover up my face because of the movement. So I'm looking directly at Juby as he opens his eyes. He frowns as he clocks me lying in his bed, wrapped up in his duvet and being very quiet.

I should think about something nice, like Lexi.

"Chas Parsons?" says Juby.

"Yes?" I answer as coolly as I can.

"What are you doing here?"

I swallow.

"Hiding from you," I say.

Juby shuts his eyes. "Fair enough," he says. I wait, expecting a fist in my head. Instead he gives a little cough and turns over.

Is this some kind of a wind-up, I wonder? At this very moment is he working out the very best way to separate my head from my body? Then I have this realization. Maybe he thinks I'm a dream. No one would be crazy enough to sneak into Juby's bed. Even his wife didn't hang around very long.

I don't know how long I lie there, it feels like ages, but it's probably only ten minutes before the snores start up again. I'd never have guessed the most beautiful sound I'd ever hear would be that of Juby snoring. However, I'm still stranded between him and the wall. It would be very brave of me to try and climb over him. Imagine what would happen if he woke up again. But I must move, I must. This is my chance. The man is unconscious for God's sake.

Gingerly I stretch out my arm, trying to free it from the folds of duvet. I can't work it properly. I've lain so still for so long; my body feels like it doesn't belong to me any more. The Coke is having another effect. I really have to pee now. The less I try to think about it, the more I need to go. *Come on*, I tell myself. *Move now.* I shift my leg and the bed gives this horrible creak. I freeze. I'm such a chicken. I should just go. *Just do it.* I can't. Oh God, Juby is moving again. He lets out this cough and settles back. This must mean he is in, what is it called? REM sleep. This is a very light sleep, when the sleeper could easily wake. So I'd better not move. If Juby doesn't choose to roll over to my side, or pull the duvet over him, and gets up fairly soon, then I'll be fine. But this is so unlikely. And I'm going to wet myself. My bladder actually hurts. The first of a series of cramps rips across my middle as I try to hold it in.

Could this get any worse?

AHHCCHHAAGGG! Juby roars in his sleep and my crotch suddenly feels wet. It's OK, he's quiet now, he's just making sleeping noises. God, this is horrible. I realize I have wet myself. The shame! But my guts don't hurt any more. At least I won't explode. But I've wet Juby's bed!

Jets of nasty old beer breath come shooting in my face as the snoring starts up again. That's it. I have to go. Now.

Quietly I unwrap myself and wriggle my limbs to make them work, hoping the tiny movements won't disturb Juby. Then I sit up and climb over Juby. At one point I am straddling him. It would get messy if he woke up now. But then my foot is on the floor, then the other, and I'm crossing the carpet and I'm out of the door. I can't look back. I'd drop dead if he was looking at me. I'm edging down the stairs, trying not to stumble because I'm shaking and fighting to keep the panic under control. But I want to scream. I run into the kitchen and turn the handle of the back door. It's locked! But then I see the key is still in the lock. I turn it and open the door. I run along the passageway. I'm nearly there. I'm flying up the front garden path and opening the gate. I'm on the street. I should relax now and amble coolly down the road, like I've nothing to hide. I can't do it. I break into a sprint and run faster than I ever have in my life. I keep running until I am out of the estate. I don't even want to go home. I run on and on, past people who all look behind to see who is chasing me. I run through the streets until I reach the churchyard. I thread my way through the tombs and flowers and finally collapse on Selby's grave.

Sixteen

I'm at home, safe, but my heart is still pounding in my chest and my head is buzzing. I'd waited at my brother's grave for ages. I was freaked out that Juby had seen me and was after me; also my trousers were wet and I wanted to give them a chance to dry. I ended up tying my jumper round my waist. I'm thankful it's only piss and not blood. Luckily Gran was well stuck into her soaps by the time I got home, and Mum was out somewhere so I managed to get up to my bedroom without my wet trousers being seen.

Now I'm lying on my bed and listening out for Juby pounding up to our house. I imagine his face, bright red with anger.

What were you doing in my bed, you little freak?

Maybe he'll wake up and think what a strange dream he's had. I think he was still asleep when he saw me. Otherwise I wouldn't be here, would I? I think about the jam jar containing either my finger or a rotten sausage in the back of the Jubys' cupboard.

I have to say, life is a lot simpler in prison. I've only been out twenty-four hours and already everything's getting complicated.

I hear footsteps on the path and hold my breath. Then I let it out. It's my mother. I recognize the shuffle as she drags her feet. The key turns in the front door and there is a clink as she puts her keys in the glass bowl on the hall table.

I fancy seeing a friendly face so I go downstairs to say hello. I get a shock when I see her eyes are all red and her make-up is criss-crossed with pale rivulets where tears have run down her cheeks.

"What's wrong?"

She looks at me through bleary eyes. "Nothing," she says. And a fresh dribble of tears pours out. "It's all the dust."

"Is it Gran? Has she said something?" I follow her into the kitchen. "You've just got to ignore her."

"Do you think I'm fat?"

"Not as fat as her. Is that what this is all about?" I take her arm and force her into a chair. "You've got to ignore her. Anyway, you're not fat, you're just well covered. It's different." I sigh. Gran is always saying *seconds on the lips, years on the hips*, whenever Mum eats anything, even an apple. And anyway, Gran's miles fatter than she is and is addicted to her junk food. "Do you want me to have a word?"

"I wanted another man's opinion," says Mum. She looks really miserable.

"What do you mean, another man?" Then it dawns on me. "It wasn't Gran, was it? It was Lenny."

Mum wipes her nose with her hand and sniffs. "He

says I remind him of an elephant seal." She looks up at me. "That's not good, is it?"

This bloke is really bugging me now. What kind of a skunk would tell a depressed female she's fat, even if she is?

"Dump him, Mum. He's not doing you any favours."

"He only says it because he cares," says Mum. "That's what men are like." She looks miserably at Gran's bowl of toffees on the table and pushes them away so violently the whole lot nearly fall off. I hope this stuff with Lenny doesn't set her off again. She's still pretty flaky. But that's why I need to protect her.

"He's just a freeloader anyway," I say.

Mum straightens up in her chair. "He is not. He's just got himself a job."

"Where? At the crematorium?"

"He's going to be a security guard at the building site, by the river."

"You mean the new yuppie flats which are going to wipe out Michael's allotment? Nice work, Lenny."

Mum ignores me. "He'll be earning a good wage, which is more than you've ever done."

"Mum, I'm fifteen. . ."

"And I wish you'd be polite to him. He can't stand rude kids.' Mum puts her head in her hands.

'Mum." But it's no good. She has set her face against me. This is a look I recognize. When she's like this, she won't hear me. She blocks me out.

Just like she always has.

*

It's Saturday, the one with the turd in the middle, and I'm late. I have to do this Youth Rehabilitation thing on Saturdays as part of my sentence. I have to meet up with some bloke called Tony and do good deeds in the community. I was told to wear wellies (I don't have any. Nobody has wellies since they were three years old and jumping into puddles for kicks) and waterproof clothes because I'm supposed to be cleaning some lock-opening mechanism by the canal.

I'm wearing my fourth favourite pair of trousers in case I'm made to do dirty work, but I'm not going out in crap shoes, NO WAY! I'm wearing the smart new trainers that Gran bought me to celebrate getting out of prison. It's drizzling so I'm wearing my puffa hoody. I like this jacket because it makes me look bigger than I am. I swear I lost weight in prison.

I see two figures waiting by the canal house. I don't take much notice of the bloke because there, in a white puffy jacket, tight white jeans and pink wellies is a very beautiful woman.

"Lexi?"

She turns to look at me. Is it me or does she look annoyed? Not the reaction I would have liked.

"I am," she replies. I'm full of questions but I need to be cool. How can Lexi have community service? I can't believe it.

"Don't ask," she says.

"You're late," says the bloke, who is probably Tony,

looking at his watch. "If this happens next week, I'll report you."

Tony's about thirty and he's scruffy with massive sideburns and a load of curly back hair spreading down to his lumberjack shirt.

"You are Chas Parsons?" he asks.

"Nope," I say. "I'm William Windsor." I watch as a tiny smile appears on Lexi's face.

"William. . .?" Tony turns over his bit of paper.

"You may call me sire," I say. "But I'd like to be treated like any other soldier." I glance sideways at Lexi. She's still smiling.

"You're joking," says Tony uncertainly.

"I never joke," I say, as Tony passes me a scrubbing brush.

He explains that there's all this machinery they use when boats want to go through the lock, and it's our job to clean it. Or what we can reach without falling in. Tony gives me a bucket of soapy water and tells me to get on with it. There's all this moss and dried-on dirt. Nice.

"You were at Bevanport, weren't you?" says Lexi, half-heartedly rubbing at a one-hundred-year old bit of moss. "You must have seen Devlin. He's in court next Tuesday. We're hoping he gets off as lightly as you."

I shrug and look over to see if Tony minds us talking, but he's sat on a bench doing a crossword.

"So how was he? He wasn't getting bullied, was he? Dad says the bullying is terrible in these places."

To my credit, I don't laugh out loud.

"He slept a lot," I say, trying very hard to control myself. "And I don't think Devil will ever be bullied in his life, do you?"

I scrub at this metal cog thing, really hard, pretending it is Devil's face.

"I suppose not," says Lexi. "But I was relieved when I found out he was going to the same place as you. I knew you'd look after him."

I nod. Images of the last time I saw Devil flash through my mind. He was lunging for me at the same time as being dragged away.

"Got your wellies in that bag?" asks Tony, suddenly appearing.

"Please," I say. "I'm not a bloody farmer."

"Mind your language," says Tony.

Lexi rolls up her sleeve and dips her brush in her bucket of water. She's got nice arms. They're tanned and not too weedy like some girls'.

"What are you looking at, Chas?" she asks.

"Lexi Juby," I say.

"Well stop it. You're putting me off." She goes back to work.

"Maybe you should work round the other side," says Tony.

I pull a face. "Aw, I'm getting real job satisfaction out of cleaning this bit."

"All right, just get on with it," says Tony.

"Are you just going to watch?" I ask him a few minutes later.

"No, I'll help," says Tony wearily. "But I don't have to. I'm not doing it all for you."

I stand closer to Lexi. I admire the energy she's putting into her work and I tell her so.

"Look," she says, "this is embarrassing enough without you making fun of me."

"I'm not making fun of you," I say.

"Yes you are," she says.

"OK, I am," I say. "I don't get much opportunity usually."

"Guys, there's work to do," Tony calls over.

I ignore him. I have turned up, more or less on time, I am holding a scrubbing brush and I am wearing last year's trousers. As far as I am concerned, I am serving my sentence and nothing more needs to be said. Lexi goes back to scrubbing. I stand right next to her and scrub at a bit she's just done.

"Are you trying to wind me up?" she says.

"Yes," I say. I point. "You want to do that bit again." I look over at Tony, who is screwing a brush head on to a pole. "Tony, I don't think Lexi is doing a very good job."

Tony ignores me and Lexi pokes me in the side with her wet brush. Physical contact! Result!

"So who's this kid you've been seeing?" I ask ever so casually.

"What kid?"

"Devil said you had a boyfriend, Connor Blacker's mate?"

"First I've heard of it," says Lexi.

Yes! Devil must have told me that story to wind me up.

This is how most of the morning carries on, me chatting up Lexi, her trying not to get dirty and Tony not doing much at all. Half the time he's on his mobile phone.

"Who's he talking to?" I ask Lexi.

"His girlfriend, she's leaving him," she says and flicks water at me.

"Maybe he's rubbish in bed," I say, and flick water back. I'm feeling pretty high now I know Lexi hasn't got a boyfriend. Yet.

"I heard that," says Tony, and turns his back on us, his ear glued to his phone.

We've run out of water so I go to the canal house to fetch some more. Tony says not to use canal water because it's too dirty and we might catch some disease from rats' piss.

"So, tell all," I say, handing Lexi a fresh bucket of water. Tony is on the phone again and not taking any notice of us.

"What?" Lexi is bored. She's not working as hard. The cuffs of her coat are wet and she looks cold.

"Why are you doing community service?"

"Mind your own business."

"No," I persist. "I want to know, must have been something fairly naughty so you couldn't be let off with a caution, and something not so bad you'd end up in the slammer."

Lexi just clicks her tongue at me.

"I never thought you were a naughty girl," I say and grin at her. To my delight she smiles back. I am getting somewhere; the old Chas charm is beginning to work. I knew I was devastating with the ladies.

"If you don't shut it," says Lexi, "I'll tell my dad you were trying to feel me up."

My jaw drops. She's a bad one. But I know she's joking. Anyway, I can't stop now, I'm on a roll.

"First offence?" I fish.

Lexi pauses.

"Second."

"Shoplifting? Smack about another girl? Get drunk in town and hit some perve?"

"Look I'm not proud of what I did," says Lexi. "I'd rather not talk about it."

Now we are getting somewhere.

"It can't be as bad as anything I've done," I say.

"I took some money from the charity box in Frankie's," she says suddenly. "I work there every Saturday. It was money for the dogs' home. I thought I needed it more than the dogs. I got seen on the security camera. I lost my job." She looks at me. "This will be on my record for ever. I'll end up on the trash heap."

"No you won't, it's nothing," I say and mean it.

"It's not nothing," she says. "I wish I hadn't done it, I've totally messed up."

I can hardly believe my ears. This girl has nicked a few pennies from a tin, how can she think that's so bad?

179

"I know what you're thinking," she says, and she throws her brush in her bucket. "You're thinking you've done things a lot worse. But I've got a conscience, unlike you. I don't want to be a bloody thief." She makes a choking noise in her throat.

"Hey." I put my hand on her arm. "You do this community service and then your slate is wiped clean. "You're under sixteen so it won't stay on your record."

I have no idea if this is true, but it seems to cheer her up a little. She looks over at Tony, who is clicking his heels and staring at the murky water.

"I thought he said he was going to help," she says and goes over to talk to him.

I watch her go. I feel weird. It's nice that she has confided in me, but now I realize she is very different to me. She has a conscience! Man. That could come between us. But then she turns round and I catch a look at her lovely bum and I know, without question, that Lexi Juby is the only woman for me.

After four hours, I'm knackered and am relieved when Tony says we can go. "Well done, you two," he says. "A good morning's work. Next week, we're at the Soapworks Art Foundation, they need some help with an exhibition. Oh and wear old clothes."

Lexi and I scowl. Neither of us would be caught dead in "old clothes".

"And be on time, you," says Tony to me.

"The name's Chas," I say. "I'd prefer it if you called me Chas, Tony." I hate it when people don't respect me, just because they're like twelve years older and haven't been caught on the wrong side of the law.

"OK, don't be late, Chas," he says.

I walk Lexi home. She asks me about prison. I keep telling myself I have no chance with her. I'm not exactly a good catch, am I? We approach her house and I start to get nervous in case Juby is looking out for his daughter.

"I'll probably see you at school," I say. I'm going to ask her out. I can feel it coming.

"OK," she says. She smiles at me.

Go on Chas do it do it do it do it.

"Bye," she says and walks up the garden path.

I haven't done it.

Seventeen

On my first day back at school, I walk in like I'm a superhero. But apart from a few questions about prison food no one seems to be particularly excited by my heroic return. I don't say anything about Lenny to anyone. I've been doing a lot of thinking about it and have decided to lay off him and Mum for a while. I still don't like it, but maybe I should give him a chance.

Connor Blacker comes up to me and asks if I think badgers are superstitious.

It's at times like these I miss Devil.

In the few weeks I've been away, everyone has been brainwashed with exam fever. I'm behind in science and technology, but thanks to the work I did in prison, I haven't got much to do in maths or English to catch up. Mr Fuller actually thanks me for the work I sent him from prison; he says I exceeded his expectations. But then he wants to know what happened to the exam papers. When I tell him they got burned I can tell he's struggling to work out if I'm telling the truth.

"You can still get the magic five, you know, Chas. It's

well within your capabilities. You just need to knuckle down. The first exam is in one week. You're a bright lad. You can still do a decent job."

"I'm not really the academic type, sir," I say, tearing at the corner of a new exams folder he's just given me.

I am about to go, when he stops me.

"We had to fight for you to come back," he says. "Don't mess it up."

I don't know what to make of the idea of anyone fighting for me. He must be mad.

At lunch time I take my carton of chips into the playing field and walk over to the group of girls sitting under the trees. The whole of Year Ten and Eleven are in exam fever. All the girls spent break and lunch time copying their exercise books into A4 files. Even some of the lads are at it.

Lexi is there with her mates. I'm terrified, but I go right up to the group and say hi to her.

"Hello, Chas," replies Lexi. "Have you come to help me with my revision?"

The other girls, Ugly Debs and Darlene Rogers giggle, but I hold my ground.

"If you like," I say. An exercise book is lying on the grass by her feet, so I pick it up. It's biology.

"We're studying reproduction," says Lexi.

"An interesting subject," say I, ignoring the sniggers from the other girls.

"Human reproduction," says Lexi. "I've got some fascinating diagrams."

"I bet you have," I say. But the moment is lost as a football, flying from nowhere, whacks me on the head.

I straighten up and see Jamie Farrow laughing his tits off on the playing field.

"Excuse me, ladies," I say, handing back the book. I charge off to inflict a bit of friendly revenge and I end up playing football for the rest of lunch.

She was definitely flirting with me. And on the way home from school, I catch up with her as we reach our estate.

"Hello, Chas," she says.

"Hello, Lexi," says I. "How's the revision going?"

"Pretty well," she says.

"Could you take Friday evening off?" I ask.

"Why?" she asks.

I'm feeling less brave every second but I have to go through with this.

"For the cinema," I say.

"I can't do this Friday, I'm revising," says Lexi.

Oh no, she's changed her mind. Maybe her dad's had a word with her about me. *You're not going out with that little turd*.

"I'll meet you the Friday after at seven thirty at the cinema," she says. "Don't be late."

We swap mobile numbers before she trots off up her path to her house.

I've done it! Not only have I spent an entire day at school without getting one detention, but I have also got a date with the foxiest woman in the school. I am a changed man.

On the morning of my first exam, Gran nearly swallows her teeth when I come downstairs at eight o'clock. I've got a maths exam. I haven't done much work for it, I've been distracted. But at least I did all that studying in prison. I don't want Mr Fuller on my case, do I?

I've been to school every day and have been keeping my head down. I can't be arsed to make the teachers want to kill me. I must be depressed or something. It's definitely not normal Chas behaviour. I'm even doing my school work. I'm right into my CDT coursework, making a camping bed which folds flat for easy transport out of cardboard. (I've never been camping in my life and if I did I wouldn't take a bed, but my teacher seemed to think it was a good idea) and I've handed in loads of maths coursework.

I keep having these flirty little conversations with Lexi at lunch times and I've walked her home every day. Connor asked me if we were going out and I just gave him a grin.

I've not seen Lenny Darling at all in the last week. I think Mum's keeping him out of my way so I don't put him off her. My spies tell me they go to one of three places: Harold's restaurant in town, the Gilded Lady pub on the posh side of town, and the bowling alley by the supermarket. I have to admit that my mum is happier than she's been for years. She even told Gran to leave her alone when Gran was going on about how Mum's new hairdo made her look like a tart. Mum deserved a slap on the back for that, but I have my own arrangements for getting on with Gran and I don't want to mess them up.

I still haven't told any of my mates about Lenny. As soon as word gets out about his past, it might make things bad for my family. There used to be this old bloke living next door to Dolores and Michael, and the rumour spread that he used to be a Nazi. Anyway, this bloke got so much graffiti and dog turds through the letterbox, he ended up moving away. He had a funny accent, and I know he came from Germany because Michael told me. But Michael also said this bloke had been evacuated during the war because he was a Jew and everyone didn't know what they were talking about. You have to keep yourself to yourself round here because it feels like everyone is looking for something to pin on you.

Gran won't let me out of the door until she's made me eat a bowl of Rice Krispies and given me a Penguin for just before the exam. I feel like a little kid.

"My grandson is sitting his maths exam," she says to herself in the hall mirror.

She's mad, that woman.

Everyone is already sitting down when I get to the sports hall. And Fuller himself is there.

"Skin of your teeth, boy, skin of your teeth," he says.

But then he pats my shoulder. "Good luck, remember to have a go at all the questions. You shouldn't find them a problem."

I wasn't nervous until then. But now that I'm sitting at my desk behind Patsy Jones the room is dead quiet and I feel queasy. God! What is happening to me? Imagine, Chas Parsons getting worried over an exam.

"Turn over the page," says Fuller, and a massive rustling fills the room. I look at the blank sheet of paper in front of me. People all around are scribbling already.

Clear your head, I tell myself. *This is important.* I imagine the look on Gran's face when I tell her I've passed my maths exam.

I turn over the page.

So, it's eight in the evening. I've got seven days until my date with Lexi, and, according to Gran, Lenny is coming to pick up Mum in five minutes. I've only seen him twice since I got released. Both times he was sat in his car, waiting for Mum. Hopefully he'll do the same tonight but even so, I lurk around upstairs, fiddling with Gran's china ornaments and flicking the curtains, just in case he decides to come in. Mum is bustling round downstairs getting ready. She's left a wet towel on the bathroom floor. I pick it up and fold it over the radiator so Gran won't have a go at her. I hear the gate hinges squeak and footsteps on the path. He must have walked or I would have heard his car. I move back the curtain ever so slightly to look at him.

He's wearing a denim jacket and a black T-shirt and jeans, and he's twisted his few straggles of hair into a wormy ponytail. With his pale skin and bony face he looks like he's just crawled out of a body bag.

As I watch, he puts his cloth man-bag on the path and stretches. Then he does a series of funny moves; lunging forward and holding out his arms, then standing dead straight with his hands clasped. I shake my head. My dad wasn't exactly a model citizen, he drank too much and was a bit trigger happy with his fists, but at least he didn't do aerobics in the garden like a nutter.

"Dickhead," I mutter.

Lenny abruptly stops his crazy moves. He looks up at the window. I skip back, but he aims this horrible grin right up at me. He can't see through the nets, can he? To my relief he turns away and examines the flowers. Gran hates gardening, but she has to have a better front than Dolores, so it's rammed with big purple, white and yellow flowers and, thanks to Michael, the grass is cut shorter than a Borstal barber's. Lenny curls his hand round a big white flower head and he yanks it off, just like that. He looks back at my window and shreds the petals one by one, letting them flutter to the ground through his fingers.

Who the hell does he think he is? If Devil did something like that, I wouldn't think anything of it. Devil does what he likes. But Lenny Darling is an adult. And adults don't go ripping up flowers in grannies' gardens.

I force open the window.

"What did you do that for?" I yell.

"It needed d-dead heading," he replies in his whispery voice. "Lots of things do round here. I rather approve of culling as an ethos."

I don't know what to say to that so I don't say anything.

"What happened to your finger?" calls Lenny.

I freeze.

"I noticed it the other day. Did you have an accident in prison?"

I don't know why I said what I did next. I think I was trying to shock him.

"My mate cut it off," I say. "He's still got it, as far as I know."

"What?" Lenny's face drops. "Someone did that to you on purpose?"

"Not exactly, we were messing around," I say. "It was collateral damage."

"Are you sure?" asks Lenny. He looks genuinely interested. "Are you being terrorized by someone, Chas?"

I grunt. "It was an accident. Devil's hand slipped." I'm not convinced this is true, but it's got nothing to do with Lenny.

"I hope you've had it seen to."

"Don't tell Mum," I say. "It will only freak her out."

Lenny grins at me. It's not nice. I decide to terminate the conversation and I slam down the window. I wait in my room until he's gone.

Eighteen

It's Friday at last. I'm dead early, but she said don't be late. So I'm hanging around like a right muppet watching all these people pile out of the Odeon. It's been a hot day and it hasn't cooled down yet. I've had a shower, shaved (not that I really need to) and I got Gran to iron my best shirt and trousers. I had a haircut yesterday; I went where I always go, the barber's next to the courts, A Close Shave. It was weird, the last time I was there was before I got sent down for nicking the jug. Me and Devil were still hanging out all the time and I was writing letters to Lenny Darling – who was still safely locked up in US maximum security. How things change. Anyway, the barber was the same bloke as always, but this time he cut my hair much shorter than usual. There's all this space above my ears before my hair starts. I look bloody stupid sideways on. I look all right from the front. But I keep pretending to scratch my ear to hide the sides.

I text Connor Blacker just for something to do.

goin out wiv lexi bet u wish u were me

I wander a little way down the street, looking in the shop windows but not really seeing anything. I'm nervous. Even though I left the shower till the last possible moment I stink of sweat.

Me and Lexi hang out all the time, but, apart from walking home from school, we're usually part of a group. She's always with her mates and I'm definitely one of the lads. Tonight is different.

I watch the traffic and the people. I check my mobile about every thirty seconds in case I've missed any messages. It wouldn't take much for me to belt home. I hate all this waiting.

Nothing has changed in the town centre for years. It's the same shops (except there's a baker's where the TV rental place used to be) the same bloke-on-a horse statue in the high street, even the same faces, only older and uglier every day. The only decent thing in this town is Lexi Juby. I'm going to leave as soon as I have an alternative. My dream job is to be a rally car driver. But that's not likely to happen. I watch an aeroplane cross the sky. I could be an air steward. I'd get to fly all round the world with lots of beautiful women. Only it is a bit of a gay job for a bloke. I pause at the travel agents' window. I saw this programme on TV a while ago about this place in Greece or somewhere where all the women get drunk and are pretty wild. That's when I decided I wanted to be a holiday rep even though I've never been abroad. I've only been to the beach once, and that was when I was eight years old with Guy and

Midge, my ex-foster parents.

I'm reading all the holiday prices.

Gran Canaria	*2 weeks £209*
Malaga	*1 week (half board) £220*
Malta	*1 week £130*

I suddenly get the urge to go somewhere. But I'm never going to have that sort of money, am I? All I get is twenty quid a week off Gran.

I'm standing there for ages, killing time and trying to stop myself watching the clock. I can't stand it. I check my mobile. 20:05.

She's not coming. She's stood me up. I bet she and Debs are all laughing themselves sick somewhere. Oh man. I bet they're all spying on me and laughing at my haircut. Maybe that's it. Maybe she took one look at my haircut and legged it off.

"Chas."

I spin round. I am half hoping it's Lexi but I know it isn't, because the voice is lisping and creepily soft. I nearly fall off the pavement when I find myself face to face with Lenny Darling.

"Waiting for someone?" asks Lenny. "Devlin Juby maybe? Your mother said you used to spend a lot of time together. Sounds like trouble. Or maybe you're waiting for your g-girlfriend."

Don't let this be happening. I breathe out. Lexi will be here any minute.

"Relax, I'm not going to kill you," says Lenny.

"What?"

"I'm being humorous," says Lenny and he cracks his skull-face into what is supposed to be a smile.

"No you're not," I mutter. I look frantically round for an escape route. But if I leave now, there's a chance I might miss her.

"Chas," Lenny shakes his head, "why should you be scared of me? I know I don't look like much at the moment, but neither would you if you'd spent the last ten years underground and in mortal dread for your life."

"I'm not scared of you," I lie.

Lenny smiles. He's wearing a suit. It's cream coloured and he's wearing a sky blue shirt underneath which is open at the neck so his pale chest pokes out.

"I'm surprised and grateful that you haven't yet divulged my unfortunate history to the entire town," says Lenny. "It makes me think better of you. I want people to get to know me as a p-person first." He puts a hand on my shoulder and I nearly wet myself. "Do you remember that eloquent question *Did you mean to m-murder that kid?* in your first letter? I thought to myself, here I have someone with startling bluntness. Some might say, damningly rude. What do you think?"

"Whatever," I say. I don't like thinking that I'm helping him out by not saying anything. I'm only keeping quiet for Mum's sake.

"I'm off to see your mum now; she's quite an

original, isn't she?" Lenny winks at me and I get a nasty prickling down my neck. "She's cooking something for me."

"Leave her alone," I say suddenly. "She's not your type and she's not well." I stare at him as long as I can, which isn't very long because his eyes are so freaky.

"She's attractive enough," he says. "Speaking of which. . ."

I follow his gaze and look over my shoulder.

"Hi Chas, who's your mate?"

It's Lexi. She's actually turned up. She's looking amazing. Her hair is straight and shiny and she's got this sparkly green eye make-up on. She's wearing a pink miniskirt, with all these ruffles, and a white vest.

"I'm Lenny Darling, a friend of the family." and he goes to shake her hand. "You might want to call me Darling."

Ugh. What a creep.

"No thanks," says Lexi.

"Come on," I say and grab her wrist and try to drag her away. But Lexi isn't the type to be dragged anywhere.

"A friend of *his* family?" she asks. "You must be mad."

"Probably," says Lenny and smiles. "And you are?"

"Lexi," she says.

"Of course, Lexi Juby, you're the sister of the infamous Devil." He looks at me. "I haven't m-met him yet."

"It's Devlin, actually," says Lexi.

194

Lenny is looking at Lexi in a really pervy way. The man's hitting on my woman now, as well as my mum.

"And I understand you're young Chas's girlfriend. What a delightful couple." His voice is like, really sarky.

"Steady on," says Lexi. "We're just mates."

"Oh?" Lenny pretends to be surprised. "Chas had led me to believe your relationship was rather more, er, i-i-intimate than that."

Bastard.

"We'll miss the film," I say and start walking off. Lexi'll never speak to me again.

"OK," nods Lenny. "I get the message. Farewell for now. I'll see you around, Lexi Juby, sister of Dev-lin. Daughter of. . .?"

"Satan," says Lexi, giving him her sweetest smile.

I put my hand on Lexi's shoulder and guide her away at a speed. When we are round the corner I realize two things. One: I am actually leading Lexi in a boyfriend kind of way. Two: I can feel the clasp on the strap of her bra. It makes me feel weak.

I remove my hand from her shoulder and grab her hand instead. We walk fast, down the street, past the police station and through the park gates.

I'm sweating again. I don't know if it's because I'm holding Lexi's hand or because I've just been face to face with Lenny Darling.

We collapse on the park bench next to the fountain.

"Who's the creepy bloke?" asks Lexi. "He could do with a block booking at Fast Tan."

"He's my mum's boyfriend," I say.

"Gross," says Lexi and she smiles at me. "Why did you freak out? You're usually Mr Cool."

"It's complicated," I say. I'm dying to tell her about him, but for Mum's sake I keep quiet.

"You can trust me," says Lexi. She takes a can of Coke from her bag, opens it and offers it to me. It's still cold. Only Lexi Juby could have a freezing cold can of Coke in her bag on a boiling June evening.

I drink half the can before giving it back. I feel better. She hasn't freaked out about me telling Lenny she was my girlfriend.

"He's not good enough for my mum," I say.

"No one likes the idea of their parents having relationships," says Lexi. She stretches out her long, brown legs. "It's psychological."

I fiddle with my phone and Lexi changes the subject.

"Devlin's been asking after you," she says. "He came home yesterday. Have you two fallen out? He's being weirder than usual."

Oh no, Devil's on the loose again. I hate to say it, but I felt much more relaxed knowing he wasn't around. Now I'm nervous. He could be anywhere.

"We had a disagreement," I say. "It can get pretty intense when you're locked up together."

"I'd have killed him," says Lexi.

"I had a go," I say and we both laugh.

We're chatting and hanging out in the park and before I know it, two hours have passed. I can't believe it, time hasn't gone this quickly since, I don't know, since before I got sent to Bevanport. Lexi tells me about Devil and how he's got a massive bruise on his face and hasn't eaten a thing since he's got home. It's hard for me to feel sorry for him. We talk about all sorts of other stuff: mostly to do with school, but every now and then she starts going on about the war or something and I have to pretend I know what she's on about.

"You look sad, what's s'matter?" asks Lexi, drawing her feet up on the bench and resting her chin on her gorgeous bare knees. "Are you worrying about your exams?"

"Exams are no sweat," I lie. I wasn't aware that I looked sad. I thought I was having the time of my life.

"I hate them," she says. "I have to pass enough to get into college. I'm going to be a psychologist."

"What's that?" Though really I am more interested in whether I am going to kiss her. We are on a date after all. Dates are for kissing. Lexi must know that.

"It's studying human behaviour," says Lexi. "Working out why we behave like we do. It's usually related to childhood."

I think I'd better kiss her in the next few minutes. Just a quick one to start, then a proper snog. I run my tongue along the roof of my mouth.

"Like, Devlin, my dear brother. Imagine being called 'Devil' by absolutely everyone since before you could even walk. He never had a chance. He's got a lot to live up to."

This is such a bizarre idea I momentarily forget about kissing.

"Hang on, you're saying Devil, I mean Devlin, is a nutter because of his name?" This psychology stuff seems a bit far-fetched to me.

"Partly," says Lexi, scratching her arm. "If I ever have kids I'm going to give them the most mainstream, boring names I can think of. It means they can be who they want."

She's lost me there. Maybe I should put my arm round her before I kiss her. I don't want to scare her off.

"OK, my brother has always been hyperactive and he could have done with a few doses of Ritalin when he was little," Lexi carries on. "But he also got depressed when my parents split up and my mum left."

"I thought your old man kicked her out?" I say, casually looping my arm on the bench behind her.

Lexi looks annoyed. "Is that what Devlin told you?"

I nod.

"I expect he tells you Dad's a right head case, right?"

I edge closer. "Isn't he?"

"Devlin says that to make everyone think he's hard too. True, my dad's not exactly a model citizen." Lexi pauses and stares into space. "Devil winds him up because he's always in trouble. And he can get really angry. But he's got his good side too."

Devil has told me in the past that Lexi is by far the favourite and can do no wrong, whereas he can't do anything right.

"Inside, Devlin misses Mum like hell," says Lexi.

Sometimes I'm glad I don't have a sister.

"So why doesn't he live with her?"

"Ha," says Lexi. "She says she can't handle him, or me. She's been saying that since we were born."

"Do you miss her?"

"Nope, she's a cow."

"My dad left me," I say thoughtfully. "What does that mean I do?"

"Aha, there you are," says Lexi. "You're searching for a father figure. That's why you're always in trouble with the police. Secretly, you love the authority."

Where does she get all this? It is probably all very interesting but I can't concentrate on psychology any more because Lexi's mouth is suddenly very close to mine and she smells so sweet that I kiss her.

"That was nice," says Lexi, when we come apart. So I kiss her again. We're sitting on the bench, kissing and kissing, and it's amazing. It's like having a fantastic meal when you're starving; no it's better than that. I forget everything when I'm kissing her; I only concentrate on how her lips feel and how good she smells. Her skin is so smooth it's incredible. I'm lost in Lexi and the evening sounds of birds singing and a jogger passing us are muffled and distant. . .

My arm is yanked back and I am dragged away. An angry, red face stares down at me and for a split second I think it is Juby-the-Killer himself and that I am about to die.

"Get off my sister, you little prick."

It's Devil. He doesn't look like a man who is missing his mummy.

"Piss off, Devlin," shrieks Lexi.

I couldn't agree more. Devil lets go of my arm and I spring up to face him.

He looks older, more tired than I remember. He seems heavier in the face and he needs a shave.

"Nice to see you too," I say. "Started any fires lately?"

"Keep your hands off my little sister," says Devil. He's all wound up like he's just done a job.

"Oh chill out," says Lexi. "Mind your own business."

"You don't know him like I do," says Devil. "He's a prick. He's been in my room."

"What are you on about?" I say, trying to stay calm.

"Don't lie," says Devil. "I know you've been through my stuff."

"How?" asks Lexi.

Devil ignores her. "Go on," he says to me. "Admit it."

"Aw, you're full of shit," I say.

This is when his fist meets my chin. I fall back on the bench and see stars. I really do. Then I get a metallic taste in my mouth and blood spills out over my chin.

Devil stands over me and I see him pull something out of his pocket. It's the jam jar from the Jubys' kitchen cupboard and floating inside is that small brown shape.

It's my finger.

"Pathetic, isn't it?" says Devil, looking down on me.

"Just like you." He shoves it back in his pocket and starts to walk off.

Then I'm mad.

When I was little and used to lose my temper, I thought I was The Incredible Hulk. There's the bit that happens first, you know, when his eyes suddenly switch to bright blue and his eyebrows come together in a massive frown. Then his muscles rip through his clothes and he goes green. I used to believe it was happening to me. I knew there was no going back. I'd start roaring and chase all the kids round the playground. I didn't usually catch anyone; I just chased anyone in my way, even if they had nothing to do with why I'd lost my temper in the first place. I must have looked pretty silly, running around roaring and chasing random people. After a few minutes I'd tire myself out and calm down. My eyes would revert back to brown, my muscles would shrink and I'd be skinny little Chas again. As I got older I realized everyone was laughing at me when I "turned", so I didn't do it any more. That's when I started nicking stuff and getting my kicks in other ways.

But as the impact of Devil's punch spreads out over my brain, I feel that old feeling. The eyes turning, the anger boiling up in me. I'm not scared of Devil any more. I jump up and nut him hard in the chest, then I let him have it, wham, wham, with both fists. I surprised him, he wasn't covering himself. I think he's winded by the way he's clutching his stomach and gasping. Devil is much bigger than me so I need every advantage I can get. So I jump on him and start thumping his back.

"Give it here," I shout.

"STOP IT, YOU CHILDREN," screams Lexi.

Devil rounds up and kicks me in the legs. I stumble, but don't fall. I lash out with one hand, but miss and overbalance. Devil kicks me to the ground. The tarmac stings my hands and knees but I get up before Devil starts his hammering. I've got this amazing energy. It's like when I nicked the lorry. I feel on fire, I don't know if it is pain or adrenalin. I turn to face Devil but he's already coming for me, swearing and shouting abuse. I cover my head and jump to the side. I think Devil is surprised by how well I'm fighting. I think he thought I would be easy, like always. But it's like all my worry about Mum and Lenny, all my feelings for Lexi, are all concentrated in my fists. WHAM! I let him have it, right in the guts. My fist makes direct contact with the area under his ribs and he keels over. He lies on the ground and I stand over him, panting.

I remember Lexi and look round for her. She's running through the park gates.

"Lexi," I roar, like I'm in a film or something but she just puts her middle finger up at me and keeps going.

Oh shit. I look down at Devil. He's breathing heavily.

"You all right, Devil?" I ask.

Devil aims a kick at my legs, but I hop out of the way. I can see the park keeper heading our way. He's talking into a mobile phone.

I look down at Devil. He's sitting himself up.

"Better go," I say. "The police will be here soon."

"Piss off," says Devil, and spits on my trainers.

I want to go for him again. He needs to be taught a lesson. But I hear the whine of police sirens and I head off over the grass, wanting to catch up with Lexi. I can't run too fast because my leg hurts. I make my way out of the park, feeling really high. For the first time in my life I actually won a fight with Devlin Juby. It's incredible. I cross the road and look down the high street, but I can't see Lexi anywhere.

It's quite late now, about ten o'clock, and she shouldn't be out on her own. It's madness, one minute I'm having the best moment of my life, i.e. kissing Lexi, the next I'm fighting her brother. Again. I tear down the high street looking all over the place. I stop for a breather and wipe my face with the back of my hand. When I look down it's covered with blood. People are giving me funny looks. Oh God, there's a police car at the end of the street. I turn and walk up an alleyway which leads past the car park. I really can't afford to get done for fighting. I decide to head home. Lexi has vanished. I circle the car park and as I cross the road I see a small figure in the distance.

"Lexi." I run to catch up; she doesn't stop, or turn round, but keeps going.

"Lexi," I pant.

"I'm not talking to you," she says. "You're just as bad as the rest of them."

"But—'

'Shut up." And she strides on ahead.

She's mad.

"Let me walk you home," I plead.

"Yes, damn right you will," she says. "But not a word."

She sounds so much like a schoolteacher I nearly laugh. But this isn't funny. My woman is mad at me.

"Lex-ie," I croon and try to stroke her hair, but she slaps my hand away and looks at me, her eyes flashing.

"If you touch me again, I'm phoning my dad," she says. "Got it?"

I nod.

So we walk home in silence. I keep thinking of things to say, but it all feels a bit lame. I want to say, *But he went for me!* or *I love you Lexi Juby*, or *It wasn't my fault.*

The fact is I have beaten up her brother. (Yeees!)

When we get to her gate she stops for a minute.

"So, is he all right?" she asks.

"Who?"

"Devlin."

"He seemed OK. He's probably the same as me." I find myself following her up the garden path.

"So you left him there?"

"Yes."

"Is he OK? Can he walk?" She suddenly looks worried.

"He'll be fine," I say. "He'll be home in five minutes."

Was he standing up by the time I left? I couldn't remember.

"I mean it," says Lexi, fumbling for her door keys. "I'm not talking to you again."

That's a bit harsh. All I did was fight her brother, and he beat me up a few weeks before.

"But Lexi. . ."

She unlocks the door, steps inside and shuts it in my face.

Nineteen

Lexi can't have her wish of never seeing me again, because the next day, as usually happens after a Friday, is Saturday and we have to attend our community service order. I've had instructions from Tony to turn up at the playground in the park and to wear, you've guessed it, old clothes.

I'm on time, but though I can see Tony sitting on a swing there's no sign of Lexi. I thought of calling for her on the way, but chickened out. There'll be plenty of time for talking this morning.

Last night, on my way home, I was pretty pissed off. I mean I was glad that I'd actually got to snog Lexi Juby and that I'd floored Devil. The showman in me wanted to phone all my mates and tell them. Or should I say, all my mates except Devil. But mostly I just felt miserable. I'd blown it with Lexi before we'd even begun. But it wasn't my fault. Devil laid the first punch.

Tony looks up from his paper when he sees me coming and slips off the swing.

"We're painting the railings," he says. "I want the whole fence done by midday or you're not going home."

Tony's trying to be a hard man today.

"Nice to see you too, Tony," I say.

I take the pot of red paint and paintbrush he is offering me and walk to the end of the railings. The park is still empty. It's only half past eight. There's fog swirling around on the grass even though the sky is blue and the sun is shining.

"Where's your friend?" asks Tony. "She's ten minutes late."

I shrug, wondering the same thing.

The old paint is peeling off the metal railings. If I paint it now, it will just flake off and look crap.

"Tony," I say. "We need to rub this down with a wire brush first."

"No we don't," says Tony, who is already painting. "Just get on with it and stop procrastinating."

"But we'll do a bad job."

"Chas, just do it."

I suppose they just want to punish us by making us work. They don't care what we actually do. It's pretty demoralizing spending ages doing something when you know it's going to turn out crap.

I'm painting my tenth upright and there are a crowd of toddlers trying to kill themselves on the slide by the time Lexi finally appears.

"At last," says Tony. "This will go on your report, you know."

Lexi ignores him and comes straight up to me. Maybe she's forgiven me. Maybe I'm going to get a lovely Lexi kiss.

"Where is he?" she asks.

She looks tired and her usually beautiful hair seems, dare I say it, unwashed. She's wearing an old pair of jogging trousers and a baggy grey sweatshirt. I'm quite shocked. Lexi is usually immaculate.

"So you're not speaking to me, then, eh?" I grin, hoping she'll smile back.

She doesn't. "Come on, I know you know something," she says.

I shake my head. "I'm ignorant, darling."

"Devlin didn't come home last night," she says.

This is when Tony hands her a paintbrush and paint and tells her to start work at the other end of the railings.

"I haven't seen him since, you know, our disagreement," I say.

"Move," orders Tony, and Lexi shuffles off, scowling at me as she goes.

"My, you are both in a good mood this morning," I say.

I dip my brush in the pot and slap the paint on the metal. Drops of red paint fall on the grass. "HE'LL BE FINE," I shout to Lexi. "DOESN'T HE STAY OUT A LOT?"

"SOMETIMES," yells back Lexi. "BUT NOT AFTER SOME NOB HAS KICKED HIS HEAD IN."

"THAT'S ENOUGH," roars Tony.

"We're both still working," I call to him. "Which is more than you're doing."

I turn back to Lexi. "SORRY, DARLING, I HAVE NO IDEA WHERE HE IS. . ."

"DON'T CALL ME DARLING," shouts Lexi.

This is when Tony throws a massive wobbler, which isn't very terrifying but I decide just to humour him for the sake of his blood pressure.

I'm not worried about Devil. He's a big lad. He can look after himself.

At tea break, Lexi goes for me again. "How hard did you hit him?" she asks.

"As hard as he hit me."

Lexi takes a sip of tea then spits it out on the grass.

"Gross, isn't it?" I say. "I think they're trying to poison us."

"I burned my tongue," says Lexi. Her eyes are full of tears. She really is worried about him.

"He'll turn up, he always does," I say, in a gentler voice. "Devil's always necking off somewhere and he hasn't been gone twenty-four hours yet."

Lexi gives me a sidelong glance. "I've just got this bad feeling." She stops and looks at me. "Dad's thinking of calling the police."

Now I am alarmed. If Juby-the-Killer is voluntarily going to call the police, he must be worried.

"Blimey," I say.

"Chas," says Lexi. "I'm going to tell my dad about the fight."

"Why?" I ask her. "It was just a scrap."

"Yes, but now my brother is missing," she says.

Is she also going to tell her dad why Devil threw the first punch?

By the end of the morning, we've painted one whole side of the railings and Tony is satisfied so he lets us go. I ask Lexi if she's going home, but she mutters something about "seeing a mate", and legs it off over the park. She's a very different person from last night. Even Tony notices.

"She's lost her sparkle," he says. "Makes my job easier, anyway."

I drop my paintbrush at his feet and walk away. I try texting Devil.

where r u waster? everyone's freakin

I get no response. It's hard for me to believe anything has happened to Devil, but I have this nagging doubt in the back of my mind. What if, when I punched him, I really did hurt him and he's dying in some ditch somewhere?

I try to convince myself that this is impossible, that I'd have to be wearing knuckledusters to hurt Devlin Juby. All the same, I wish he'd turn up.

Twenty

At home, I lurk in the hall outside the kitchen, listening.

Mum's not alone; she's got Lenny with her. Again. That's like, twice in three days. What do they talk about? I can't think of anything they have in common. Lenny sounds tired. His voice is louder than usual.

"Caroline, I really don't need to hear this now."

Is he having a go at her?

I walk in.

Mum's bustling around making tea and there's a plate of those horrible yellow and pink square cakes on the counter. Lenny looks crap. He's unshaven and wearing a tartan shirt and what must be security guard trousers. His breath stinks of booze and his boots are covered in mud. He's trailed loads of crap all over the kitchen floor. That's well disrespectful that is.

"Look at that," I say to Mum, indicating the floor. "He's worse than me."

Lenny doesn't even bother to look up. "Are you initiating a conversation, my erudite ex-correspondent? Or are you also about to throw some f-foul accusation at me?"

What's he on about?

"Chas," says Mum, fussing with the mugs. "I've not seen you for ages." She's jumpy.

Lenny helps himself to three cakes and sits himself at the kitchen table. He's so at home it makes me mad.

"Mum," I say, ignoring Lenny. "Devil's missing."

"And that's a bad thing?" butts in Lenny.

Cheeky.

"Juby's going round the neighbours talking to everyone," I lie. "So if you don't want to see him, you'd better go out."

Mum sets down her tea. "Devil's dad can be a bit aggressive," she tells Lenny.

"So I gather," he replies, staring into space. He's not listening. He's miles away.

"Lenny's taking me out," says Mum proudly. "We're going to the Gilded Lady, for dinner."

Lenny really does look crap.

"What's the matter with you?" I can't help asking. "You've not seen Devil, have you?"

"Chas, don't start," says Mum, looking nervously at Lenny.

Lenny stares at my mother. "Your son doesn't like me, Caroline."

"I'm so sorry," says Mum, giving me the evils.

"Where's Gran?" I ask, not looking at Lenny. I don't like the way he talks to Mum.

"At Dolores's."

Lenny stands up. He goes to the sink and splashes

212

cold water over his face, but catches his hand on the tap. A thin line of blood appears on his skin and he swears.

"Been on the bottle for long?" I ask.

"Chas," says Mum. She looks like she is going to either cry or hit me.

Lenny takes a massive swig of tea and slams down the mug.

"I'm out of sorts because I've been up all night. My work colleague has inexplicably fallen sick and I've had to cover. During my shift, my thoughtful employers decided I would be better employed in some emergency courier activity for them, which involved a drive to Bristol at four o'clock in the morning, and finally, during the rest of my marathon shift, which is never the most stimulating of occupations, I was visited for questioning by the p-police over the disappearance of Devlin Juby."

OH MY GOD, I can hardly believe I'm hearing this. Devil's hardly been gone a day and already the police are sniffing around.

"It's a routine thing," he says, "for someone with a background as colourful as mine. However, as you may be able to imagine, and I may be crediting you with more intelligence than you could ever possess, police interrogations do not evoke happy memories for me." He has a swig of tea and I notice his hand is trembling. As far as I know, Lenny has never even met Devil.

I stare at him. "So the cops reckon you did something to Devil?"

Lenny snorts. "I can't imagine how anyone could hurt a teenager," he says turning to my mum. "They are uniformly so s-sensitive and charming."

"Don't bother talking to him," says Mum. "He's not worth the effort."

Her words make me feel sick and I have to look away. I hate the way she sucks up to him.

"Shall we depart?" asks Lenny. "I'm obviously not wanted here and rude children make me ill."

I'm not children. I'll be sixteen in three weeks.

Mum opens and then shuts her mouth.

"I'll get my coat," she says.

"It's warm," says Lenny. "You won't need one." He swallows the last of his cake. "Prison doesn't seem to have made much of an impression on your son. He has no respect for his elders at all." He wipes his mouth with the back of his hand. "Has he ever had any discipline in his life?"

"Oh, get lost. You're not my dad," I mutter.

I feel Lenny's eyes on me.

"Oh no," he says. "I really don't ever want to be your dad."

Mum and Lenny have been gone for about an hour when my mobile bleeps. It's a text message from Lexi.

no devlin.
dad on his way

At least she cares enough to give me a warning. I hide all the kitchen knives and make sure my mobile is in my pocket. I turn on all the lights and open the windows, so when I scream, the neighbours will hear. I feel like I'm one of the kids in that old film, *The Lost Boys*, when they are running around, boarding up the house at sunset before the vampires arrive.

I sit at the kitchen table and wait. I want to run. But I can't hide for ever, can I? I have to sort this out. I'm hoping I'll be able to make it up as I go along. I clench my teeth as I hear the front gate click and heavy feet pounding up the path.

BANG BANG BANG.

He's here.

I open the door before he breaks it down. Juby fills the hallway. He's wearing an immaculate white T-shirt and his muscles stick out through it. He's got so much stubble, it's practically a beard.

"Where's your mum?" he growls.

"Out," I say, stepping back as Juby comes towards me. I feel puny next to him, like a little kid. He smells of fresh sweat and it makes me feel ill.

"Where?"

I shrug. I'm not going to involve her.

"Grandmother?"

"Out," I say. I so hope he doesn't remember me being in his room.

Juby pushes past me to look in the sitting room, then he pokes his head round the kitchen door.

215

He puts a heavy hand on my shoulder and propels me into the kitchen. He pushes me into a chair and sits opposite me. I can't believe this is happening to me.

"You were fighting with Devil in the park last night, yes?"

It's not a kitchen any more, it's an interrogation room.

I shrug. It's all out now. Everyone's going to know. I can't stop looking at Juby's hands. They're huge. He could smash me to pieces.

"Why?"

I say nothing.

Juby reaches over and grabs my arm. It hurts.

"I'm serious."

Just then the front door opens, there's the sound of pattering feet and a small, wrinkly ball of fire flies into the room screeching and snarling.

"GET OUT OF MY HOUSE, YOU GREAT BULLY! THE POLICE ARE ON THEIR WAY."

"Gran, leave it," I say.

"OUT," she screams and aims a kick at Juby's shin.

"Mrs Rack, I'm worried about my son and – ouch. . ."

Juby tries to protect his head as Gran goes for him with her frying pan.

"YOU COME IN HERE, INTIMIDATING MY GRANDSON, GET OUT!!!"

Juby is on his feet. "Jesus, I'm not here to make trouble."

"ARE YOU DEAF?" Wham. She whacks him again with the pan and Juby is backing towards the door.

"My son—"

"OUT."

Then things get all confusing because suddenly Lexi is in the room and is pulling Juby out by his arm.

"Dad, you might give her a heart attack. Come on."

"I'LL GIVE YOU A HEART ATTACK MORE LIKE."

Juby backs down the steps on to the path. "My son is missing."

"GOOD THING TOO. YOUR SON IS A BAD INFLUENCE ON MY GRANDSON. THEY SHOULD LOCK HIM UP AND THROW AWAY THE KEY."

Juby tries once more. "For God's sake—"

"GET OUT!"

Juby's standing on the pavement outside the garden gate, but he doesn't want to leave. But Gran comes back out with a carton of eggs and starts throwing them at him. One hits him right in the middle of his bald shiny head. Yellow slime runs down his face. Lexi drags at his arm and he backs away down the street, as he sees Gran aiming another egg.

"Stay away from my grandson," screams Gran. She chucks the egg and it falls just short of the garden gate. She's getting another one out of the box when I grab her arm.

"Gran, he's gone."

Gran grins at me, her face is all pink and hot and her eyes are sparkling.

"I hate eggs anyway, disgusting things. I can't think why I let Caroline bring them in the house."

I take the box from my gran's hands and guide her back into the house. I sit her on her favourite chair in the sitting room and drag the pouffe over for her to put her feet up. I go next door to make her a cup of tea.

"Gran," I say, putting the tea on her table. "I thought you were at Dolores's?"

"My sixth sense told me to come back," says Gran. She takes a sip of tea and lets out a giggle. "And anyway, I haven't had the opportunity to throw an egg for years." She's really pleased with herself. "I'm not scared of Juby. I've know him since he was a baby. And no man barges into my house. Your father found that one out." She leans forwards in the chair. "Come on, Chas, tell me what's going on." I can see her pink scalp through her hair. "You're not doing anything against the law are you?" She grabs my wrist. "If you're involved with drugs you can pack your bags."

"Gran, cool it." I shake her off and then surprise her by kissing her papery old cheek. "Would your beloved grandson get involved in anything like that?"

Gran's on a high all night. But I know Juby will be back. I go upstairs and get out my maths book. I stare at the page, unable to concentrate. I slam the book shut and hear Gran laughing to herself downstairs.

At least somebody's happy.

I go to bed early but I can't sleep. I keep thinking about Lexi and how worried she is about Devil. Trust him to vanish and mess everything up just when I was getting somewhere with her.

I wish my brothers were around. They'd find Devil. Selby would be twenty-five by now if he hadn't gone overboard sniffing lighter fluid, or glue or whatever it was. And Stephen might as well be dead. He's not come home for years and years. I wish he would walk through the front door right now and come and talk to me.

I hear a male voice outside and I stop breathing. Maybe it's Stephen. Maybe he's come home. He'll help me find Devil. I'm not having him go anywhere near Lexi though, he's too good looking. I sit up on the bed and begin to feel a bit excited. What if it really is him? Why not? He's due for a visit. Downstairs, a woman is speaking. It's Mum. Her voice is funny like she's been crying. It's not Stephen. I'm disappointed right down to my guts. I hear a sob. She's crying. What's he said to her now?

"Just GO," Mum shrieks and the door slams. I hear the garden gate click as Lenny leaves. A lovers' tiff! Fantastic! Now maybe she'll dump him. But Mum's sobbing carries up the stairs. I should go and mop her up as Gran went to bed hours ago. But then Mum thunders up the stairs and bursts into my room.

"I HATE you," she screams, running to the bed and shaking me.

"What?" I pull away and stand facing her from the other side of the bed. Her eye make-up is smeared down her cheeks and her hair is falling out of its clip.

"He doesn't want to . . . *sob* . . . see me . . . any more . . . *sob* . . . he says . . . family conflict . . . my son . . . *sob* . . . impossible. . .'

Oh God. She's losing it.

"You deliberately . . . *sob* . . . set out to do this," says Mum. She collapses on the bed. "Didn't you?"

"Mum."

"You don't want me to be happy." She wails and bursts into tears all over again. "I'm alone again."

"You're too good for him," I say and mean it. I never really thought he liked her anyway. He didn't look at her the right way.

"That's what they all say," says Mum, wiping her eyes. She sits there crying and I don't know what to do. If I tried hugging her, she'd probably hit me. To my relief Gran comes in looking tired and tiny in her purple quilted dressing gown.

"All right then, poppet," she says in the voice she only ever uses when Mum is like this. "Has he let you down? They all do, trust me. Come on, let's get you a drink." She puts an arm under my mother and sits her up. I'm about to say something when Gran shakes her head and puts a finger to her lips.

"What's wrong with me?" cries Mum.

"You're fine, lovely. It's him with the problem." Talking and whispering, Gran manages to persuade Mum out of my room and into her own. I stare at the tear stains on my rumpled duvet. This is all my fault. She was doing so well, now everything's going wrong.

To my amazement I hear Mum laughing a little from next door. It's like Gran gets an attitude transplant when Mum's ill, she's so good with her. Then, when Mum's on the mend, bam! Gran's back to being the old cow she really is.

I get into bed, turn out the lamp and put my fingers in my ears.

Twenty-one

It's Monday. I go to school and do my science exam. Like Mum, I spent most of yesterday in bed. I ventured out to the shop once and saw police cars outside the Jubys' house. I hope it's not bad news. I tried texting Lexi but she didn't reply.

After my exam I feel weak. I don't think I'm going to pass. My heart wasn't in it. I've got one more left – the second maths exam – tomorrow afternoon. I decide to hang around at lunch time to catch up with some mates but I keep finding myself on my own. No one is being especially unfriendly, but it feels like my old sparring partners are keeping their distance. Take Connor, for example. He nods at me and asks if I've ever seen a cat's belly button, but as soon as one of his chess-club buddies appears he can't get shot of me quickly enough. And a footy game starts up but I don't join in. It doesn't feel right. Lexi isn't in school. I'm walking down the corridor on my way to see Mr Fuller when Ugly Debs blanks me.

"Debs," I say. "What's up?"

She keeps walking and I jog after her.

"What's all this unfriendly act about, hey? Don't tell me you're not in love with me any more?"

Debs stops, and spins round. She's quite pink and looks almost attractive.

"I don't talk to psychos," she says.

"What?" I catch her arm.

"What happened to Devil after you beat him up?" she asks. I drop her arm and step back, shocked by the hate in her voice. I watch her bounce off up the corridor, unable to believe my ears.

How did she know about the fight? Is this why all the kids are acting strange? Blimey, nobody likes me any more. Even my own mother isn't speaking to me.

Fuller steps out of a classroom.

"You're late," he says. "We need to talk about the exam." And he leads me off to his office and goes on about attempting all the questions and not giving up and having a good weekend of revision and that he glanced over my first exam paper and it looked like I'd passed.

"Chas?" he says. "Are you listening to me?"

I nod.

"Just remember," says Fuller. "Turn up tomorrow at two p.m. We're impressed that you've turned up to the rest of your exams and done your coursework, though admittedly some of it is pretty ropey."

He goes on like this for a while before he lets me go.

"You'd better be here tomorrow," says Fuller. "Or else."

I drift out of school and nearly get knocked over by a white van man because I forget to look when I'm crossing the road.

"Stupid kid," shouts the driver. I make it to the pavement and feel like crying.

At home, I lie on the bed for ages, listening to music to try and blank out the world, but then the door swings open and Gran stands there, looking none too pleased.

"You've got a visitor," she says.

My heart sinks as I run through the list of those eager to talk with me.

Lenny Darling? Juby? The police?

I stop outside my mother's room and listen. Silence. She hasn't come out since last night. I go downstairs and prepare myself for another ordeal.

It's Lexi.

It may be shallow of me to notice this, but she's looking hot. Her eyes look incredible, they're so serious and sexy and. . .

"We need to talk," she says. She looks at Gran, who is flicking a duster over the cabinets. "In private."

"Let's go upstairs," I say, winking at Gran, who snorts.

"Leave the door open," says Gran. "There'll be no hanky-panky in my house."

I wish.

I run up before Lexi, kick the dirty clothes under the bed and open the window but Lexi doesn't mention the mess.

"We've just had the police around again," she says. "You've got some talking to do."

I feel the grin slip off my face. "Me, why?"

"I overheard them talking in the garden. I think you're going to be arrested."

I stare at her. "I don't know anything."

"I find that hard to believe." Lexi sits on my bed and folds her arms.

(She's on my bed, she's on MY bed.)

"OK, I'll tell you what I have learned today and you can fill in the rest. First they were saying something about a fight in prison? Devlin burned all your exam work?"

"Oh that. It was just a scrap," I say. I smell her perfume. It makes me think of vanilla fudge.

Lexi stares at me intently. "Dad says the screws found you going for him with a chair."

"Actually he went for me with the chair," I say. I think this is true anyway. I don't like the way this is going.

"The police were looking around our house and they found your fingerprints everywhere."

The police have had my fingerprints on file since I was nine years old.

"But I used to go round all the time," I protest.

"Even in my dad's room?" says Lexi, raising an eyebrow.

I shut my mouth. I can't have Lexi finding out about me hiding in her dad's bed. I *can't.*

"There's something else I need you to explain before the police take you away," says Lexi. "They found Devil's mobile in the park and guess what?"

"I'm all ears," I say wearily.

"They found your fingerprint on it. And they say it's very recent."

I don't believe what I'm hearing. I don't remember ever touching Devil's phone.

"Did you borrow it?" asks Lexi.

"No," I say. I'm getting fed up. All I did was give Devil a well-deserved punch. I can't believe I'm getting all this grief.

I look across at Lexi. She's holding herself carefully, like she's getting ready to spring up and run off in case I jump on her and murder her as well.

"Well?" she asks.

I shrug. "Looks like you've sentenced me already." I want her to go. I want to lie on my bed and shut my eyes.

"Chas, the reason I'm telling you all this is because I care about you. I want to give you a chance to explain it all to me." Lexi puts her hand on my knee and my skin feels on fire. "Besides, when the police take you away I won't get to find out anything."

"I know nothing about the mobile," I say. Lexi takes away her hand. I reckon she's left behind a red palm print. "But I did go round your house a couple of weeks ago." I look up at her. "I wanted my finger back."

"And?" Lexi waits.

"And nothing. That's all. I didn't find it."

"You're not helping," says Lexi. She fingers my duvet.

226

I don't know what else to say. I look out of the window. Will they come for me tonight?

"Is there anything you're not telling me?" asks Lexi.

I'm tempted to do a runner until all this blows over.

"What do you think has happened to my brother?" she asks. "Really."

I blow out my breath and scratch my head.

"I honestly don't know," I say. "Look, I don't know what all the fuss is about. This is Devil we're talking about. Not some defenceless little kid." I'm about to go on about how someone would have to be crazy to abduct Devil, he's such a mean kid, but something tells me Lexi wouldn't appreciate it. Daringly, I stroke her hand. "He'll be back."

A round of sobbing erupts from the next room.

"What's that?" Lexi leaps off the bed.

"Only my mother," I say. "She got dumped. She's not taking it very well."

"What? Dumped by that creepy bloke I met outside the cinema?" Lexi settles herself back on the bed and winces as Mum lets out a little yowl.

I nod. "I don't think he ever really liked her. But she thought he was fan-tastic."

"Who is he? I've not seen him around."

Should I tell her? I don't see why not. It might even distract her from obsessing about Devil for a few minutes.

"It's complicated."

"You said that before about him," says Lexi.

227

I let out a lungful of air. "All right," I say. "I'll tell you about Lenny Darling."

I start by telling her about the pen-pal website and how I wrote letters. I miss out the bit about me pretending to be my mother. It doesn't make me look good. I'll explain later if I have to. Lexi raises her eyebrows every now and then and once she murmurs, "You odd boy," under her breath.

I tell her about me being in prison and getting that letter from Lenny.

"How did he know where you were?" she asks.

So I tell her about him meeting up with my mum, and them getting on, and. . .

"Hang on," says Lexi. "Why did you write to him in the first place?"

I go quiet. I have to think about that one. "I suppose I thought it would be funny," I say. "I wanted to know what a killer would be like."

"I wouldn't," said Lexi.

Sensible girl.

"Your mum's going out with someone who escaped from Death Row?"

"He didn't escape," I say. "He was freed. And they're not going out any more."

Lexi stretches.

"So what is he supposed to have done?"

I tell her about the boy on the beach, how he was drowned, but that recently it had been revealed he'd had a heart condition, and how Lenny spent nine years of his life on Death Row. I like the way Lexi listens to me, though I must sound like I am making all of this up.

"It's creepy," says Lexi when I'm finished. "But he's been freed." Lexi looks at her watch and asks ever so casually, "Do the police know about Lenny?"

"He's been in for questioning today," I say. "They know all about him."

Gran is bustling around on the landing and slamming the airing cupboard door. She's pretending to put away washing.

"That should do it, Gran," I call out.

"Do what?" Gran sticks her head round the door and clocks us, sitting on the bed.

"Your first great-grandchild should be on the way." Despite everything, I can't resist winding her up. Gran stares at me and clicks her tongue in annoyance. She wags her finger at me.

"Don't worry," says Lexi wearily. "He's being stupid."

"He'd better," says Gran, and goes back to her rummaging.

"Nob," says Lexi.

I hang my head. She's right.

"I still don't get why you wrote to him in the first place," says Lexi.

"I must just be a bit sad," I say, suddenly feeling fed up. This isn't making me look good.

"Nah," says Lexi. "There must be another reason."

I must look confused.

"Everyone always does things for a reason. It's psychology," says Lexi.

Ah, we're back to psychology.

"Can I see one of his letters?"

I don't see how this will help but soon enough, I'm grovelling in my sock drawer for the letters. I fish one out. It's the first he wrote me.

"Let me see," says Lexi. I hand it over, explaining only now how I pretended to be my mother. I watch her scan the page.

"He writes funny," says Lexi, when she's read it. "And I don't like how you've obviously told him about me. Look at this bit, '*Fallible creatures, young women, so you must keep an eye on their behaviour. One question, did you say her surname was Tuby or Juby?*'" She looks at me in disgust. "Ugh, Chas, what else did you say about me?"

I can't remember.

"Did you tell him my surname was Juby, not Tuby?"

"Um, yeah," I say. I can't remember what I wrote. Does she think I've got a photographic memory? Besides, I've got more important things to worry about right now.

"He's got a weird way of saying things," says Lexi. "And I don't like the fact he's talking about my family."

"So a Death Row convict hasn't got a proper grip on his grammar, so what?" I say grumpily. Am I really about to get pulled in?

"I'm following up leads," says Lexi. "Before the police

remove the evidence." She glances out of my window like she's expecting to see The Stealth and Panda Polly charging up the garden path.

"Let me see the other letters."

I get up off the bed and rifle through my drawers. I can only find three. The last one isn't with the others. If she can make anything of them, good luck to her. I'm trying to think who she is reminding me of. There's a cough from the landing and I realize. When she's being all bossy like this, Lexi Juby is very like my dear gran.

"I'd better go. Dad's well jumpy about me since Devlin went missing. I need to borrow these." Lexi scoops the letters into her bag and looks at me. "I should pack yourself an overnight bag, Chas. The police will be here soon and I'm pretty sure you're their number one suspect."

Lexi lets herself out. I go to the window on the landing and watch her run up the garden path and along the street. I'm chuffed she came to warn me but I don't know what to do next. I don't want to wait for the police to arrive. What if they decide I really am to blame? What if I get remanded in custody again? What if I get sent back to Bevanport? It would kill me.

I'm pacing round my room wondering what the hell to do when I hear a siren in the distance. Then I panic, even though I know the sound is coming from an ambulance. I have to go. Now. I can't hang around here a minute longer. I'm not waiting around for the Old Bill to catch up with me. If Devil can disapear, so can I. I'm going to have to miss the maths exam, but anything is better than being sent back to prison. I fumble under the bed for my rucksack and pack some T-shirts and socks. I chuck in my mobile, a torch, all the cash I can find (about ten quid) and my baseball hat. I'm shaking. I keep thinking about my cell at Bevanport, the broken bog, the plastic mattress and the painted brick walls I'd stared at for hours on end. I'm not going back there. Downstairs, I raid the cupboard and load my bag with biscuits, cakes, Coke and nuts.

"What are you up to?" asks Gran, bursting into the kitchen.

"Later, Gran." I bend down and give her a kiss. I don't know when I'll see her again, maybe tomorrow, maybe never.

"Don't break my heart, Chas," she calls as I step out the door.

I pause.

"You've never got a heart in there have you, Gran?" And I'm off, running down the garden path and out the gate. I turn right, so I'll avoid the main drag of the estate. I'm nearly at the end of my road when I see something out of the corner of my eye. I duck behind a car and look back at my house. A police car has just drawn up outside. Shit! I scuttle like a crab behind parked cars until I reach a back alley. Then I leg it. I don't think the cops saw me. I pass a few kids I vaguely know but I ignore them. I'm on my own. It's a warm, windy night and my T-shirt is sticking to me. I feel full of energy. I can go anywhere, do anything. This must be how Stephen felt when he went off to Scotland. I could hitch up there and find him. Or I could make my way to the seaside. I could try and hitch a lift on the car ferry to Ireland, lie about my age and get a job somewhere. But what about Lexi? At the end of the alley, I hesitate. One way will lead me to the centre of the estate: the shops, the bus shelter, the road into town. The other will take me through more residential streets and to the canal.

I end up at the allotments, in Michael's shed.

Twenty-two

Michael hides the key to his shed under a plant pot. I've told him it's a crap hiding place but he says if someone wanted to get into his shed, they wouldn't need a key anyway as it's so easy to break in.

The shed is rammed full of Michael's tools and bamboo and bags of compost. He's also got a deckchair, a camping stove, teabags, coffee, a tin of biscuits and a bag of barley sugars. There's a pint of milk sitting on a shelf. I take a sniff but it's well past it so I put it outside the door. I feel strange, kind of sketchy. I keep hearing rustlings and funny noises and I have to keep looking out the door to check no one is prowling around. It's dark by now and I'm a bit jumpy. Lenny works just over the fence doing his security work, but I'm not too worried about him. It's the police I need to steer clear of. I'm not going back to Bevanport for something I didn't do. I don't know what I'm going to do tomorrow, or the day after. But I can't handle everything at the moment and just want to be out of it for a while.

I brew myself some black coffee and settle in the deckchair. I keep thinking of my bed. I shift around, trying to get comfortable and the whole thing nearly tips over. I can't sleep. The shed doesn't let in much air and the window is jammed shut, but I don't fancy opening the door. Anyone might be about. Now I'm not moving, I can hear all the night noises. The generators from the building site next door are buzzing away, but over them I hear the trees at the bottom of the allotments along by the canal creaking and rustling in the wind. There's a dog barking somewhere, a car revving up some way off, and in the distance, a faint banging. If I listen very hard, I imagine I can hear people's voices coming in on gusts of wind.

I must have drifted off because I nearly fall off the deckchair when my mobile rings. I fumble around my pockets but don't find it before it goes silent. I check the screen. The call was from Lexi and, according to the time on the screen, I've been in the shed for over two hours.

A bleep tells me I have a text message.

wher r u? must c u.

It's also from Lexi. But if I tell her where I am, is she going to set her dad or the coppers on me?

Another message arrives.

chas i must cu now!

There was a time when I would have died for a message like that from Lexi Juby. Now, however, I'm suspicious.

I text, what?

The phone rings and I answer straight away.

"Chas, I've got to see you. I found something. Chas? Are you there?"

"I'm here," I say.

"Where are you, Chas?"

"Do you have to see me now? It's pretty late."

"I'm walking out the door. Tell me where to come."

I breathe out and pray she's not got her old man with her.

"Chas? I'm running out of credit."

"I'll meet you by the allotment gates," I say.

"See you in a minute." Lexi rings off.

What can be so important she has to see me right now? I come out of the shed into the night. It's pretty blowy out here now. Michael's beanpoles and plants are moving around and the massive fence separating the allotments from the building site creaks and groans in the wind. I don't use my torch. The lamps surrounding the building site light up the whole area. The torch only draws attention to me. I step on to the path and walk past the allotments. I wait in the shadows near the gate. I'm as jumpy as hell. I mean, look at me! I'm a nearly-sixteen-year-old kid, who is being tracked by the police and persecuted by his mates because they think I've done something bad to my best mate. All this would make anyone nervous. I wish I had my brothers with me. I wish Selby and Stephen were standing next to me. We'd be invincible. We'd be scared of nothing.

It's dark by this hedge, but I'm still scared someone is watching me. I imagine the coppers are on my tail. Maybe they've got a dozen men in black, all wriggling closer and closer every second with their infrared goggles, all trained on me. Any minute I'm going to be bundled on to the ground and dragged along by my legs. Where is Lexi? She should be here by now, I've been waiting ages. A cracking sound in the greenery makes me hold my breath. But nothing happens. Eventually I have to let out my breath and it comes out way too noisily.

"Chas?" A soft voice whispers my name from the other side of the hedge and my teeth clamp painfully on my lip.

"Is that you? What are you doing breathing like an old perv?"

A figure comes into view and fiddles with the catch on the gate.

"Hello, Lexi." I tongue my lip to see if it's bleeding.

"How do I get in?"

I am tempted to tell her she has to climb the gate. She is wearing a very tight pair of jeans and this would be a sight no boy should miss. However, like I may have mentioned before, the old Chaster zing is missing, and I settle for telling her there's a hole in the fence a few metres along.

"Bugger that," she says. "Come with me, I've got something to show you."

"Lexi, I don't want to go anywhere . . . the police."

"There are no police. I just want to take you to the bridge."

Lexi Juby wants to take me to the canal and show me something. Is she going to try it on? *Now?* No. This can't be right. There's too much madness going on. But Lexi is a mad sort of girl. Maybe she wants to have me before I'm dragged away by the law. I'm confused, but I crawl through the hole in the fence and join her. Even in the dark I can tell she's hot and flustered.

"Lexi," I say, calmer now. "What's all this?"

"You wait. It'll be worth it," says Lexi. She pulls at my hand. "Hurry up."

I allow myself to be dragged along. The bridge is well known for being a place where friendly couples get together after dark. It's dead romantic, the flowing canal, water dripping off the bricks, the thunder of juggernauts hammering overhead.

"What's going on over there?" Lexi points at the building-site fence. "That wasn't there before, was it?"

"They're building luxury flats. There's been building work going on since the spring." Maybe girls don't notice things like that. "Michael's going to lose his allotment," I tell her. "Soon there will be flats all over here."

"Nice place to live," says Lexi. "By the river."

"But the allotments?"

"Houses are more important than old men's beans," says Lexi.

"But what if a family of fluffly rabbits gets squashed by the bull dozers—'

"Shut it," interrupts Lexi. "I thought I heard something."

I fall silent. This isn't the kind of talk I'd expect from a woman in seduction mode. However, Lexi isn't like a lot of girls.

"Shouldn't you be giggling and agreeing with me about everything?" I say, just to see how she reacts.

"Shouldn't you be sticking your head up your bum?" says Lexi, cupping her ears to hear better. I watch her standing there, her hair blowing round her face.

"The canal?" I remind her.

"It's all right. I was just hearing things." Lexi starts off again. "Come on."

We hurry down the lane then cut down the footpath to reach the towpath. I wish I'd had a wash before I'd left. I give my armpit a sneaky sniff. I'm minging. All that fear and panic has come out in my pits. Also I haven't brushed my teeth and I haven't got any gum.

There's nobody by the bridge. This is a relief. I was a tiny bit worried Lexi would have her dad waiting for me or something. Lexi walks right under the bridge and I follow. When we reach the middle she stops and looks up at me. Is she going to kiss me?

"Look at this." Lexi switches on a torch and shines it at the far wall. Now I'm confused. I can't decide whether to kiss her, or turn round and look at whatever it is she's showing me. I decide to kiss her. I make the right shape with my mouth and zoom in.

"Chas, you wazzock, look," orders Lexi, pushing me

off. She spins me round and I follow the beam of light.

I read the familiar names:

J.JUBY
NAPPY PARSONS

"So?" I say, feeling a little disappointed even though I wasn't convinced Lexi was going to try anything. Not really.

Lexi lowers the torch. There are more names scrawled below my dad's. Names I've seen for years but never taken any notice of.

FRANKYJOHN
SCOOTER
BILLY BOY

"I don't get it, what's so special about. . ." My voice trails off as Lexi shifts the torch again. The beam of light picks out some letters made almost unreadable by moss and slime.

LENNY DARLING

For once I have nothing to say.

Twenty-three

"*I* knew I'd heard the name before," says Lexi, a tad smug.

It's difficult to get my head round this. One minute I think I'm about to get off with Lexi, the next I'm looking at a tag Lenny may or may not have done, like, a million years ago.

"So there's history," says Lexi. "He probably knew my dad when they were kids." She looks at me. "And yours."

I get this horrible creepy feeling then. Lenny knew Juby and my dad?

"Maybe we should talk to your dad," I say slowly. I can't talk to mine. He could be anywhere in the world. Anywhere where there's a booze shop and a park bench anyway.

"We should," says Lexi. "But when I found this I went home, and there was a note from Dad. It said "gone out". She fiddles with the torch switch. "He could be anywhere, and he's not answering his phone."

The wind blows harder and I shove my hands in my pockets. It's a warm night but I'm cold. I can't shake off the feeling that I'm caught up in something bad and I'm way out of my depth. I also feel bloody stupid. Lexi had no intention of getting off with me. I must have been mad. I want to go home but I can't. The police are after me. I don't want all this hassle.

"It was when I saw his name written on the letters," says Lexi. "I knew I'd seen it somewhere before. And there's something else. I know it."

I don't know how this all connects with Devil, or me. Lexi sits on the low wall that runs along the back of the towpath and gets some papers out of her pocket. She switches on the torch. It's the letters from Lenny.

"Look," she says.

She's showing me the signature at the bottom of the page.

"Look at the 'L'," says Lexi.

I look. It has the same loop around the bottom as the "L" on the wall. Lexi takes back the page and holds the torch close, studying the letter.

The wind whips around us. I sigh and kick my feet against the wall. I don't want to stay here looking at the graffiti. It freaks me out. I'm also fed up standing under this bridge.

"Lexi. . ."

"Shhh."

I roll my eyes and walk up and down. I'm hungry and tired. Every now and then the light from Lexi's torch flickers over the wall and I catch sight of it again.

LENNY DARLING

Lenny knew my dad? I listen as cars roar overhead. I don't like thinking about my dad. He must be the worst father on the planet. He's a liar and a thief and a loser. He's also never around, which is a good thing. I try to imagine him at my age, scrambling up to tag his name on the wall. Did Lenny give him a leg-up? Does Mum know about this? Maybe I should call her and ask her. But then I think of how she has spent the last forty-eight hours in bed and refusing all food. No, she needs to be left alone for now.

"Lexi. . ."

"Shut up, Chas. I'm on to something." She gets out a pen and starts scribbling.

She definitely doesn't fancy me or she wouldn't talk to me like this. I walk a little way from the bridge down the towpath. I'm tempted to keep going. I don't, of course. I walk back. She's still scribbling and muttering.

And then she says, "Oh."

"Found out something else, Sherlock?" Listen to me. I sound really pissed off.

"No, somebody's coming. Let's go." She points out the light from a cigarette beyond the bridge back along the towpath.

It's most likely someone I don't know, walking a dog, but I'm not hanging around long enough to find out.

"Why don't you come back to mine?" asks Lexi, stuffing the letters into her pocket. "The police won't be looking for you there."

I give her a look.

"You can sleep in Devlin's bed," she says.

I'm not going into Juby's house. If that man sees me in his own environment, it might trigger memories of me hiding in his bed. I persuade Lexi to come back with me to the allotments until we work out what to do. To my relief she agrees. I don't think she wants to go home anyway. We slip along by the canal and up the footpath. We walk quickly, alert for any sirens or police cars, or anything. The footpath turns into the private lane and we make it to the hole in the allotment fence in less than ten minutes.

Lexi follows me through the hole.

"You're not going to make me sit in a cabbage patch, are you?"

"Come on." I take Lexi by the arm and lead her along the path to Michael's plot. I help her down the steps.

"The shed, right?"

I nod. What does she expect. The Ritz?

I open the door and hang my torch from the nail in the roof. I offer her the deckchair and she collapses into it.

I decide to brew us a cup of coffee while we work out what to do. I open the door of the shed, lift the camping stove from the shelf and turn the screw. I hold my lighter to the filament and it takes. I put the whole thing on the grass outside. I don't want to add arson to my troubles. For a minute, I think the wind is going to blow it out. I put a saucepan on the flame and fill it with water from the tap by the path.

The wind is warm against my skin. The place smells of vegetables and earth and I think I can hear a humming coming from the direction of Michael's bee boxes. I find an old blanket in Michael's allotment and spread it on the damp grass by the shed.

"Let's sit outside," I say and Lexi joins me on the blanket. She's got Lenny's letters out again. Her arm touches mine but she doesn't move away. Her torch flickers on the pages.

I feel a bit better now we're away from the bridge. I'm safer here. Only Michael works his allotment now, and I think he's away. Besides, no one gardens at midnight.

The kettle boils and I make two mugs of coffee. I hand Lexi hers but she puts it straight on the grass with a gasp which makes me think I've burnt her.

"Look at this." She shoves one of Lenny's letters at me.

"It's a letter," I say helpfully. Should I tell her to put the torch out? Lenny might be guarding the building site. He'd grass me up in a second. He'd love it if I got nicked.

"No, look."

In the torchlight I make out that she has ringed the first letter in every sentence in biro.

"*He's insane*," mutters Lexi.

It's horrible to feel stupid, especially in front of the woman I love. Unfortunately for me it is a feeling I'm getting used to.

"I don't get it," I admit.

245

"Look at this one." She's marked the next letter the same way. "Chas, you knob-head, look!" She hands me the pen. "Write down the first letter of every sentence," she orders.

I don't see what the point of this is, but I don't know what else to do. I'm learning not to disobey Lexi. I copy down the letters on the back of my hand.

"Look at it," she demands. "I thought Devlin was thick, not you."

Obediently I hold my hand to the light.

DYOUTHINKIMAFOOLISEEYOUY

"Ignore the first and last letters," says Lexi, beginning to sound weary.

"OHMYGOD!" I drop the letter like it is burning hot. "Lexi , it says. . ."

"I know what it says," says Lexi, putting her foot on the letter before it blows away. "I don't like it."

"It can't be a coincidence," I say, when I've got my breath back.

"No," says Lexi coolly.

"It's a hidden message," I say, still unable to believe it. How could Lenny be so, so, I don't know, sneaky?

"Chas," says Lexi. "Forget the BTEC in travel and tourism, you're headed for Oxbridge, mate."

"What?"

"Nothing. Do you want to see the other letters?"

"He's done it to others?"

"Let's work it out."

So I take the second letter and Lexi works on the third.

"Shit," I say, when I've worked out the next letter.

LEAVEMEALONE

I show Lexi my hand and look at her in awe. "How did you know to do this?"

Lexi scratches her head with her long nails. "There's something unnatural about how he phrases things."

"You're a clever lady," I say. I look again at the letters. It's there, as clear as anything. Hidden messages.

"You should see this one," says Lexi, giving me the third letter. "It's well creepy."

The message in the second letter was bad enough. *Leave me alone.* I suddenly feel bad. But I only lied about who I was because the pen-pal organization wouldn't let a kid write letters. I wasn't taking the piss or anything. Or was I? Maybe Lenny thought I was laughing at him the whole time and thought I found his situation funny. I take the third letter.

IFOUNDYOUIAMNOTAFRAID

Not afraid of what?

"So, do we go to the cops with this?" Lexi asks. "It doesn't let you off the hook; you haven't explained about the fingerprint on Devil's phone yet." She gives me a searching look but I don't say anything because I'm as confused as she is.

"But what's this got to do with Devil?"

"It's another lead."

It goes against my genes to voluntarily walk into a police station. I'll get the shakes as soon as we step into the car park. They'll question me over Devil and the fingerprint.

"Sorry, Lexi," I say. "I'm not going down the police station. They'll bang me up and ask questions later."

"You might be more comfortable in a cell than in that," says Lexi nodding at the shed.

"No I bloody wouldn't," I say, and watch as Lexi taps a message in her phone.

"Shit, I'm out of credit, can I borrow your phone?" She holds out her hand expectantly.

"Who are you calling?" I feel I have a right to know in the circumstances.

"I'm trying Dad again," says Lexi.

As she messes around with my phone, I try to work out the best thing to do. I don't want to gambol round to the police with the letters like a little lamb and turn myself in. I'm the chief suspect. I might get framed and end up inside for years and years!

Lexi doesn't get a response.

"I think Lenny has come back here for a reason," says Lexi, giving me back the phone. "Something to do with his past." She looked at me. "I think Devil is involved but I don't know how or why."

"We'll find him, Lexi," I say. "Your brother's invincible."

I'm about to get up when I feel a pair of arms around me.

'I need a cuddle,' says Lexi. 'I wish I could do something.'

I hold her close. Maybe she does like me after all.

We sit in the dark, like vampires. I can't wait for all this Devil/Lenny business to be over so we can get to know each other properly. It's hard to believe Devil is related to this woman.The wind ripples her hair over her shoulders. Oh no, she's pulling away. Maybe I've got bad breath or. . .?

"Tell me everything you know about Lenny," says Lexi.

So I tell her what I know about his past but she waves at me.

"I know all this. Tell me what he's like now."

I describe how he talks down to me like he thinks I'm thick. I say how my mum was into him, but that I didn't think he ever really liked her.'

"Maybe he was using her to get at you," says Lexi.

I don't like the idea of this so I carry on talking and telling her about his job.

"He's a security guard? Next door?" Lexi twists round to look at the fence. "You're kidding. Why didn't you tell me?"

I shake my head. Why's she so excited? She jumps up, spilling the coffee all over Michael's blanket.

"We've got to take a look round," she says.

"Why?" I ask. I'm quite happy where I am. "Lenny might be here right now."

I hope this will put her off.

Lexi stares at me.

"Then we definitely have to go in," she says. She races up Michael's allotment to the path. She wades through waist-high grass and brambles to the building-site fence, which is made of huge metal panels bolted together. She smacks her hands on it and makes no impact at all.

"How are we going to get in?" She looks at me. "Come on, you're the burglar."

"Not really, not any more," I mutter. Is this what she thinks of me? That's terrible. Maybe that's how everyone sees me. A thief. A low-down scumbag. I don't see myself like that at all. Most of the time I'm a law-abiding citizen. I go to school and make jokes with my grandma. It's only every now and then that I do something really naughty, like steal a lorry for instance. And after Bevanport, I wonder if I'll ever do anything like that again. Or at least, if I do, I'll make damn sure I don't get caught.

"Lexi, what's the point?" I pant, chasing after her. I don't want to get nicked for breaking and entering as well as everything else.

"I'd have thought that was obvious," says Lexi.

She turns away and hurries along the fence, testing each panel. But they're all solid. I follow her, dragging my feet. What is she going to do when she comes face to face with Lenny Darling?

250

"*Oh, hello, have you seen my brother?*"

We move along, until we have reached the end of the allotments. The fence then veers off, edging the private lane up to the site entrance.

"Lexi," I begin, as she vanishes through the hole in the fence out into the lane.

"I just want to look," she snaps. "I'll go on my own if I have to."

I follow her through the hole and she steps close to me.

"If it was your brother who was missing, would you just sit around and not do anything?"

"All right, all right."

I follow her down the lane to the site entrance, wishing I was back in Michael's shed.

Two white doors stand ten feet high, covered in safety posters and padlocked together. Two huge lamps tower over the gates. I can't break padlocks. Devil can. That's the reason I took him on my jobs. He's good at that sort of thing.

"Ready?" asks Lexi. I put my finger to my lips as I spy an old lady and a dog coming towards us. Lexi grabs my head and puts her mouth on mine. There are some bonuses to all this. The old lady tuts as she passes. When she's gone Lexi pulls away far too quickly for my liking. It would be much better if we just stayed here snogging.

Lexi goes to fiddle with the padlock and gives a squeak. I assume she's caught her finger on something so I hurry over. She holds the padlock up, a massive grin on her face.

"How did you. . .?"

"Basic engineering," says Lexi, and goes to open the door. She's not the innocent she seems.

"Wait," I say. "There'll be security guards, maybe dogs."

"Come on." Lexi pulls open the door and slips inside. I can't let her go in there on her own.

The first thing I see when I'm the other side of the doors is a Portakabin with a light on inside. I signal to Lexi to wait and I sneak up to the window to look inside.

There's a mug on the table and a half-eaten biscuit. A screen saver jumps over the computer monitor. Six TVs are mounted on the wall, all of them showing different site locations. I'm freaked to see a figure flashing across one of the screens.

"Lexi," I whisper. "Where are you going?"

"Over here." She waves from behind a pile of plastic piping.

I wish she'd keep her voice down. Even if Lenny isn't working the night shift somebody is. And he won't be far away. I follow Lexi across the site, trying to keep my head down. A huge generator buzzes away. I hope the noise drowns us out. There's stuff everywhere: flapping tape, rows of wires, stacks of concrete blocks and piles of stones. There are huge pits in the ground and massive heaps of soil. Every blade of grass has been obliterated.

I notice a small St George flag fluttering against the windscreen of an empty JCB and a small flash of the old Chas hits me. Imagine joyriding that! Lexi is charging on so I struggle out and follow her. I catch her up as she picks her way through the mud between a dumper truck and a digger and put my hand on her arm.

"Where are we going?"

"Everywhere." She looks completely mad. Maybe she's just getting a kick out of running all over a building site on a windy night.

"Lexi, we've got to keep our heads down," I say. "Look, let's just go a little bit further, then leave."

But there's no stopping a Juby. She's off again, looking behind machines and lifting metal sheets and generally poking around. Swearing under my breath I follow her and stumble, falling on my palms and narrowly missing a wicked-looking metal spike. Lexi stops when we reach the far fence. She puts her hand on the metal.

The wind blows harder and a cold drop of rain runs down the back of my neck.

"Let's go, Lexi."

She bangs her palms on the fence and I bite my lip. Does she want us to get caught? It's all right for her. She only has to flutter her eyelashes and the worst that will happen to her is another Saturday in her old clothes with Tony-*The-Guardian*-reader. Me? I'll be swept off to Bevanport.

I step on something which feels nasty. There's a wet

sock stuck to my boot. I peel it off. It's tied in a knot and has something inside. I hold it to my nose and retch. It's poo! How gross is that? It must be a dog owner who has thrown a turd over the fence. I drop the sock and wipe my hands on my trousers. I feel contaminated.

More rain, and I'm only wearing a T-shirt and jeans. I left my jumper in Michael's shed.

"I'm leaving," I tell Lexi. I mean it. I'm fed up.

"Wait," she says.

I shut my eyes. Why has this woman got such a hold over me?

I hear rain landing on the machinery.

"Lexi. . .'"

"I can hear something," she says, putting her head on one side. I can't hear anything except the generators and the wind and the rain.

"Lexi. . ."

But then I hear it too, a faint tapping. It sounds close, but far away. But I don't care. All I want to do is get out of here.

Lexi walks ahead a few paces, then looks up. I follow her gaze. She's looking up the long column of one of the tower cranes.

"*Devil*," screeches Lexi.

High up in the air, a figure stands in silhouette against the glass of the cabin.

Twenty-four

The figure waves and the wind blows so hard we see the cabin sway from side to side.

"It's him," screams Lexi. She can't tear her eyes away. The rain runs down her face, making her hair stick together and go blacker than ever. It could be anyone up there. I turn to talk to Lexi but she is already belting over the uneven ground to the boarded-up base of the crane.

"Why hasn't he come down by himself?" I ask, sounding a bit harsh. I'm not good with heights. I've never been one of these kids who can balance along bridges or go bungee jumping or whatever. So I'm not exactly overjoyed to see Lexi Juby jumping up and down on the concrete pad and trying to get a leg over the hoardings of a tower crane.

"Lexi, look how the tower is wobbling. It doesn't look safe."

"What?" Lexi stops bouncing and gives me a dirty look. "That's why we've got to get him down." She leaps up and manages to grab the top of the boards, but the wood is wet and she can't hold her weight with one hand. She slips off, giving a little yowl. She crumples on the ground and I rush over.

255

"Shit," she says, licking her hand. It's bleeding. The cut looks quite deep. It's hard to tell. It's too dark.

I wonder if I'd be like this for my brother. If Stephen knew I was in trouble now for instance, would he come back to help?

Turn the boat around, Captain, and sail for England. My little brother is about to fall off a tower crane in Bexton. We must abandon this money-spinning deep-sea prawn fishing trip and go save him.

We find a large wooden door, ten feet high and stuck with DANGER – KEEP OUT posters, and it's swinging wide open. Like an invitation. I hesitate, then follow Lexi in. I'm surrounded on four sides by towering wooden walls. Massive steel girders are bolted into the ground. A thin wire hood surrounds the ladder, which rises perhaps twelve feet before it reaches a platform. Then there's another ladder, and another. There's so many platforms I can't see them all. Just looking up makes me giddy.

"It's a long way up, Lexi," I say, trying not to sound as nervous as I feel.

But she's off, scrambling up the rungs in her white trainers. I take a deep beath, and follow.

In normal circumstances I would enjoy this fantastic view of Lexi's arse. And, I admit, while I'm climbing the first ladder I tell myself that this whole thing has its advantages. We reach the first platform and come out above the hoardings into the rain and wind. I'm thinking about a bit of a rest, maybe a tactic talk, but

Lexi is already racing up the second ladder. I look down through the metal grid floor. The concrete pad the crane is bolted into is only twelve feet or so beneath my feet. And so far, I'm feeling fine.

I smooth back my wet hair, and climb the next ladder. Lexi doesn't stop at the next platform, or the next. It's only when I'm getting seriously tired and wet and cold, that I shout to her.

"Can we stop a minute?" She's already on the next ladder. Her feet ring out on the metal rungs. It's not safe for her on her own. I have to stick with her.

"I'm not stopping," calls down Lexi. "You can catch me up."

I pull myself up to the next bar. The metal rungs are cold, wet and a couple of times I've missed my footing and slipped right off.

It is suicide for someone with vertigo to look down, but I have to. It's like a compulsion. Also, it's interesting. The diggers and dumper trucks already look like toys. I can see the whole site, ringed with lamps and lashed by rain. I look for any sign of security, but there's no people, no dogs, nothing. My arms are aching as I pull myself up to the next platform. I collapse on the grid, holding on the sides as the wind blows hard, and I feel the whole thing move. I groan. I don't want to die yet. I've got too many plans. Besides, I need to sort out Lenny and stop Gran and Mum from murdering each other. Lexi is charging ahead. My God, that girl is fit. I reckon we must be about halfway up. It feels like we've been climbing for ages, but it's probably only been five minutes. The metal frame of the tower doesn't protect me from the rain. My T-shirt is stuck to me and my jeans are cold and heavy. My trainers have no grip left and squeak whenever I tread. The things I do for a woman. And she doesn't even appreciate it. When I've got my breath back, I sigh, and put my foot on the first rung. A gust of wind wobbles the tower again and I grip hard to the sides.

"Lexi, wait," I shout.

She doesn't answer. The Jubys are not known for their obedience.

I swear and start to climb. My hands are so cold, they feel sore. I make a mental note: if I ever climb one of these things again, wear gloves. My palms and fingertips are getting skinned alive. It makes it harder to grip. Relax, I tell myself, if I fall, I'll only go as far as the next platform. I wouldn't even break a leg.

I hear a thudding noise.

"Shit."

"Lexi? You all right?"

There's a pause and I wipe the rain out of my eyes, and hurry up the ladder, forgetting for a moment about the height and the wet and my sore hands.

I reach the next platform and look up. Lexi is halfway up the next ladder, her arms locked round one of the rungs and cradling her head. But she's upright, she's in one piece, and there's no Lenny Darling beating her up.

"Lexi?"

"Let me recover," she snaps. I stand there. I want to stroke her shoe but she'd probably kick me.

A few seconds go by before she unclasps her head and looks at me. It's dark up here, so I can't really see properly. But I think I can make out a black smear on her forehead.

"I slipped," she said. "I smacked my head on the ladder."

"Come down, and have a rest, only for a few minutes." I'm worried in case she gets dizzy and passes out.

To my surprise, Lexi agrees.

"But I'm not coming down," she says. "I'll have a rest on the next level up." And she drags herself up the rungs. I wait until she is clear of the ladder before I climb. I don't want her dead weight falling on me if she faints.

When she's made it I haul myself up after her and sit on the platform. We're very high and can see the bottom of the crane driver's cabin. It doesn't sit still, but sways, slowly, back and forth in the wind. It makes me feel queasy. I don't look down, but edge over to Lexi. (This high up, I have to do everything in small, controlled movements.)

"Got a tissue?" she asks. "My head's bleeding."

I shake my head. I haven't got anything on me except my clothes, my wallet and my phone.

My phone.

"Lexi." I find I am talking in a quiet voice, this is because, despite the wind and rain, I'm worried that whoever is in the cabin can hear us. We need to be the ones who are the surprise. "Lexi, why don't we call the police?" Listen to me. I must have got altitude sickness. "If Devil is trapped up here we'll need help to get him out. The cabin is bound to be locked. And if it's Lenny. . ." My voice trails off. I have a vision of two small bodies falling through the air. I clear my throat. "And if it's Lenny, then we're buggered."

I have another, even nastier fear, I hardly want to admit, even to myself. Devil and I didn't exactly part on good terms. No one in their right minds would want to be up a tower, God knows how high, with Devlin Juby when he has a grudge match against them.

I don't trust him. If Lenny doesn't murder me, Devil might.

I sit close to Lexi. "Let's call someone."

Just then there's a loud crack, and a bolt of lightning streaks across the sky. It is followed by a deep rumble of thunder.

"Bugger this," I say. I may not have the snappiest ciruit board, but even I know that being up a tall, metal tower in a thunder and lightning storm is not very clever.

"Eek," says Lexi. Then: "Give us your phone."

I fish it out of my pocket and hold it up. I think I'll phone the police first. But Lexi has other ideas. "I'll try Dad," she says reaching for it.

"Where's your phone?" I ask, holding it out of her reach. I can't have this messed up.

"Run out of credit, remember?"

"I'm calling the police, Lexi." I never thought I'd hear myself say that.

"Chas. . ."

Just then another flash of lightning illuminates the whole building site, and in that split second three things happen.

1. Lexi, in a move which reminds me of her brother, makes a grab for my phone.

2. Startled by Lexi and the lightning, I let the phone slip from my fingers and it falls through the gridded platform and crashes down through the levels, ringing on the metal.

3. I see a figure running over the ground towards us.

"Shit," I say. "Shit, shit, shit."

"Back to plan A," says Lexi, pulling herself to her feet.

"We could go get it," I say, without much hope. "I heard it land. I bet it's only a few ladders down."

"Go for it," says Lexi. "But I'm not waiting."

I tell her about the figure I saw.

"I can't see anything," she says, looking down at the building site.

"That's because I saw him when the lightning lit up the ground." I'm trying to stay calm.

"In that case, I'm definitely going up," says Lexi. "You reckon it was Lenny, right?"

I shake my head. I don't know. It could be anyone.

261

"Devlin's up here," she says, tying back her hair. "I know it."

She walks carefully over the platform, holding the sides because of the wind, and begins to climb the next section.

I don't know what I should do. My mobile will be very useful. It might save our lives, but on the other hand, there's Lexi disppearing up to meet God knows what on her own. If anything bad happens to her, how will I live with myself? How will I tell everyone that I let her go on alone, with a bleeding head, while I went to fetch my phone?

A chill creeps up my back as far, far below, I hear the faint *clink clink* of heavy boots on metal rungs.

Twenty-five

I'm frozen in my little corner of the tower. Thick bundles of wire run vertically up the column and the rain is smashing on to the metal. Overhead, the arm of the crane reaches out over the building site, with a chain and huge hook swaying back and forth in the wind.

Move it.

I'm swarming up the ladder after Lexi. Every so often, I stop and listen. There's two pairs of feet; one set belonging to Lexi, who is moving much more slowly now. The other set is getting closer and closer and seeming to fly up the ladders, *tap tap tap tap*, like the man is an Olympic athlete. This makes me feel a bit better. Lenny has been locked away for nine years. He can't be that fit. No, this must be someone used to climbing a tower crane. In a minute we're going to get an earful from a crane driver. But why would a crane driver be out in this weather? I climb a few more steps, then I hear something.

Someone is shouting, not far above my head. And it sounds like Devlin Juby.

"GET ME OUTTA HERE!"

He's alive!

I fly up the last ladder and crawl through this trapdoor type hole on to the top of the tower and, oh wow. . .

It's dark but I can just make out the ledge on which we're standing. It juts out from the body of the crane and there's nothing between me and the ground except the metal grille floor and sixty-odd feet of air. The jib stretches out before us and above is more tower and more machinery. Behind is a shortish arm, loaded with massive metal weights and pulleys. There's a drum, not six feet away, which is coiled with thick steel rope. We're a long way up. The rain blows hard into my face. I think of those figures toppling through the sky. I hear the *tap tap tap* of boots below us.

"Listen," I say to Lexi. But she's tottering towards the cabin door. A strong smell of urine comes off it.

"Devlin, is that you?" she calls, steadying herself on the barrier as the wind blows her off balance.

"Lex?" The voice breaks in astonishment.

"We've come to get you out."

"Hurry up, there's lightning!"

Devil never did like thunderstorms. There's not much room on our ledge, and the barrier to stop us walking off the edge only comes up to my waist. I hold on so tightly to the bars that my fingers go dead. I don't look down.

"Let me out," screams Devil.

The footsteps are getting closer and closer. I look

down and see a pair of white hands only metres below, climbing deftly up the ladder, one rung after another.

"There's a lock," says Lexi, her fingers fumbling over the door. "Ohmygod, the key is in it."

"Let me out," howls Devil.

Lexi turns the key just as a head wearing a peaked hat pops through the trapdoor.

"Let us in," I scream as a security guard pulls himself up. He rolls his body out on to the ledge.

"Lenny," I gasp. For a minute I didn't recognize him. But it really is him.

Lenny scrambles for a handhold and my mouth drops open when I see a gun in his hand. A gun!

"Lenny, what's all. . ." I begin, but Lexi flings open the door and she drags me inside. We fall heavily against Devil, who is pushing to get out. With difficulty, we manage to shut the door. There's no room in here. There's just a chair, some controls and a glowing roof light. Lexi crouches in the chair and Devil and I are wedged up against each other next to the door. It is like trying to fit us all in a phone box.

"Let me out," shouts Devil, going for the handle.

"Leave it, he's got a gun!" I shout and realize we left the key in the door on the outside.

"Devlin," says Lexi. "Are you all right?"

He's wearing a dirty red England shirt and black tracksuit trousers. He's got so much stubble it's practically a beard. He looks pale, hungry and very pissed off. He also stinks. The smell of his BO fills the tiny cabin and it's hard to breathe. My hip is jammed painfully into the back of the seat, and my neck is bent to one side because there's not enough head space, but there's nowhere else to go. I'm badly shaken. It's Lenny out there . . . Lenny! And from the look of it, he bloody well wants to hurt us.

"What happened to your head?" asks Devil, looking at his sister. "'S bleeding."

"Nothing," says Lexi.

I feel the door handle turning and grab it and hold it up. Devil sees what is happening and pushes his hand under mine. Together we prevent Lenny getting in, and after only a few attempts, he gives up and the handle goes slack. We keep our hands on it though.

"Why are you doing this?" screams Lexi.

Everything is quiet, except the drumming of rain on the cabin roof. A belt of wind makes the cabin rock and sway and I have to clutch at Devil's stinking football shirt to stop myself falling. Then there's another huge gust of wind and I fly over the seat towards the glass front of the cabin. My nose is pressed against the window and again I clock the amount of air space between me and the ground. Half the floor in this thing is made of glass, so it's like the cabin is sitting on thin air.

Devil and Lexi are back on the door handle. There's no room behind the chair so I have to crouch on the glass floor at the front.

BANG BANG.

The hammering on the door makes us all jump.

"Child-ren, let me in. The gun is just p-p-part of my uniform." Lenny's voice slurs and stammers, like he's been drinking.

This is really happening. Maybe he got hold of a gun somehow through his security contacts.

"We're not letting you in, you bloody nutter." Lexi smacks her hand on the door.

"What did you do to him?" I ask Devil.

Devil shrugs. "Search me," he says. "He tricked me up here."

Lexi is unusually quiet. I hope she hasn't got concussion or anything. We need her brains.

"Child-ren," Lenny's voice is horribly close. "C-c-come out here. 'S over now."

Does he think we're stupid? Maybe if I try and talk to him, he might see reason.

"Lenny," I call, winking at the others. "It's me, Chas. What's happening?" I mean it. Despite everything, the tag under the bridge, the letters, my own eyes, I can't believe this is really happening.

'Chas. Talk to your f-f-friends. Get them to come out.' He sounds like he's pleading.

There's an almighty crack, the whole sky lights up and the whole tower shakes. I must be close to death. I feel as jumpy as a rat in a food processor.

"Have we been hit?" asks Devil.

"It was close," whispers Lexi. "I'm going out to see what he wants. We can't stay here."

"Don't," I tell her. I look over at Devil for back-up but he doesn't say anything.

"What's the alternative? Starve to death in here? I'm going out. No one's going to shoot anybody."

"No," I say, aware nothing can stop Lexi if she puts her mind to it.

"Yes, yes, out you come. This is all a . . . a . . . misunderstanding."

"You still there?" I say angrily. "I hoped you'd got hit by lightning."

"I'm not comfortable," says Lenny. "I'm a little n-n-nervous around strong electrical charges."

"Don't go, Lexi," says Devil unexpectedly. "He's insane."

Lexi slumps back in her chair. I am relieved but a bit annoyed. Why does she listen to Devil but not me?

We hear the key turning in the lock on the other side of the door.

"Listen to this," says Lenny.

We go quiet but don't hear anything except the wind and the rain.

"That was the key falling down the ladder shaft," says Lenny. "Disgusting ch-ch-children."

We hear his feet on the bars as he climbs down. The sound gets fainter and fainter.

"Right," I say, rubbing my hands together. "Anyone got a plan?"

It's still raining but the thunder has moved off. The rain dribbles down the window. I rub a space in the steamed-up glass and see a streak of lightning over the hills beyond the town. Devil has wedged himself on the floor in the space behind the driver's seat and looks quite comfortable, but I'm aching and cramped and don't know how much longer I can stand it in here.

"Does Dad know I'm here?" asks Devil.

"Nope," says Lexi, pressing a tissue against her head. She has her head resting on her knees, her feet tucked up on the seat. She looks tiny. She opens her bag and takes out a can of Coke.

"Give us that," says Devil.

"How long have you been here?" I ask as Lexi passes him the can. He tips it up and swallows in great big gulps. He finishes the can, crushes it between his fingers and squeezes it out of a small slatted window near the roof of the cabin.

"Three nights, not including tonight," says Devil.

I reach into my rucksack, pull out another can and hand it to him.

"I had a bit of a headache, Friday night," says Devil, draining the second can. Lexi gives me a dirty look and I roll my eyes. Devil belches. I can't see very well in this light but he looks skinnier than usual and have I mentioned the smell coming off him? It's worse than a changing room full of football players with indigestion.

"You stink," I say kindly.

"I know," says Devil. "It gets boiling in here in the daytime. Like being shut in a bloody greenhouse, only

269

I can't break the glass. It's reinforced, see?" He looks at Lexi. "Got any food?"

"Nope," says Lexi. She's so cool. It's like she does this sort of thing every day. And Devil's in pretty good shape for a man shut in a small box on top of a thin scaffold for three days. Maybe they're used to this sort of thing. Maybe life with Juby is full of terrifying experiences. I'm the one who is sweating and shivering. I'm the one who is most likely to pass out from lack of oxygen and fear. I give Devil a couple of cakes from my bag. I don't give him all my food though. I don't know how long we'll be in here. I try and tune in my brain so I can process what Devil is saying.

"On Friday night I was in a bad mood you know, because of Mr Thinks-He's-So-Hard." He nods at me and I shrink back against the glass, hoping he's not going to launch a revenge attack.

"I ran into the Farrow clone." He means one of the Farrow twins. "I asked him to lend me some money, but he wouldn't. We had words."

"Devlin," says Lexi.

"He's always annoyed me, that kid," says Devil. "I only wanted some money for a kebab."

"Which was it?" I ask.

"Jamie," says Devil. "Little prick."

Poor Jamie. I can just imagine the scene. I wonder why he hadn't said anything when Devil was reported missing. Did I see him in school this morning?

"Anyway, after I'd had the run-in with Jamie, I met

this bloke in the park and he said, 'You're Juby, right?' And I said yes what was it to him? and he says he's an old friend of Dad's and he offered to buy me a kebab. I wasn't scared if he was a perv or anything because I could have knocked his head off if I'd wanted. And I was hungry. He was telling me about all the stuff he'd been up to and said I probably wouldn't want to hear about most of it, because I was most likely a lad who kept on the right side of the law. I said not to worry, it helped pass the time while I ate my kebab. And he was talking about a train heist, no shit. And how he once infiltrated the Bank of England by working as a cleaner."

I listen as Devil babbles on, unable to stop himself. He's not talking to me. He's talking to Lexi, who seems to have forgotten I'm here even though my groin is only inches from her face. I look at the controls of the machine and spy a walkie-talkie radio. I grab it and mess around but it's dead.

"He tells me he's got keys to the new building site, and it's deserted cos of a disagreement between the contractors and the planning people, or something, and would I like a look round? He's like, hinting heavily that he's got keys and stuff. And like I said, I wasn't scared of him. He's really weedy, man. And posh. I kept telling myself, no paedo would fancy me anyway. I look like a bloke. And if he was queer, well, I'd just batter him one round the head, no harm done."

I've never heard Devil talk this much. He ought to be

locked away more often. Maybe this is like therapy for him. Actually I might change my mind on that one. He was locked away with me and it nearly killed us both.

"So we're in that Portakabin down there, and he's showing me all the security monitors and walkie-talkie radios and stuff. I was going to nick me a radio mike but then he says, 'Wanna go up in one of them?' And he nods at the crane. I admit I was a bit suss. So I goes, 'Why? You're not a queer are you?' and he goes, 'No, I like ladies,' and he says he's going out with Mr Muppet here's mother, and hadn't Chas told me about Lenny Darling the ex-con, yet? And I goes, 'No.' But I feel safer, knowing he's one of us. And he says he just gets dead bored working here as a security guard and he didn't see why one of Chas's mates shouldn't have a look round."

"But how did he know who you were?" asks Lexi, interrupting.

Devil shrugs. "I must be famous."

"Does it still hurt?" I ask Lexi, looking at the cut on her head.

"I'm talking," says Devil in a dangerous voice. "We're climbing the ladder and he goes first, and it's wicked. You can see for miles from up here."

We know that, we're up here with you, I think.

"It's a long way up," says Devil.

I stop myself from snorting. *Devil,* I want to say. *We've just done it. We know!* He's so thick!

"And when we get up the top he goes, 'Wanna steer it?'"

272

Now this I can understand. Imagine operating one of these beauties. But where would you start? I think I can see four long chains dangling from the arm, attached to a metal thing and a big hook. I'd like to make it swing.

"Did you start it up?" I ask.

"He unlocked the door, and I went in, and he locked the door on me before I'd realized," says Devil.

"Has he hurt you?" asks Lexi.

"He's starved me and robbed me," says Devil. "When I get out of here I'm gonna kick his ass."

Oh God, is this what Lenny is going to do to us? Maybe he's going to keep us all locked in here until we eat each other, like famished gerbils.

"In what way, robbed?" asks Lexi nervously.

"He's had my phone out of my jacket," says Devil. "He must have done it in the café." Devil gives me a funny look. "He took something else too."

"What?" I ask. But Lexi seems to know what he is going to say.

"Chas's finger," she says.

Devil sticks out his bottom lip. "I was planning on giving it back. It was annoying me. But then I found him groping you." He glares at me.

"Oh leave it out," says Lexi. "I was groping him."

"What's my finger got to do with anything?" I ask, totally confused now.

Lexi pats my shoulder. "Do keep up, mastermind. You've been framed."

I must look as stupid as I feel because she goes on to

273

explain. "Lenny took Devil's mobile and your finger. The mobile was then found in the park with your fingerprint on it."

"What?"

"Fingerprint," says Lexi. "Chas, it's a good job you've got looks. I don't know how far you'd get just using your brains."

The truth finally dawns on me. Did Lenny. . .? Did Lenny use my decapitated fingerprint to frame me?

"The . . . the . . . dirty. . ."

"Yes," says Lexi. "That explains it." She grins at me and taps the bottom of her chin and I hastily shut my mouth.

I can't believe it. Surely my finger would have been too manky to make a print? Obviously not. But what have I ever done to him? "That's low," I finally manage to say.

"As low as writing to someone on Death Row just for a laugh?" asks Lexi.

We're all quiet after that. I shift my legs, trying to make myself more comfortable in the tiny space, trying to take all of it in. I look sideways at Lexi, wondering what is going through her head.

Did she just say I was good looking or was that my imagination?

The cabin is about six feet by four. The whole front is made of glass, even the floor and half the roof. I guess the driver has to be able to see what he is doing in one of these things. The glass stops about halfway along the side walls and gives way to this yellowish metal, but the side walls have slatted windows running along the top. The back wall is made of metal, with the door and a small window in it. There's a small light, like in the roof of a car, above the controls, which, miraculously, is working. The roof is a creamy metal and I can see every rivet. It's like being in a sardine can. There's a tiny square hatch in the centre of the ceiling. I can't see how you'd open it. As I look at it I feel a pressure build in the pit of my stomach. Imagine climbing through that, on to the roof. It would be terrifying.

"Have you tried opening that?" I ask Devil, gesturing to the hatch.

He nods. "I've tried everything, mate, smashing the glass, breaking down the door. But I'm still here, aint I?"

The walls and door are covered in scuff marks and dents where Devil has been booting them.

"Don't use this bottle for anything," says Devil, taking a plastic water bottle from the space under the driver's seat. "I use it to empty my piss out of the window."

I exchange a glance with Lexi. I know what she's thinking. He's been stuck in here for three days.

"I had to take a dump in my sock," he says, suddenly grinning. "I tied a knot in it, and I pushed it out of the window."

"I can't do that," says Lexi in a small voice. "I'm only wearing *trainer socks*."

I eye my shoe and want to retch. I'll throw it away when I get out of here.

We all jump as the cabin is filled with a tinny electronic calypso ring tone.

Lexi dives into her pocket and bites her lip as she holds it to her ear. "Hello?"

"GET ME OUTTA HERE," roars Devil, making a grab for the phone, but Lexi swings away.

"Hello?" she asks in a funny little voice and my heart sinks. She puts her hand on her forehead and slumps in her chair. She turns to me and mouths, "It's Lenny. He's using your phone."

Devil makes a grab for the phone and knocks it out of her hands and to the floor. He scrambles to pick it up and holds it to his ear. "Let us out, you. . ." His voice trails away. "Gone dead," he tells us as he punches some numbers into the keypad.

"No credit, Devlin," says Lexi in an annoying voice, like she's talking to a little kid. "Don't you think I'd have called someone if there was? Beside, the batteries are nearly flat."

I wonder what Lenny is thinking now he knows we've got a phone. He doesn't know we have no credit. He might think the entire South-West police force is charging over here. Does this mean he'll just abandon us and disappear? We couldn't stay even one night in here with all three of us. There's no room to lie down and it's so cramped I'm sitting with one arse cheek on top of the other.

"Crap, innit," says Devil.

This is the first nearly friendly thing he has said to me

276

in about a month so I nod, telling myself that no way should I wind up Devlin Juby while we are stuck in this machine.

Lexi starts asking me more about Lenny.

"I thought he was mad with you, you know, for all your letters. But why Devil?" She shivers and I want to put my arm round her but I'm nervous about Devil. Last time he saw me cuddle his sister he tried to kill me. "What's going to happen to us?" Lexi murmurs.

It's so not like her to sound scared. I forget about Devil and I lever myself up on one leg to give her a hug. I flash a look at Devil. *Don't try anything*. But he stares out of the window.

"What does he say when he brings you food?" asks Lexi, when I have let her go and am squashed back into my corner.

"How does he get it in here?" I interrupt.

"Same way it goes out," says Devil. "He shoves it through the top window, there."

"But why us?" asks Lexi.

I watch her, sitting there, thinking away. I'm not worried about why we're here, I just want to work out how we are going to escape. But that's Lexi for you. She has to know the reasons for everything.

"He's just a nutter," I say. "This is the sort of thing he enjoys. Look at those messages in his letters."

"What messages?" Devil leans forward. He gives me a hungry look. "Are you sure you haven't got anything else to eat?"

"The letters he wrote to me." I pass him a handful of biscuits from my bag. "You saw them when we were at Bevanport. He was writing hidden messages in them. Lexi worked it out."

"Got one here," says Devil through a mouthful of biscuit. He turns out his pockets and loads of stuff comes out; receipts, chocolate wrappers, rolling papers, matches, coins. And my missing Lenny letter.

I don't know what to think.

"Where did you get that?"

"In Bevanport. I wanted to know what you were up to, only you came back when I was looking at it. So I stuffed it in my pocket. Don't know why I've still got it."

"Give it here," says Lexi, and snatches it out of his hands. "Got a pen?" We shake our heads. She flattens out the sheets, and holds them up to the little roof light.

"What's all this?" asks Devil.

"Hidden messages," I say.

"I had that paper all lined up to wipe my bum next time," says Devil, nodding at the letter.

Lexi reaches over and draws each letter in the condensation on the window.

We watch in silence.

JAMESWILLDIE

"Well that's all right," I say. "I don't know anyone

278

called James." This is good news. I just wish Lenny would concentrate on this James bloke instead of us.

Lexi and Devil are quiet.

"I don't get it," Lexi finally whispers. She sounds like she is going to burst into tears.

"What's the matter?" I ask.

"James is Dad's name," she says.

Then the idea that has been forming comes to the surface. Maybe we're not actually that important to Lenny at all. That's why he hasn't killed us, or done anything to us. It's a big step for my brain to make, but I think I'm on to something.

"Maybe it's not us he wants," I say slowly. "Maybe we're just the bait."

Twenty-six

We've been shut in here for at least an hour. But the storm has mostly gone and we're not being blown all over the sky. It's well scary the way the cabin sways when the wind blows. I keep imagining the crane toppling over. There's a flashing beacon right on the very top of the crane. I guess it's there to stop aeroplanes flying into us. Lexi's sitting on the driver's chair, her head in her knees, thinking. Devil is squashed up on the ledge next to her seat. Every thirty seconds or so, he swears and thumps the glass with his fist. I'm crouched on the glass floor right out front, close to Lexi's legs. There's so little space, I have to have one arm up above my head. I'm wondering if it's worth trying to get behind Lexi's chair, next to the door, but can't work out how I'm going to get there without stepping on someone's head.

Lexi and Devil are waiting for an explanation about us being bait, but I can't give one. It's just a hunch.

I'm surprised Devil hasn't managed to escape. He's been in here for three days. I can't be in here that long. I remember how I felt, years ago, locked up in the attic. How I crashed through the roof and landed on my foster parents' bed. If I can break out of an attic aged eight, surely I can bust my way out of a glass and tin box aged nearly sixteen?

"Let me sit in the chair," growls Devil, and Lexi lifts her head from her knees. She looks round for a place to go and decides that behind the chair is the best place. That's my chance gone. It's quite a job, moving people round in a space which is meant for one. It means Lexi's leg is pressed close to mine at one point. Look at me, I can't be that scared, I'm still crazy about Lexi. I can't let Lenny murder her. We have to get out. Breaking the window is the obvious answer but it's tough, reinforced glass. It will take a lot of effort to break it, and we don't have any tools. I'm worried about breaking through, then tumbling out, with nothing between me and the ground except a couple of seconds of free falling. The cabin is perched on a kind of ledge and if we did manage to break the glass we'd have to try and climb round to the side and scramble on the platform. It would be hard, especially in the dark. I look at the door. Devil says he's spent most of this time trying to pick the lock. If he can't do it, I certainly can't. And Lexi would have done it by now if she could. We're going to have to break it down using all our combined strength. How hard can it be? It's not like it's built to keep people out, or in. It ought to be easy.

I examine the cab as best as I can in the tiny space, looking for any hidden cupboards or drawers where we might find something useful. I'm feeling down behind the seat (with Devil swearing at me for having my shoulder in his face) when my fingers find a pouch about halfway down. I pull out a newspaper, a crumpled bank statement belonging to a bloke called Andrew Heard and a small screwdriver.

I replace the newspaper and bank statement, hoping we're out of here before I have to wipe my bum with them, and work my way round to the door. I smile apologetically at Lexi as my body presses her into the wall. I slide the sharp end of the screwdriver between the door and the frame and give it a shove. The screwdriver slides out. I try again. And again. The door doesn't budge.

"Let me have a go," says Devil, shoving me out of the way. I sit back on the chair and watch. I have a vision of Devil losing his rag and chucking the tool out of the window but I let him try. Ah, the comfort of sitting in a proper chair when you've been wedged between cold glass and a metal control box for over an hour.

The next twenty minutes feel just like old times. With our new tool Devil and me try to break the door lock, the glass; we even stand on the chair and have a go at the hatch in the roof. It feels good to actually be doing something, and since Devil has eaten all my biscuits (not all, he gave Lexi half of one) he's acting quite perky.

Lexi glances at us as she fiddles with her phone, trying to send text messages, over and over again. "Why don't you unscrew the door?" she asks.

Devil and I look at each other, then at the door. The hinges are inside. The screw head on the tool is star-shaped and the screws in the door have slit heads. But it might be possible.

"Clever girl," I say and give her a kiss. Devil has already set to work. He works so hard at the first screw I'm worried he'll break the thread. His hand slips and bashes against the hinge. He swears and sucks his wrist, so I whip the screwdriver off him and get going on the hinge at the bottom of the door. The tool keeps slipping from the grooves in the screws. But when I hold it at exactly the right angle, I get a bit of traction.

After what seems like ages, the screw finally budges. By now, Devil wants another go but I don't let him. I don't want him messing it up, and a few minutes later I'm unscrewing the rest of it by hand.

I give it to Lexi.

"Souvenir," I say, instead of the obvious, *Do ya want a screw?* Best not cause any friction at this stage. There are five screws left and this one has taken me about ten minutes. I set to work on the next one. Lexi watches as I scrabble about, the screwdriver slipping and hitting the wall. She hunts through her bag, fetches out a make-up bag and orders me out of the way.

"Lexi," we need to get out of here before Lenny comes back."

"Just let me try," she says.

I sit back on the chair and Devil curls his lanky body up on the ledge next to me as Lexi works away at the hinge. We give each other a brotherly look. She's probably having a go with her lipstick.

But then Lexi is holding out a screw in the palm of her hand. I look at the hinge in disbelief. She's done it in three minutes flat.

"Souvenir?" she smiles sweetly and waves a metal nail file at me. "I don't know about you but I'd like to be out of here before Christmas."

We've got three screws out and are starting work on the fourth when I spot a beam of torchlight playing over the ground, far below.

"Something's happening," I say. A figure at the end of the torch beam steps into the light pool cast from the overhead lamps.

It's Lenny.

He's walking fast, and we watch as he climbs up into the cab of a JCB.

There's a roar from the ground as an engine starts up and I squeeze over to look. As we watch, the bucket on the JCB is lifted, then lowered and lifted again and stretched right out. Then it retracts. The machine trundles close to the tower. I think Lenny is driving because I can make out the peaked hat. What's he up to now?

"Is it him?" whispers Lexi.

The bucket slams into the ground and tremors run up my legs. I don't know how this thing stays up. I remember walking on concrete before we climbed up the ladders. It was like the whole thing was bolted into this concrete pad. He couldn't dig us up, could he? The arm of the digger is raised high in the air as the machine crawls even closer. The vibrations buzz under our feet.

We watch in slience as Lenny tears down the wooden hoardings round the base of our crane. He does the job in just a few minutes. It's scary to see how the massive boards crumple like cardboard under the weight of the bucket.

"Nearly done," says Lexi. "This last screw is a. . ."

AAARRRGGHHHH! We are thrown sideways, hitting the wall as the cabin shakes.

"Don't tell me that was the wind," says Lexi, pulling herself up.

Lenny retracts the bucket from the side of the tower and swings it back ready to make another blow.

"He's trying to knock us over," screams Devil.

The impact from another smash sends us flying.

I land with my nose in the window and my head under Devil's armpit.

"You all right, mate?" asks Devil as I straighten up, rubbing my nose. It's sticky and prickling with pain and my hands are covered with blood. Lenny has drawn blood. He really is trying to kill us.

"Fine, ta," I say coolly. We see the next blow coming and Lenny has timed it badly or something because the cab only gives a little shudder, similiar to a few hours ago when the wind was blowing. And I thought that was bad.

Lexi takes advantage of the lull to get to work on the screw.

"Done it," she screams as the next slam sends her flying into my arms. We smack against the wall and the breath is knocked out of me.

"Thanks," says Lexi. "You're a good cushion."

In any other situation I would love to hear those words, but standing here, gasping, with every last breath knocked out of me, I feel weak and useless.

Then the cabin is filled with the sound of white noise as the radio crackles into life. Maybe the JCB jiggled some connection. I grab the reciever and push down the button.

"Hello, hello? Can anyone hear me? We're trapped up here. You've got to help us."

I let go of the button. No response. I try again.

"We're trapped on the crane by Bexton allotments. If anyone can hear this you've got to get help. Hello?"

I wait a few seconds, biting my lip, then there's a change in the noise as someone breathes over the radio.

"*I copy.*" The voice is distorted.

"Help us," I splutter.

"*I didn't mean it to go this f-f-far.*" It's a man's voice. He's upset.

"What?" My voice squeaks like a choirboy hitting puberty.

Devil grabs the mike off me. 'Let us out, you sick tosser. I'm going to kill you when I get out of here.'

The voice changes. There's no stammer now.

"*You murdered me years ago . . . Juby scum.*"

We stare at each other stunned.

The radio goes dead.

"Get the door," shouts Devil. I'm left panting against the glass front of the cabin, wondering if it can take the strain as Devil and Lexi brace themselves against the back of the chair, and start booting the door.

There's a thud and a crash as it topples to the platform outside.

They've done it.

"I'm outta here," says Devil, but I lean over to grab his arm.

"Wait! What happens if you're out there when the JCB bucket hits the tower? You'd go flying off the side."

"We can't stay here," says Lexi.

"Take some of that, you prick," screams Devil. He's outside on the platform, holding the door above his head. Without pausing, he throws it over the barrier. I have to admit, it's a nice move. The door slams into the roof of the JCB and slips off on to the ground.

"Shot!" I say.

"Great," says Lexi. "Now he knows we've got the door off, and there's nothing between us and his gun."

Ouch. I didn't think of that. Neither did Devil because he's already climbing down. He's got some balls, I'll give him that. If Lenny hits the tower, will Devil be able to hang on to the ladder? I can't move from the cab as long as I know there's a chance I might fall off the platform. It's a long way down. I may have mentioned this before. It's strange, but I haven't been properly scared until now. There hasn't been time. But now, with the door off, and the likelihood of me having to go outside, I'm cacking myself.

"Breathe," says Lexi, patting me. "It helps you to live."

I follow her advice and take a deep breath. OK, I'm OK. I edge away from the window towards the door and see Lenny climbing out of the cab and jumping to the ground. He kicks at the door lying in the mud at his feet, and looks up.

What did he mean? *You killed me years ago . . . Juby scum.*

I suck in my cheeks as Lenny runs to our tower.

"He's coming up," I say.

Lexi steps outside, lies flat on the platform and sticks her head down the ladder opening.

"DEV-LIN, HE'S COMING UP. REMEMBER HE'S GOT A GUN."

BANG!

Way below, something hard pings off the tower frame.

I hover in the doorway. I'm less likely to get shot in the cabin, but if Lenny gets up here, I'm a sitting duck.

There is the sound of someone crashing up the ladder.

"Shit," says Devil, reappearing on the platform.

Panic is filling my head. This is no good. I need to

288

think clearly. My eye falls upon the screwdriver, lying abandoned on the floor of the cab. I look at the second crane, standing some way off in the middle of the site. Its back end with the massive counterweights seems to hover in the air.

I look at the arm of our crane, out to the side, with its pulleys and trolleys and cables. I have an idea.

Can I do it?

I've picked up the screwdriver and I'm prising off the plastic covering behind the ignition. It comes off fairly easy. This ought to be easier than a car, there's no steering lock for a start, or immobilizer. I look at the bundles of wires all taped together. Surely the principles are the same?

I could do this using brute force and the screwdriver. If I smash the key mechanism, I can use the screwdriver to turn the switch. But I don't want to smash things up, because once you break things, there's no going back if it doesn't work. No, what I need to do, is work out which are the ignition wires. I wonder if they are the same colour as in cars (though they are different in newer makes of car, in older cars, most ignition wires are red). I find what I hope are the ignition wires; they are red and are attatched to the ignition switch. I yank them out. It feels good to be doing something I know about. Now I need to find the starter motor circuit. This is a two-man job. I need to attach the ignition wires together at the same time someone sorts out the starter motor circuit. I need an expert in car nicking.

Devil appears, panting in the doorway. "He tried to shoot me," he says in outrage.

"Ah, Devil," I say. "Just the man I need."

He sees what I am doing and a slow grin breaks out over his face.

"Cool as," he says, and he's squeezing in next to me, fumbling round for the wires. We're squashed in there bickering over which wire belongs with which and who is going to do what when a cool voice from the doorway says:

"And what is the point of this? It's not like you're going to drive it away, is it?" Lexi is not impressed. She goes outside and starts shouting for help.

Devil looks at me. "She has a point, Chas. What are we going to do, try and make him dizzy?"

"We're going to use it to help us escape," I say. I nod at Devil and as he brings his wires together I press the exposed ends of my ignition wires against each other. There's rumble, and a judder, and from behind us, a motor starts up.

"Oh yes," I say, squishing my wires together so they stay. "Let's give it some." I shove Devil aside and fumble for the gear levers next to me. I have no idea what they do. I try to follow the diagram printed on the casing but it's really complicated. And I keep getting distracted by Lexi's yelling. I'm pulling back the lever on my left and hoping that the arm is going to spin round. Instead, the trolley which runs along the underside of the arm comes speeding up the arm towards us. It comes so fast the chains fly out behind and when I let go of the lever they slam into the tower.

"Ooops," I say. "At least we know what that one does."

"Hurry up." Lexi comes in, clearing her throat. "I can hear him."

"You two had better start going along the arm," I say calmly. "I'll move it over, so that it overlaps the back of the other crane. Then you just have to drop down on to it, climb down, and you'll be safe." It sounded like a good plan, only I don't know if the arm will definitely reach, or if I can move it in the first place. But it's better than doing nothing. All the time I'm talking I'm fiddling with the levers and gears, trying to work out what the hell I'm doing. I press a yellow button just for the hell of it and at once a row of lights start twinkling the length of the arm.

"I want to steer it," says Devil, giving me his dangerous look.

"I'll catch up. Go!"

Devil wavers in the doorway. If he hadn't already been shut in here for three days I think he might have given me more trouble. As it is, we both know he is desperate to get out.

"I don't like leaving you here," says Lexi. "He's got a gun, you know. If we all stay, maybe we can overpower him. . ." Her voice trails off.

"Go," I say, and she leans in and kisses me. "Only hold on tight," I shout after them. "It might be a bit jerky."

I watch as Lexi and Devil climb even higher above me as I fiddle with the controls. They've reached the top of the ladder and stand, about eight feet above my head. This is where the arm is attatched to the tower. Devil steps out first. He's got guts that boy, I'll give him that. There's a narrow strip of mesh running inside the length of the arm. I don't know if it is supposed to be walked on. The arm is constructed like the tower; triangles of steel forming a hollow column. I watch as Lexi edges her way on to the mesh. I'm glad they're inside the arm. At least there is a small barrier between them and space.

"Don't put your full weight on that," I yell. "It might not be safe, hold on to the sides."

Lexi sticks up her thumb. Just watching her makes me feel dizzy.

There's another reason I'm still here in the cab while the others are edging along the crane. I don't know if I'm more scared of Lenny and his gun, or facing that drop.

I twist the lever on my right to the side and the cab judders and moves. As I watch the arm swings round with me.

"Wow," I gasp. The whole thing is moving, and Lexi and Devil are clinging to it like bugs. Awesome. I'm turning it back now, trying to keep steady. I don't want to shake my mates off. Devil and Lexi are making good progress along the arm. They're sticking close together. I wonder if I'll ever catch them up. I manoeuvre the arm so that from where I am sitting it looks as if it is hanging directly over the counterbalance of the second tower crane. Then I stop it. This is all I can do. I pull apart the ignition wires, jump out of the seat and step out of the cabin. I stop and listen. Sure enough, I hear feet clanking up the rungs. I reckon he's got, what, three more ladders to climb. He's slowing down. He's getting tired. And what's the rush? He thinks we're trapped. I hope he hasn't spotted the others yet. I hope I haven't turned them into sitting ducks.

I have to follow them. I have to climb the next ladder and step on to the arm. I have to. The wind blows and a chill goes down my back. I can't do it. It's cold up here, out in the open air. The lights from the town glow orange. I see the dim outline of the hills beyond the town. There's thousands of people down there, all asleep in their beds and unaware that Chas Parsons is stranded up in the sky looking down on them.

I can't move yet. Just another minute. It would be stupid to try anything when I'm shaking this much. Maybe I could somehow hide in the cab. Even as I think it, I know it's impossible. I have to go up. Lenny is very close. I watch the hatch, biting my lip, willing myself to move, but I'm glued to the rail. I can't move. I watch in horror as a pair of pale fingers grope around the floor and Lenny Darling pulls himself up to the platform outside the cab.

He aims the gun at me and I freeze.

I must be seeing things. He's got *tears* running down his face. Every so often he uses his arm to wipe them away. And even up here in the wind and the rain I can smell the alcohol fumes coming off him.

I'm so scared I can't move. He just has to pull his finger back and I'll be dead.

"Lenny," I finally manage to speak and my voice sounds like it doesn't belong to me. It's coming from somewhere outside my head. "What's this about?"

"S-s-sorry," says Lenny and to my amazement he gives a sob. "I've dreamed of this moment. For years and years. B-b-but it's awful." He goes to wipe his nose and the movement knocks his hat off. Then he makes these moaning noises which remind me of my mum when she's in a bad way.

He's still managing to train the gun on me though.

How did I come to be here? When they find me, a bullet hole through my head, I'll have a really surprised look on my face. I feel so strange. Like I'm watching myself.

"You found me again, Nappy. Like in my night-mares. You held out your hand to me and you offered me poisoned meat." Lenny's voice twists into a little yelp.

"I'm not Nappy," I manage to say. "I'm Chas. Nappy was my dad's nickname."

"S-s-sorry," he says and shuts his eyes. "I can't go back to that place. You'll put me there if I let you live." He's crying so hard I'm surprised he can see.

I wonder if my life ought to be flashing before me. I see my body falling through the air.

"Oh God," I say.

"I shouldn't have c-c-come back," says Lenny. He bursts into a fresh fit of crying. "Too many memories. But I couldn't stay away. The letters called me. There was nowhere else to go." He snots into the arms of his coat. I ought to say something to talk him down, but I don't know what. I can't take my eyes off the finger holding the trigger.

"They t-t-terrorized me. They made me what I am. I was their victim for years. They reduced me and took away my life."

I edge towards the ladder.

"Who terrorized you?" I whisper, but I think I know the answer.

All of a sudden Lenny stops crying. He strokes the barrel of the gun.

"You did, Nappy," he says in a harsh voice. "You and Juby. You broke me down until I couldn't stay at school any more. You ate away at me until there was nothing left. Nothing but a ghost. Look at me." He frowns. "LOOK AT ME."

I obey. The rain is running off his bald head and down his face, mixing with the tears and snot. He's so thin it's hard to see how he can be alive.

"Don't I look like a ghost?"

I nod, not wanting to upset him. "But I'm not Nappy," I whisper again. "I'm Chas."

"Your father breathes through you," says Lenny. "You found me when I was at my lowest, and wrote me cruel, lying letters. You savaged me even after all these years."

"Sorry," I say.

"And J-J-Juby. I found him kneeling on a boy's chest, forcing this into his mouth." Lenny makes a sudden movement and I shut my eyes, expecting the worst, but Lenny throws something at me. It's small and light and smells of vinegar. I see it roll over the wet metal and stop by the barrier.

My finger.

Devil tried to force it into Jamie's mouth? Urrgh. He didn't tell us about that.

"Each generation carries on the evil. But not any more." Lenny bites his lip so deeply I see the top row of his teeth. "I'm sorry," he says, shutting his eyes. "I never meant it to be like this. But I can't have witnesses. I can't go back."

I stop breathing as his finger tenses round the trigger.

He fires.

Twenty-seven

The bullet slams into the ladder next to my head. I don't hang around. I'm off up the ladder before he's had time to recover. It gets colder and windier with every step. I expect to feel a bullet embedding itself in me any minute.

Oh God, I'm really high. I'm nearly at the top, in the crow's nest. I can see the whole world from up here. I step out on to the first rung of the arm. I'm too scared to walk on the mesh bit. It looks too flimsy. The lights underneath help, but it's still hard to see my feet. I try and convince myself I am walking on one of those ladders that stretch from one post to another in a children's playground. The problem is I need to look down to see where I'm putting my feet. But if I look down I see the ground. The rungs are spaced quite far apart. I could fall through. Easy.

"Nappy," sobs Lenny, somewhere below. "I have to end this."

"Bugger off," screams Lexi from somewhere along the arm. "Leave him alone."

I close my mind to Lenny Darling. I have to take this slowly. Very slowly. I force myself to unlock my arms from the girder I'm hugging and reach for the next. I lift my foot delicately and tread over thin air before I place it on the next rung. Now I just have to do this about a hundred times without slipping or freaking, or looking down.

I'm doing it, I'm making good progress until I come up against a massive drum of cable blocking my way. In order to get past, I'll have to climb over. I groan, imagining it uncoiling when I'm on top of it. I see myself falling, falling. I shut my eyes and grip the bars tighter. I can't go any further. My head is pounding. Oh God. Please don't let me faint. I'm going to be sick. Darkness. Oh shit. I retch and a string of vomit flies out of my mouth and splatters against the struts. This doesn't make me feel better. I shut my eyes again. My arms are loosening from the bars. They won't hold on any more.

I've had it.

"Chas," a voice whispers close to my ear. "What are you playing at, man?"

"Can't go on," I manage to whisper. I mean it.

"Come on, nobbins, we're gonna make it."

I force open one eye. Devil's ugly face looms at me from the other side of the drum cable.

"You look like shit." He frowns. "Better get a shifty on. Mr Psycho is on his way."

I don't bother to look behind me, but grit my teeth and will myself to hold on.

"Don't lose it, Chas boy," says Devil. "Lexi will

298

never let me forget it if you go and fall off." He hauls himself halfway over the cables. "Cummon, muppet." He offers me his hand. What choices. Either stay here and get done in by Lenny, fall off out of terror, or put my life in the hands of Devlin Juby. How did it come to this? Four or five hours ago I was dozing in Michael's shed, thinking dirty thoughts about Lexi Juby. Now look at me: I'm drenched, freezing and terrified. I really shouldn't hang around with the Juby family any more.

I grit my teeth and grab Devil's hand and he guides me over the drum. It's wet and slippery. My knee shoots out from under me and I'm about to nut the cables. I'm a goner. Devil yanks me up.

I've done it. I'm over the drum.

"Hurry up," says Devil and he picks his way along the arm like he's Spider-Man.

Now I'm over and I'm still alive I feel better and force myself to let go of the upright I'm clinging to and step on to the next rung. And the next. I feel numb now. I'm like a machine. After a few minutes I'm together enough to look up and see what the others are doing. Lexi has reached the end. From the cab it looked like the end of the arm was directly over the back of crane two, but now I can see it falls short. I can't see by how much. This doesn't stop us all moving forward, away from Lenny and his gun.

There's a shout from the ground and against my instincts, I look down. But instead of going dizzy and dopey I gasp. I recognize the figure from his bald head.

Standing in the light of the overhead lamps is none other than Juby-the-Killer.

"Where are you?" he belows.

"Dad," shouts Lexi. "We're up here."

Juby looks up but he can't see us. "Are you all right?" he shouts.

"Yeah."

We all duck as we hear the crack of a bullet. Juby throws himself flat on the ground.

"Let them go," he roars. "I know who you are."

"I hate you," screams Lenny. He sounds terrified.

I hear a clink, clink, clink noise; the sound of someone's boots on the ladder. Lenny's slowly, slowly going down.

"You killed me, James Juby." Lenny's voice is awful. He sounds like he's being tortured.

"Don't hurt my kids," shouts Juby.

Or their friends, I think to myself.

I watch as Juby hurries behind the JCB. How did he know to come here? Has he brought a gun too? I hope I don't get caught in the crossfire. I'm crouched here shivering, when I notice a couple of figures clambering back towards me.

"It's too far to jump,' says Lexi.

'Come on, let's get off this thing," says Devil.

Oh shit. They want me to go back over that drum cable, along the arm to the crane.

300

"I'm all right here, thanks," I say.

"Come on." And Lexi puts her arm through mine. "We'll go together."

I'm feeling seriously wobbly and even more unsure of my balance now Lexi has such a firm grip on me. I need to do it my way. Then Devil grabs my other arm.

"It's easier if you step on this," he says, guiding me on to the mesh strip. "Go on, it's safe."

Stuck between these two I have no choice, so very shakily I place one foot then the other on the mesh walkway. Eek. There's only a quarter of an inch of metal between me and oblivion. Lexi goes over the drum first and grabs my hand as Devil shoves me over. At one point I am sitting astride the thing, with the wind blowing into my face but before I can get too dizzy, Devil has shoved me over into Lexi's arms. Then Devil climbs over like he's vaulting a dustbin. I edge along, wishing they'd let go of me so I could cling on to the sides, but this way is quicker than clambering round every upright. We reach the tower platform much quicker on the way back. Lexi lets go of my arm and crawls up. I follow, then Devil. I cling to the tower. I can't believe how solid and safe it feels after being out on that arm. Remind me never to become a crane driver.

"I'm going to end this." Lenny's halfway down the crane now.

"Dad, he's mad. He'll shoot you," shouts Devil.

There's another gunshot and I swear I see a spark as the bullet pings off the wing of the JCB.

301

I decide to sit tight. Juby might have a gun as well. But Lexi is already on her way down.

"Lexi," I hiss. "Stay here."

"No way," she says, and she's off down the ladder. I don't want to sit up here on my own, so I follow, hoping my shaking legs don't let me down. We've reached the cab when Lexi grabs my arm. "Look," she says, "look, look."

Way down in the distance, we see a trail of blue flashing lights speeding towards us along the dark streets.

"I never thought I'd be pleased to see that," I say. Movement on the ground catches my eye and I look and see Lenny is on the ground, creeping towards the JCB.

"Dad," screams Lexi. "Dad, he's coming."

This is where I have another of my ideas. I haven't thought it through or anything, I never do. I just like the feel of it, like something promising is going to come out. I step into the cabin, and rewire the ignition. I beckon Lexi into the cab to come and help me, and show her how to connect the starter motor circuit. I'm feeling better. The cab feels like the safest place on earth compared to being stuck out on that arm.

"But I'm going down," says Lexi.

"It'll only take a second," I say. "I might be able to do something."

She bends and connects the wires. In seconds the crane is up and running again. Lexi nods at me and is off down the ladder. I don't hold her back. You can't stop a Juby. Slowly, slowly I bring the jib round, and watch as the metal chains swing in the air. I manoeuvre the arm so that it is directly over the JCB. The chains are attached to a metal anchor-shaped thing, which in turn is connected to a massive metal hook. I fiddle with the knobs and gears until there is a groan and a screech and the trolley runs along the arm and suddenly the hook drops. It goes lower and lower till it reaches the ground. This is where my plan runs out. I suppose I was thinking Juby could grab the hook and I'd swing him safely up into the air, like James Bond. But it's not happening. Come to think of it, I'm not even sure how I get the hook back into the air. But even as I try and work it out two figures fly out of the darkness at each other. Lenny gives out an awful scream and for a split second I almost feel sorry for him. I wouldn't want to be in a fight with Juby, even if I did have a loaded gun. I watch the figures roll in the mud. They struggle on for ages but from up here it isn't clear what's happening. BANG. A second gunshot bounces off the fence. Suddenly Lenny breaks free and runs back behind the JCB. He doesn't seem to have a plan. Maybe he's lost his gun. But Juby is still lying in the mud. I stop breathing. Has he been hit? No, he's sitting up. Now he's crawling behind an oil drum. He must be injured. I bite my lip as Lenny sneaks out the other side of the JCB, holding his arm outstretched. Oh no! He's still got the gun and he's going to shoot. I rush out of the cabin to the platform. I lean over the railing, not caring about the drop. "Look out," I scream. "He's coming for you."

As Lenny and Juby look up in my direction a third figure flies out from nowhere and jumps on Lenny from behind. It's Devil. I hear a dull thud as he clunks Lenny on the head with something. Lenny goes limp and Devil shrieks with delight as he grabs the gun. I can't see very well, but it looks like he only has it for one second before his old man has taken it off him. But Juby hasn't finished yet. He waves up at me, lifts Lenny up and grabs the hook which is dangling nearby. He wedges the hook under Lenny's belt.

"Take her up," he shouts.

I climb back into the seat and fiddle with the lever which I believe operates the pulleys. To my delight the cables tighten, then slowly lift Lenny into the air. When I reckon he is about thirty feet above the ground, I halt the mechanism and switch off the engine. Then I take a deep breath and climb down the tower. I take my time because my legs are shaky. As I climb I watch Lexi run to Devil and hug him. I see five panda cars draw up outside the gates and loads of police pour in through the gates, flashing torches and shouting.

By the time I reach the ground they're everywhere. It's like an infestation. I haven't seen so many policemen since my mum dragged me off on a peace rally when I was four years old.

I sit on a pile of stones with my head in my hands. I'm exhausted and my legs won't work any more. I watch as

Juby slaps his son on the back and Lexi stands there, talking, talking, talking. Panda Polly is trying to ask them something but she can't get a word in. Juby gives his daughter a quick hug and ruffles Devil's hair. This is almost the most shocking thing I've seen all night. I bang my feet on the ground to try and get some blood running in them. There's a thin cry from the crane as Lenny comes round. He starts thrashing around in the air.

"KEEP STILL OR YOU'LL FALL," shouts a policeman. He uses his mega phone but there's really no need. Cops love an excuse to use their equipment.

"Ah, there you are."

I look up. It's me old mate, The Stealth. He asks me if I'm OK, then nods up at Lenny, who is swinging in the breeze.

"Can you get him down again because we need to arrest him."

I shake my head and give him a winning smile, trying hard to act like my normal self, when inside I feel like a puddle. "Sorry, officer. I can't."

Stealth frowns. "Why not?"

"I haven't got a licence to drive one of them," I say and give him a grin. "You're not encouraging me to break the law are you, officer?"

The Stealth breathes out slowly and I give him a smile. I ask him the time and he tells me it's three thirty-three in the morning.

"Well if it's all right with you, officer, I'd like a lift home," I say. "I've got an exam tomorrow."

Twenty-eight

Me and Lexi are walking over the bridge. She's holding a pot of yellow flowers which look like alien daisies in one hand, and holding my hand with the other. It's been three days since we went up that crane and found Devil locked in the cab. Three days since Lenny Darling tried to murder us.

Lexi tells me how her dad sat her and Devil down and told them all about Lenny Darling and him. Juby apparently was straight faced as he talked about how he used to pick on this kid at school. This kid was tall and skinny, and shy, and spoke weird. Juby said he could be a bit of a bully in those days and couldn't leave this kid alone, even when it was obvious the kid was really suffering.

Lexi doesn't want to tell me any more but I make her.

Juby and his gang (which included my dad) lay in wait for Lenny every day after school. They stole his clothes, they hit him, they abused him and hurt him. They ridiculed anyone who tried to be kind to him. Then they started having a go at him in school, at lunch time, breaks, whenever they saw him. He was like their project. It gave them something to do. They did this for two years. And every day Lenny grew more distant, spoke less and avoided other kids. Lexi then said that her dad told her he'd done something really bad to Lenny, something he didn't want to talk about. But Lenny was found nearly drowned in the canal and he never came back to school again.

Then everyone forgot about Lenny Darling.

Years later he ended up on Death Row, convicted of drowning a fifteen-year-old boy. Then little old me wrote to him, fascinated by the fact he was from my area and unknowingly dropping my surname and the name "Juby" into the letter. It must have sent Lenny bananas.

Juby said he was out on Monday night, but he eventually picked up a message saying if he wanted to see his son alive again, he had to come to the building site, unarmed and not tell a soul. The message said if he told the police, Devil would die. (This bit really freaks me out.) But the cops were already on their way. A dog walker had seen the lights on the crane and heard Lexi shouting.

"But I don't get it," I say. "If he wanted to do your dad over, why didn't he just go round your house with his gun, why bother going to all the trouble of kidnapping Devil?"

"Too dodgy," says Lexi. "You can't fart on our estate without everyone knowing. The building site is a perfect place to do away with someone. Besides, Panda

307

Polly says he didn't intend to kill anyone, not at first, but then he saw Devil with Jamie and it acted as a trigger. It made him flip out. But once he'd got Devil in the crane, he didn't know what to do with him. He'd left Juby the message earlier and was expecting him to arrive: he was going to do him in. But Dad didn't get the message until much later. In the meantime we turned up and Lenny panicked."

We walk along the road close to the building site. Whatever dispute was going on is over and machines clank and roar from behind the fence. The crane moves a massive concrete pipe through the air. I can just make out the tiny figure of the driver inside the cab. I watch the crane lower the pipe out of sight.

"But why didn't the police cotton on when they had him in for questioning?" I ask.

"He never was in for questioning. That was a lie," says Lexi. "Chas, if you spoke to Panda Polly properly, she might tell you stuff too."

"Whatever," I say. I'm not quite ready for cosy chats with the law just yet. Though I'm going to have to in the next few weeks.

"Lots of people didn't want to see Lenny freed, you know," says Lexi. "But they had to let him go because it would have unlawful to hold him any longer. His sentence had been reduced in the light of the new evidence and he'd already served the time. But there were all these letters from psychiatrists and stuff, urging them to keep him locked up. But they couldn't, so they deported him back here quicker than anything, glad to get shot of him."

We walk through several more residential streets, then cut across the back of the park to get to the church. The graveyard is deserted. I lead Lexi through the overgrown grass and headstones until we reach Selby's grave.

"Here." Lexi unzips my rucksack and hands me a small red gardening trowel.

She sets the flowers close to the headstone and settles back to watch. I start scraping the gravel, ever so delicately at first, but after checking no one else is watching I gouge a great scoop of soil and gravel out of my brother's grave.

"Take it steady," says Lexi. "There's no one here."

When I've dug a decent hole I sit back and look at it.

"Is it deep enough?" I ask.

"Go deeper," says Lexi. "We don't want to worry about dogs."

So I scoop more soft soil and pile it to the side. Eventually Lexi agrees I've done enough and I reach in my rucksack for my school pencil case. I unzip it and draw out a wad of cotton wool.

"Let's see," says Lexi.

I hesitate. I don't want to put her off. But then she holds out her hand so I unwrap the cotton wool and tip my severed finger into her open palm.

"Hmmm," says Lexi. I don't give her a chance to say anything else. I take back my finger and plant it in the bottom of the hole. Lexi passes me the daisies and I tip them out of their pot and push the roots into the soil. I firm the earth up around them like I've seen Michael do with his cabbage plants at his allotment.

"Cool," says Lexi.

I like this. A little bit of me is with my brother, rotting away into the ground, just like him. It feels right. We sit there for ages, just staring at the plant and me wondering if it's wrong to snog your girlfriend on your brother's grave. I don't reckon Selby would mind. I wouldn't. Talking of brothers. . .

"How's Devil?" I ask. "Recovered?"

"He's still at Mum's," says Lexi. 'But the novelty value will wear off soon, I imagine. She hasn't got the stamina to cope with him, unlike Dad."

"So he'll be back?" I ask.

Lexi nods. "Oh yes."

I squeeze Lexi's hand and she squeezes mine right back. Then she starts running her fingers over my hand. She finds my half-finger and strokes it. At first I feel weird. I've always tried to hide away my stub. And it's only just healed. But after a few minutes I realize I'm enjoying this. A lot. I hope her brother doesn't appear.

Then she kisses me and I forget about Devil.

It's my first day at college. I'm due to pick up Lexi at eight thirty a.m., then we're going to catch the bus. She's starting her last year at school and I'm starting my BTEC in travel and tourism at college. I'm wearing all new clothes, right down to my boxers. I've got this really cool T-shirt and some smart new trousers. My trainers are crispy new. Gran gave me £120 and I've blown the lot. But I look great.

I'm too nervous to eat any breakfast. I'm saying bye to Gran and Mum and am about to step out the door when I see the post lying on the doormat. There's a postcard on top of the pile with a picture of a hairy cow on the front. I turn it over and read.

Dear All,
Run out of prawns. Am coming home. Don't let
Gran cook anything special.
Stephen

At last.

I'm just about to call Gran to *come and look at this* when I clock the next letter, a small brown envelope with familiar handwriting. I look behind to see if Gran's watching, but she's busy in the kitchen. I step outside, shut the door behind me and sit on the doorstep.

My hands are shaking as I tear open the envelope.

Dartmoor Prison
Princetown

Dear Chas,
I expect you thought you'd heard the last of me.
Lucky you, I'm still around, even if I am
incarcerated in conditions a Death Row inmate

wouldn't envy. Lucky you being able to walk outside and breathe the fresh air. Get yourself to court on 6th of November, that's when they're holding my trial. Exeter will be the city which decides my fate, whether I am to be freed, transported back to the States for a retrial or imprisoned here. Take heart, Chas, I forgive you for your voyeuristic ways. Regrettably I realize you never had any compassion for my plight, just a childish fascination with the macabre. Even so, you are only young, and therefore not accountable for your actions. Very honestly, Chas, I forgive you from the bottom of my heart. Even so, you must watch your behaviour as nothing winds some people up more than rude, disobedient children. Nothing is more pleasing than a silent child.

Get yourself some new friends and a few social graces and you'll go a long way.

Enjoy life, Chas, it's always shorter than you may think.

Yours truthfully,

Lenny Darling.

"Well that's all right then," I say to myself.